WILL

WILL

Shane Neilson

ENFIELD
&WIZENTY

Enfield & Wizenty
(an imprint of Great Plains Publications)
345-955 Portage Avenue
Winnipeg, MB R3G 0P9
www.greatplains.mb.ca

Great Plains Publications gratefully acknowledges the financial support provided for its publishing program by the Government of Canada through the Canada Book Fund; the Canada Council for the Arts; the Province of Manitoba through the Book Publishing Tax Credit and the Book Publisher Marketing Assistance Program; and the Manitoba Arts Council.

Design & Typography by Relish Design Studio Inc.
Printed in Canada by Friesens

LIBRARY AND ARCHIVES CANADA CATALOGUING IN PUBLICATION

Neilson, Shane, 1975-, author
     Will : stories / Shane Neilson.

Issued in print and electronic formats.
ISBN 978-1-926531-77-9 (bound).--ISBN 978-1-926531-78-6

(epub).--ISBN 978-1-926531-79-3 (mobi)

     I. Title.

PS8577.E33735W54 2013   C813'.6   C2013-904139-7

                              C2013-904140-0

FSC
www.fsc.org
MIX
Paper from
responsible sources
FSC® C016245

ENVIRONMENTAL BENEFITS STATEMENT

Great Plains Publications saved the following resources by printing the pages of this book on chlorine free paper made with 100% post-consumer waste.

TREES	WATER	ENERGY	SOLID WASTE	GREENHOUSE GASES
8	3,511	3	236	647
FULLY GROWN	GALLONS	MILLION BTUs	POUNDS	POUNDS

Environmental impact estimates were made using the Environmental Paper Network Paper Calculator 3.2. For more information visit www.papercalculator.org.

For the fictions

"The more you love a memory, the stronger and stranger it is."
—Vladimir Nabokov, *Strong Opinions*

TABLE OF CONTENTS

MEDICINE IS A MIRROR

THE ENTIRELY BEAUTIFUL

Next to the piano stool lies a pillow, a mat. The window open to the god there is; snow today. Still in his Spider Man diaper, the two-year-old boy climbs the stool, begins to beat out the alphabet song on the ivory, a single undeviating note for each letter, a syncopated D. He makes a screamed abecedary, all the way to P, and the man's behind the boy, his hands held in readiness. The man ushers the boy down to the mat with no illusions of angels and no awareness of dream procedures. The only feeling is the boy's feeling: thrash and remove. The boy seizes.

The man marks the time, begins the count. Forty minutes since the last one. Out the window snow can't restore his belief in God or love, though the white semblance tells him that random beauty beckons when he least needs it and needs something else: reliable, homely safety. The piano recovers sound, as silent as if it were never played.

One minute.

"Stop, please stop," the man asks nothing, no one. The boy arcs as if he's a tiny oarsman, beating ceaselessly against an electrical tide, the creature struck down, touched by God, rendered more beautiful than the man's plea. Blood-tinged drool bathes the boy's teeth. The man imagines every one of the boy's cells aching, nerve and muscle, though all he feels might be nothing.

Two minutes.

The man never played piano in his life but in a sudden hatred, he begins to fantasize about a Rachmaninoff fugue from a score he'd heard but once in a film some twenty years ago, a film about an ill boy and a therapeutic piano. The man imagines himself astride the stool, his son juddering on the floor while he plays the whole score from memory with just a single note: D. Instead, the man looks back to the window. Outdoors, God hurls snowflakes past the sky's consciousness; the evanescent glass pane predicts that no one visible or invisible can see the drama of the man or the boy, that no one cares. The man's fugue ends with an image of his wife cutting across the window returning home from work, a beautiful shadow making him look again in surprise. No. She was never there.

Three minutes.

His boy could be dying. As martyr to the extraordinary, the man chases each second, willing his watch to stop, praying that death has not come. Time for another plea! He looks from his son—bleeding freely from the mouth now—and fixes his eyes upon a distant chimney emitting a plume of grey smoke. He looks to the height of this plume, as high as it can reach, where it ambiguously dissipates. He begins to pray insanely.

Our father, if you were here, I'd take your throat and cut it out.
In your open throat I'd shove hospital bracelets, drug bottles,
my son's toys, this piano, the bloody mat, the bloody pillow....

Four minutes.

The ticking watch is enough to pull him out of curses, which, through their vehemence, are forms of prayer. He replaces the pillow underneath the boy's moving head as he curses again, perfecting the prayer to the only god he's ever known:

The churches! The spires! The priests! The pews, the parishioners! The doctors! The hospitals! I would thrust my hand in your throat and pull down every pillar I could find! Can you be defiled? Fuck you! I'll place my quivering son on the mat you love your lambs served on. With that offering,

would you then stand and return home? Out the window!
I'll throw you out the fucking window!

The boy moves from little arcs to large arcs, pulling harder and harder, a great oarsman. Farther and farther to go. There are many states of unconsciousness: dream, daydream, dead sleep, semi-wakefulness, the slippage into sleep, drug opacity, coma. The man imagines what seizures are like: an active idiocy, a marathon to an unreachable shore. By this time, his son has expended enough energy to row ten kilometres.

Five minutes.

IV bags; drugs; black-uniformed men; a siren the boy'd be thrilled to hear, if he were able to hear it; a stretcher. The needle won't go in, it goes in, but it blows, so another needle must go in, but it can't go in. "Is your son dehydrated?" a paramedic asks.

"Would sips of water make this easier?" the man sarcastically responds. The man couldn't encourage his son to drink too much. Seizures came when eating and drinking, food and the liquid flowing into his son's lungs. "He drank as much as he could."

Blue like water, like sky, white like catheter tip, like snow. The paramedic slips a catheter up the boy's nose, injecting a snowy substance.

Seven minutes.

The man hears a dispatcher speak over the radio: a heart attack at the mall, a fall from a height in the west end, a bee-sting anaphylaxis. The paramedic riding in back keeps apologizing. *Sorry* for when the IV won't go in; *sorry* for when it does; *sorry* for when it promptly stops working; *sorry* for when he takes it out; *sorry* for when he cleans up the blood escaping from the punctures; *sorry* for the catheter inserted in the nose, and *sorry* for the white liquid he injects.

Even in the ambulance there are windows: one rectangle with small bars to reinforce the glass, and at the front of the ambulance, another window. The driver slams his fists on the dashboard, enraged at unyielding traffic. No one wants to get out of the way. Everyone has his own personal emergency.

Eleven minutes.

Another *sorry*. The paramedic has nothing left to do, all his magicks wielded. The boy is as safe as he can be made: oxygen bathes his face and mouth, monitors attest to a beating heart and working lungs. He's pink, but red at the mouth. The paramedic needs saving himself, like the man and the boy. The paramedic must watch the boy just as the man has to watch the boy. The method is to prepare for the worst as best one can. To have a mat. A pillow. The paramedic knows that, just like the man does. It's the paramedic's business to know. In response to the latest apology, the man says, "Thank you."

The paramedic replies, "It's amazing that you can be so calm at a time like this. It really helps, you know?"

Twelve minutes.

The ambulance becomes a battering ram: the driver plays chicken with sluggish traffic. The boy erupts up, crashes back down, straining against the buckles and belts. It's getting worse. Yet, the man thinks, how is dying worse?

Thirteen minutes.

Sorry.

The ambulance occupants step out into blue sky and white precipitation. The paramedics wheel the boy to where four women wait, standing inside the bay doors. All wear blue scrubs, holding their sides in the cold, one of them distinguished by a yellow sweater. The man watches the women lift his son from the stretcher. The paramedics pull out the stretcher from underneath him and take it back. The women set his son down on a gurney. A pillow, a mat.

The woman in the yellow sweater talks to the sorrowful paramedic, glancing at the boy as the paramedic runs down the history. She finally turns to the man and says, "I'm the doctor here. Follow us."

Sixteen minutes.

The trauma room is a more spacious version of the ambulance interior: the same instruments and implements, only room to fit more personnel. And now there *are* more. The man stands at the foot of the bed as a multitude of nurses descends on every limb, trying to get access. "I've got a vein!" shouts one, and the swarm becomes static as if it is a freeze-dance the boy loves; the liturgical nurse works the needle into the arm, everyone praying that this be the right chance, the right place, the right technique, the right hands. Above the diviner, another nurse holds the upper part of the limb steady, though not still; below the diviner the same. The only person moving is the boy, and he is being held not to move.

Flashback! say a few nurses in appreciative amazement, blood rushing past the white catheter and into the barrel of the IV. The diviner looks to the man with a smile. "I got it," she says. "Blood." Then another says, after pushing a button, "It won't run." The ritual starts again.

A bag-valve-mask is pressed to his face, eighteen minutes.

A white substance is rubbed onto his gums, nineteen minutes.

A syringe-tip is shoved into his rectum, twenty-three minutes.

An IV goes in, flashback, and runs. Twenty-four minutes.

The doctor begins to talk to the man, there being things to do and, those things being obvious, she now has time to talk. As she speaks, the man suffers a second fugue: the doctor starts to sing, in a surprising baritone, the words to Johnny Cash's "25 Minutes to Go." *They're buildin' a gallows outside my cell. I got 25 minutes to go.*

There are no windows in the trauma bay.

The man assents to everything, there being no choice in such situations. Any drug, any measure, yes; the room quietens for the man as he nods his head while thinking about the doomed prisoner in Cash's song, nearing the end of his life, having done something terrible, nobody caring enough to keep him alive.

With the IV in place, the doctor wants to use something to induce a coma. "We need to put in a breathing tube," she says in a rich drawl.

I'm waitin' for the pardon gonna set me free. With nine more minutes to go.

The sorrowful paramedic walks in, having cleaned up the blood from the ambulance floor, having restocked the ambulance's shelves of the equipment used to save the man's son. The paramedic stands at the perimeter of the room, where angels and effectiveness and prayer are best kept safe from use. The numerology of doom: when the patients are this young, this many people stand in attendance. Another emergency rushes down the corridor, perhaps the heart attack, the fall, or the sting; the team wheeling the limp, blanketed mass jostles the paramedic. Absent-mindedly, he takes a step farther into the trauma room and mumbles, "Sorry."

I can see the mountains. I can see the skies. Three more minutes to go.

The boy stops seizing.

The man calls his wife at work.

"We're at the hospital again. It's bad—he'll want to see you when he wakes up."

"Is he going to die?" she asks.

The man, worried about this prospect most of all, doesn't actually know how to answer the question. "He's just stopped, I don't know if he'll start again."

"Okay, I'm coming."

The clock doesn't matter anymore. After a time, his wife arrives. The boy sleeps drug-sleep and reprieve-sleep. The man doesn't know if the boy will be the boy again. Will the boy still be able to walk, talk, and learn? Will he fall in love with a woman? The man fixes on this: whether the boy will grow up and fall in love with a woman. But then the man wonders if the boy will ever wake up. It is timeless, this not-moving.

She goes first to her son. She touches his face. The boy can't feel her; he doesn't move. She stares, registering the physical fact of him, then sits down on a chair the man found for her on the opposite side of the bed. "How long this time?" she asks.

"Twenty-seven minutes."

His wife looks lost.

"I let it go the five minutes, like the neurologist told us. Then I called the ambulance."

"You okay?" she asks.

When asked about how he is, the man feels like he's being asked to pray to a deity he's long refused. This marriage is the same: it is about being with the boy while she is not, about watching the boy seize when she cannot. Such witness does things to anyone, mother or father, and renders each witness separate. The man watched the boy seize by himself for months and felt sad, but eventually he watches the boy as the only one who watches. He feels betrayed, but all he says is to her is, "Yes."

"Can I get you anything?" she asks.

Emergency department staff already asked him that. The doctor was the first to ask, once it was clear his son might live; the nurses asked, even bringing him a coffee and some cookies from their pantry after he refused. The man thanked but didn't eat or drink.

"No."

Months ago the neurologist told them both to pack a "hospital bag" for the boy should an emergency like this occur. The doctors said this with the hope that the hospital bag might not be necessary. In the bag are diapers, spare medication, clothes, and toys. The man packed the bag as soon as they'd come home from the doctor that day. The last thing he packed was an anthology of love poetry, something he received as a gift a long time ago. A woman gave him the book as a gift; his wife? The book sat on the bookshelf for years, unread. The man reaches into the bag for the book of poems. It reads as if the target market were young lovers, adolescents perhaps; the poems are pigeonholed in silly categories. The man opens the book to a section called *And he's talking bout' burnin' but I'm so cold.*

None of the love poems that this section contains had yet been read in the trauma room, though all had been enacted. The man chooses "Lullaby" by W. H. Auden to be his final fugue. He begins:

> Lay your sleeping head, my love,
> Human on my faithless arm;
> Time and fevers burn away
> Individual beauty from
> Thoughtful children, and the grave
> Proves the child ephemeral:
> But in my arms till break of day
> Let the living creature lie,
> Mortal, guilty, but to me
> The entirely beautiful.

Does the man agree? Is agreement important? Is there something mortal in his son? He looks at his wife, his own arm. No—he doesn't agree, refusal coming out of him as his one great talent. The grave proves nothing. Auden's arm is a scythe. His son is a love greater than the kind of time and fever Auden proposes. The man erupts in a belief for the entirely broken and this lack of consolation is why his wife holds out her arm to the broken man, calling him to rest.

THIS IS MINE

The duct tape wrapped around the doorsill is mine. So's the orange carpet bleached from sunlight pounding though the windows. The copper frames encircling the wedding pictures are mine—my wedding too, my pictures. The tractor trailer noise coming from the highway—mine. *Fuck the truckers*, my husband, Roy, says. Roy's mine, ha. *Fuck the truckers* he shouts as the big rumbling goes up and down the road, either replenishing Tim Horton's with treats, fruits, napkins, and paper bags, or taking away. Roy says *Fuck the truckers* especially to trucks parked on the side of the road in front of the drive-through coffee shop, paunchy old men that need to piss or purchase a pailful of coffee. *Council never should have let Tim's come in here*, Roy says. I don't know if he's right. I get coffee there sometimes, when I can afford it.

We rent the basement apartment to a boarder. If I didn't have the boarder, I wouldn't be buying coffee at all. I'd be working in the Tim's! Here I sit in the lap of luxury, the outskirts of Saint John, in a small two-story on a wooded drive. Roy screams *Fuck the truckers* in the middle of the night, still asleep, when a truck gets the windows resonating. The pockmarked floor and the streaked kitchen table tell how long I've been married: forever. So, why am I talking to you?

'Cause Roy's not here. He's helping his friend Jimmy move, you know how friends are. They call and you help them. Jimmy's in Moncton and Roy says the move'll take all weekend. I wish he was here though. Roy knows I wish he was here, that's probably why he's gone. Roy keeps me busy while I'm off on the stress leave. He's my pet project, you could say.

What do I say now that mother's dead? That she died, and that's why I cry every day? It's not so simple as that. I still cry, especially mornings. Before she went, her breathing was so irregular I never even knew if she stopped breathing, the return of her breathing was like a bad surprise. Twenty seconds would go by without a breath and then she'd give a big suck, pant two or three times, and then stop again for a half-minute. This went on for hours because the drugs for keeping her comfortable didn't keep her comfortable, nothing stopped that big suck. The big suck had to stop all on its own.

Is it possible for a dying person to be "comfortable?" My mother must have had something she still had to do or say to somebody, who knows what it was, and it kept her clinging, gasping, *uncomfortable*. And whatever it was had nothing to do with me, she had lots of time to say whatever she wanted to with me by her side.

Can't say enough about those palliative nurses though, they were unbelievable good, they were a comfort to me at least. People are my drug, ha.

Yes, busy. I keep busy too. It's not all listening to Roy scream *Fuck the truckers* around here for me. Work's lined up after the long weekend. Being off work only makes things worse, more time for me to moan and wonder if mother wanted to say she was wrong. I say she had lots of time, but maybe she was putting it off and then she wasn't able to talk but still had the desire, you know what I mean?

I've cleaned this old place three times since mother died, and I still can't get the all the stains out. You'd think we're slovenly people, but we're not. Maybe I just notice the mess more now, that's all I've got to do, spot the mess and try to clean it.

One of the nurses, Jeannine her name was, gave me a book by Kübler-Ross. I didn't tell Jeannine I didn't get my grade twelve, that I'm the black sheep. Though Jeannine looked to be the type that might have cared that I fell in love with Roy in grade eleven, even though Roy was twenty years older. Jeannine might have cared that mother *almost* disowned me, though the old woman couldn't quite bring herself to do that completely. Instead, mother sneered whenever she saw my husband or heard his name spoken. Whatever mother had to say about men and love, she never told me a whit more of it when she knew I was going to marry Roy.

Mother showed up for the wedding and smiled, soldiering through her daughter's grand day. She didn't sneer the entire time, which was nice. Her picture with me wearing the white dress is up on the mantelpiece, see for yourself. It's strange and sad, but her pulling it together for one day probably kept me by her bed when she was dying, probably kept the door open for me to wait, and wait, and wait for her to say something she'd never be able or want to say. The words I wanted were words of apology, but what I wanted, really, was mother herself.

Yes, Kübler-Ross wrote the book on grief, ha! I tried to read the first chapter right there at mother's bedside, but that felt like flying overhead in a hot-air balloon: down there, a distant death bed of an old woman, grief! Land-ho. I do remember a line of the first chapter from the time of that reading, though, the line's something I can't get rid of: "Therefore death in itself is associated as a bad act, a frightening happening, something that in itself calls for retribution and punishment." Yes, that's just how mother worked, for sure—bad, punishment, retribution. I associate those three words with her. And now "death" too. With that line of Kübler-Ross running through my head, I screamed *Keep busy* out loud to the walls when Roy wasn't around. *Keep busy.* Roy wasn't around much, still isn't. He likes to help people.

Don't mind the dog, little Maxie just loves it when people come. So excited, Maxie is. *Yes.* But give her five minutes and if you don't pet her belly she'll growl. *No Maxie. No. No growl, no. No, ha!* I should write a book like the ones they give out at palliative care. A dog is great for anybody who loses something, a dog's little life of treats and misbehaviour takes the mind right off death, mine included.

Before mother died, she made me promise we wouldn't go after the doctor. Dr. Catolli misdiagnosed her, see. He said the scans were clear after the chemo when the cancer was all through her, even after the horrible drugs, *still all through her the cancer was*. Can you believe that? Dr. Catolli gave mother at least five years to live, he did, with me right in the room to hear! And she was dead in three months. And though she was cheated of the rest of her life, so to speak, you couldn't get a bit of anger from her! It was like she already read the Kübler-Ross book Jeannine gave me, like she accepted she would die. Maybe mother did read the book—you know the size of the library in her house. But it really was as if mother had learned the ways of the meek. Even when I was crying and heard the news from her and felt way beyond anger, possessed of a rage, aghast, as if that quack Catolli was killing her with his bare hands at that very moment, mother wouldn't agree, she wouldn't say an unkind word. Too churchy, mother was. Cross her and she excommunicates you. Grace got mother in the end, ha!

She tried to iron things out with me a little. In the bed before the big stroke that stole her speech, she told me running away from home she came to understand, but that took a long while. The Roy part, she told me in the bed too that she'd never get over it. She said he was a good man, he was, but not the right man for me. She didn't look at me when she said that, not like when she punished me. At that moment I felt like she was Dr. Catolli looking at the cancer on the screen and announcing, "Everything's good." Everything wasn't good, and everything isn't good with me right now.

I wish she would have realized that everything was good on my wedding day. I fired back with that when she said her bit about Roy. But mother wouldn't budge and a few days later the stroke, and a few days later her breathing the big suck, big suck, gaaaaarp, big suck, and Christ that went on forever.

When I left the hospital the night she tried to forgive me about Roy, which is what she was doing, not apologizing, not trying to own up to her part, still making a power play, I realized that in some permanent way, to her mind, I had done bad things to *her*—run away, married scandalously. She wondered if she did the right thing, concluded she had, and wanted to make me feel guilty all over again. That sounded good on the drive home to Roy, but when I got home and looked Roy in the face I wondered if this was as close as she came to offering me forgiveness. I'm still not sure if I wanted it then, or if I still want it now. What I wanted was for her not to die. That's what all children want.

Roy comes up with ideas. "I got an idea, Raylene," he said one day he caught me looking out the window, crying. "Maybe you should read that book the nurse gave you, the Koobler-Boobler book."

I raised an eyebrow. "Roy, are *you* making book recommendations now? The only things you read are cereal boxes and road signs." This was always the way with me and Roy. I was smarter, and I could say so. I had to quit school for him. But Roy protects me, he always has. That's the deal. I got the equivalency years later, and then the nurse's aid certificate from the college in Bathurst.

I didn't listen to Roy and go back to the hospital and ask Jeannine for the Koobler-Boobler because I thought somebody dying at the palliative care might need it more, or somebody watching their mother, father, sister, brother, or child die. But I broke down a few days later and drove to the public library. I took the book out and I never told Roy, don't you go and tell him either.

When I got to page fifty-nine of the Koobler-Boobler, I asked Roy about his own mother's death fifteen years ago. The crotchety old bag died suddenly, no time to commemorate her, and then who would want to, the bitch. "Did you think you were lucky, Roy, your mother dying so sudden?" I asked him. "Or am I the lucky one with the time I spent with my mother before she was gone?"

"Not lucky, not lucky," he said, and he wouldn't say anymore. Who did he mean, himself, or me, or both of us? Fuck, how did you grieve the old bag's death, Roy? YOUR WIFE IS ASKING YOU! But when he left the house for a few weeks, I understood that I was asking because I didn't notice how he grieved at the time. Or didn't I care. Was that it?

When Roy came back, and I apologized, he said something that surprised me, something that reminded me of my mother. Roy said the best and worst possible thing at once. "I didn't really know love until I met you. Then things hurt more. I loved you and that helped me forgive mom for stuff I used to hold onto. I learned I couldn't love anybody and still hold onto things, there were too many things to hold onto." Some days I wait for Roy to say a single word. Some days I needle him until he talks. Some days he fills me up like a well and it's a long time since I've drunk what he's given me dry.

Roy works seasonally. He isn't much around the house, but when he's here, I feel better. That's how it works for us. The skinny boarder is after calling him for weeks to fix a simple thing, and if the thing isn't fixed he jumps up and down on my porch and calls me a slum lord, even though his Metallica T-shirt has stains, and the shirt is black. Black is hard to stain. Once he's insulted me, he makes an ultimatum, "Fix it today or else!" I just shrug my shoulders and say "You can go. No problem. Forget about this month's rent, dear, but be gone by the end of the month."

Roy knows when it's *time*, though. He didn't complain about how long I spent with mother. In the beginning with Roy after I ran away, I half-believed my mother was right some days and thought I was a fool. But Roy knows what I need. Sometimes it's to be left alone, and other times I need him to come to me, and rarer still I need him to let me go to him.

Look at the picture of me at the altar: all of eighteen, a wisp. If you asked me then what would happen, I would have answered *I don't know* and if you asked my mother what was going to happen I'm afraid of what she would have said. But now she's dead. Roy tells me he knew she didn't like him but that he always liked her despite that. "I would have felt the same in her position," he said. "I got you and she lost you. It didn't have to be that way but it was that way for her."

When Roy said that, I was on page 102 of Koobler-Boobler. I told Roy to just stop talking, to shut up. That was a time I needed to be left alone. You see that my wedding dress was second-hand, an off-white. Roy couldn't afford to rent a tuxedo, all he had was that dark suit. We had no honeymoon, I went straight to school as a nurse's aide. Roy drifted just like my mother predicted. But here we are, still together.

The more I read the Koobler-Boobler, the less I thought about how things could have been better with my mother. I'm sure that's the point. But the strange thing is that I thought more about Roy. Now I constantly think of Roy dying. He had the heart attack five years ago, remember. Before that, I used to think Roy was permanent. Having given up so much to be with him, he couldn't be anything but permanent! I prayed Roy would come through, that all those lines and tubes were just temporary, that all he needed when he walked out of the hospital was a baby aspirin a day. I needed him. I wanted a phone I could call his comatose brain and say, "Hey Roy, I'm the boarder in your heart and I want this heart repaired."

When the ICU doctor asked "Do you want us to do CPR if Roy's heart stops?" I thought I was auditioning for a TV soap. "Yes doctor," I wanted to say, my hand pulling down the neckline of my blouse, "You don't let my Roybeam die, y'hear!"

At page 150 of Koobler-Boobler, I imagined losing Roy a thousand ways: heart attack (again), traffic accident (caused by heart attack). Right now he's helping a friend move—will a piano fall on him? When he comes back home to fix the boarder's propane tank, will the tank blow up in his face? When I told my doctor, Dr. Sirin, about my worries and asked him why I had them, he said, "This is the same reason I put you on sick leave. The reason is grief." That made me mad, but it strikes me now that he was right.

I will go back to work to clean surgical instruments, to fetch what the surgeons need before they ask for it. I will be the cleaning mistress of the autoclave. I'll still have thoughts about Roy like *Did Roy remember to take his aspirin today?* Too much of that kind of thinking and the surgeons will get cross because I can't find their doodads in time. I'll cry, and everyone will think I am crying over my mother when the real reason I will be crying is selfishness. *Don't leave me, Roybeam, don't you leave me.*

Koobler-Boobler died before I read her book, but if she were alive and in front of me I'd ask her this: am I mourning my mother, or am I afraid, just like everybody else, that I will die alone?

Back at work I'll finger the hemostats, mosquito clamps, and vascular clamps. I'll daymare about Roy decapitated in a freak accident with cables, or Roy as a surgeon, throwing an instrument at me from across the OR. When I tell Dr. Sirin, the closest person I have to a real-life Koobler-Boobler, my fears, he says that I may have the post-traumatic stress.

I smarten up then. "Oh, Dr. Sirin, I had better be careful then. I'll think instead of how work will be fun!" Why talk to doctors anyway? He's a smart one, that Dr. Sirin. He keeps quiet for the most part, meaning I'm always waiting for him to tell me that I am not ready to go back.

Is it grief to want a different life? I want undone choices, clear New Brunswick skies, and eternal love. Say that to a doctor, even a good one like Sirin, and they'll chuck you in the bin. So instead I say, "I'll be fine, the other girls at work will help me. I can push buttons. I can pour disinfectant into a sink. I know where everything is. I can find whatever anyone needs."

Koobler-Boobler wrote that grief is insistent and stage-skipping. Mother was a reader, devouring everything from *Leaves of Grass* to *The Second Sex*. She was Catholic devout but that never stopped her from reading. She left her basement library to the public library in Newcastle, I don't know how they'll fit all those books in, more books in her house than in that library in the first place. All the town had to do is go and get the books, that was the deal. The town sent the biggest of their trucks to do the job.

The last book I read for pleasure was just before I left grade eleven and ran away with Roy. The books after that were textbooks, nursing manuals. I felt fake, reading even though I didn't finish school. But mother didn't finish school either, just to grade seven before she had to help out in the fields.

I wish I picked through mother's books before the librarian took them away. I might have learned that mother read Koobler-Boobler, for example. Now all mother's books are scattered through the general collection. Maybe I'm better off not knowing. How would I have felt if I found that book with my mother's discrete signature in the upper right corner of the inside cover?

On the mantle, there, is the picture of my mother, Roy, and me at the wedding reception. Roy wears his cheap, dank trousers and charcoal sports jacket. I wear a yellow sun dress. Mother wears a grey blouse and long skirt. Her neck is weighed down with a large pearl brooch. The look on my mother's face doesn't look like grief. She looks as if she were letting something go from her hands, but had yet to feel relief in her muscles and her eyes.

Yes, Maxie Max. Yes.

UNIVERSAL PRECAUTIONS

"I'll fucking kill you, you fat slut," John Doe screamed at our charge nurse. I thought I had a drug for that outburst. But after the Haldol went in he punched Mandy, his primary nurse, full in the face, breaking her nose. I wanted to wring his neck, whisper in his ear "I have a drug that will fucking kill you, you skinny addict fuck." I wanted to lift him out of the instant slum of his bed and slam him through the wall, but he was eighty years old. *Only* eighty years old or an *almighty* eighty—what didn't kill him made him stronger.

I put the IV in Mandy's arm myself. O Mandy in tight blue hospital greens with the granny panty lines showing through, you look like candy, do you taste that way? Into the intravenous line I inject diazepam, one of the drugs John Doe licks like candy. A knockout knocked out on the bed, next I inject ten ccs of lidocaine in the nasal fracture. Returning Mandy's nose to its previous angular perfection might require the ministrations of a slick plastic surgeon months down the road, as funded by workmen's comp (the doctor in the suit and tie will whisper in her ear, *Mandy you will be beautiful once more*), but *crunch*, the bones are back in crude alignment. I think John Doe, like all the men of this world, has taken a shine to our Mandy here. He might bash her again. So I tell Mike the Gorilla to go get the physical restraints.

Gorilla and I grab the upper limbs. Two nurses sit on his legs. Why do I always feel this process is sexual? Bondage, I suppose. The nurses are pissed, John Doe should be old enough to understand that he can only fuck with people for so long before they'll make you pay, they get you back better than you could ever get them.

The problem now is that John Doe *likes* the nurses sitting on his legs. "Why sit on me all the way down there, come up to me face now girls, it's a lot better, the view is nice." Men are all the same. The piece of shit tries to bite me and Gorilla, until Bert the New Paramedic grabs John Doe's head in a lock. Mandy's up now, the knockout—ha, I kill me—drug's worn off, She cinches the arm belts around his wrists—tight. She moves to the leg belts where the two nurses simulate smoking a crack pipe. Mandy laughs as the belts go around John Doe's ankles—extra tight. Mandy looks that snapping turtle in the eyes while pushing back his ugly head, the belt wrapped around his forehead and jaw. A drop of Mandy's blood trickles out of her nose, falling into John Doe's roaring, undentured mouth.

All ninety furious pounds of John Doe are now trussed to the gurney. *The situation is controlled*, as we say in the trade. He writhes the few millimetres of give against the cloth. John Doe's head shakes, he's foaming mad—completely, utterly gone. The chemical restraints from twenty minutes ago failed because the old bugger's liver gobbled up each drug I gave through the intravenous. He cut each substance down like a thresher to wheat. Drugs only make John Doe angry, drugs don't settle him. They make him stronger because he's indestructible. Textbooks have taught me John Doe exhibits "the paradoxical response" but John Doe, I don't know. He was made for high potencies and high doses, gasoline for the machine.

John Doe came in my ER without identification. We still don't know his name. He shook from rock. Bert found him in the middle of Queen Street, seizing from a bad OD. When we cut open his filthy blue jeans, black from the gutter and the rain, we gowned and gloved for fear of disease, taking universal precautions. We found what looked like a name and a phone number, GORD GRANDSON 634-3357, tattooed in blue on his thigh. The number was inked over top of a green mermaid's gigantic breasts. The mermaid gazes lewdly in the direction of John Doe's groin.

Mandy sees the number, figures she'll try. Asking for Mr. Grandson, she gets Gord, John Doe's grandson. "Yeah—Izzy's had it bad for years," Gord tells her. "Happened when grandmother died. He went from rum to crack, got acquainted with it in the rooming house."

"Does he have any other medical problems we should know about?" Mandy asks, touching her nose, feeling its new configuration. *Mandy, my darling, a thousand ships, do not worry, and a thousand more.*

"Izzy's losing his mind too, right? Not just from the drugs and whatnot. He wanders. My sister's a nurse in St. John's and she says he has the dementia. One day I took him to a tattoo parlour and got him a tattoo of my phone number in case people like you found him. I wanted to put it on his wrist like those Medic-Alert bracelets, 'cause you guys look there, right? But Izzy would only let the artist put the number on the mermaid's tits. 'For a good time call,' he kept laughing as the numbers went on. 'For a good time call.'"

"Any allergies, or surgeries, or medications?" Mandy persists.

"No. But I don't know. Health Sciences in St. John's knows. See, he's famous in St. John's—it's where he lives, all the hospital people and doctors and such know him there. Always in the fucking Health Sciences, all the time, always reminding them he's not dead. But when he travels around the island he can really get fucking lost."

"What happened today with Izzy?" Mandy asks, the blood in her sinuses forcing her to mouth-breathe.

"It's more what happened this week. He was short of breath all week. He told me he had chest pain on and off but he was doing a lot of drugs and so was I. Maybe a little more short of breath I suppose. I'm from Gander, I picked Izzy up in St. John's and we drove to Corner Brook for Linda's wedding. Linda's my sister, Izzy's granddaughter. Izzy was halfway through a forty-ouncer and who knows how many bumps, only the lord above, when he said the pain came on. It looked like he had it real bad too. Fuck, that wedding. My sister's a skank. Izzy still made the actions to the YMCA song, though, he's tough, huffing and puffing and coughing. He was on the C when he grabbed his chest like he'd been shot. Then he left the reception hall. I figured he needed some air. Guess I should have tattooed his name next to my phone number, he might have come up in your systems or something. Well I was half-cut when I got the idea, and when I got to the parlour –"

"What's his full name?"

"His real name's Ishmael Dunbracken, but he's Izzy to us."

Izzy lies in the bed, face flushed, not speaking. "Can you point to where it hurts?" I ask. Izzy spits yellow on my coat. *You are a fuck, Izzy, I have good drugs, I'm just getting to know you and the dose you need. The dose can always go higher. All drugs have a lethal dosage. Dead, you will be stronger than ever. Propofol, Izzy. Propofol.*

Mandy of the tight-fitting greens approaches with a Kleenex and a sultry smile. "Dr. Walsh, do you need a spit shield?" she asks while dabbing my white coat, her accent thick and musical. It's still hard for me to tell, but I think Mandy might be from St. Anthony. She turns to Izzy and sing-songs, "I've talked to Gord. He says he'll be here after he makes the Mary Brown's. He says he'll save you a leg."

Gord arrives. "It's your mainlander accent, doc. Where you from? Izzy can't understand anything but the Newfinese. *And* he's deaf. He watches other people do YMCA to know what letter's on deck, hilarious." Looking at Mandy's chest, he says, "That fucking wedding DJ was *loud*." Leaning in to Izzy's restrained head, flicking the tragus of Izzy's right ear, Gord says "Do you think you could get the workman's comp to move their asses? They're something slow figurin' out whether to pay for the hearing aids on account of the bomb factory noise back in the Second World War."

"What?" Mandy and I say together.

"He worked in a factory out Ontario way as a young man. Made bombs or some such. Couldn't hear worth a damn after that, I guess."

"Just ask him where it hurts," I say. Later, I write *history related by a family member* in the chart. *Patient and family member unreliable historians.*

I fill a styrofoam cup with water. "Gord, tell him he needs to take this. It's baby aspirins."

Izzy looks at me, and then back at Gord. His grandson says in the Newfinese, "Aspirin. Doctor says."

Izzy's suspicious but he takes the pill on his tongue and chews, choking back the water chaser. Mandy walks away as I auscult his heart through his thin chest. His lungs sound free of pneumonia—bad alcoholics aspirate, I always check. Pleased, Gord declares, "Izzy saw the doctor two weeks ago for the methadone. Doctor said his heart was as good as the day he was born." Izzy makes a face at Gord. Can he hear, or is he lip reading? "Do you think you could give him some of the methadone, doc, he's due," Gord concludes.

Mandy comes back to hand me the EKG printout. The closest I get to being a fortune teller is when I interpret these jumps and swoops on pink graph paper. Izzy is having a heart attack, and no fucking shit. I see big tombstoning ST segments. The EKG sheet tracing the air from my moving hand, I try to explain this current disaster to Gord and Izzy. TIME IS MUSCLE I want to scream in frustration, TIME IS MUSCLE.

The old man puffs away in mild respiratory distress. His mask is off to the side, shoving rich oxygen towards his ear. I put the tracing on Izzy's chest and adjust the mask back to the proper position.

"He's having a heart attack," I say to Gord Grandson, giving up on talking to them both together. To Izzy I scream, beating the left side of my chest, "You're having a heart attack!" Before Mandy and I walked into the emerg bay to receive Izzy from Bert's ambulance, I said to her, looking at her full mouth, "Thar she blows."

Izzy, sweating profusely, wears a baffled expression. Gord Grandson translates my mainlandese to, "Doctor's saying your heart is attacked."

Before I can correct Gord Grandson, Izzy growls, "*My* doctor said *my* heart is fine."

At times like these, I usually don a top hat and tap-dance. I put on what I call "the show." I unveil the EKG and its evil alien ink pecks to the resistant patient and say in a stentorian voice, "There is no doubt. Look at this very, very, very concerning pattern. The blood flow to your heart is being cut off. Time is muscle." When the doctor says it's bad, non-medical jackass, it's really bad. I drop science voodoo on people like Izzy. Crack is not helping, Izzy, your heart or your mind.

Izzy shakes his head. "My heart is good as the day I was born." Emboldened by the self-apparent truth of the statement, he screams, "DAY I WAS BORN!"

"It's true," Gord says. "I was there. Two weeks ago, when he got the methadone. A big fancy doctor in a white coat said to grandfather, 'Izzy, your heart is good. Takes a licking, keeps on ticking.' He even knocked on grandfather's chest as he said it."

I contradict Izzy in even-more-cloying mainlandese. I say, "You're. having. a. heart attack. You. could. die. You. need. to. stay. in. the. hospital. You. need. treatment."

"Grandson, get me the fuck out of this hole."

From where he's sitting, Gord Grandson begins to untie Izzy's right arm. In just two seconds, the IV in the dorsum of Izzy's hand is lost. "Gord, what the hell are you doing?" I ask.

"Just a stitch, grandson," Izzy coos. "Just a stitch is all it is. Let's go and have some of that Mary Brown's." Izzy's sweating like he's in a sauna, which indeed might be the heat of the flames of hell coming closer and closer.

"Get out of here," I order Gord, swatting his hand away from Izzy's left arm. "Your grandfather could die—he's having a heart attack." But Gord gets up to pull out the old man's rancid clothes from where they're stored in a plastic bag under the bed.

"Security!" I yell.

The Beefy Monkeys come and remove Gord from hospital premises. They rip the bag of shit-soaked clothes from Gord's hands. As he's dragged away, Gord screams, "They're after stealing your clothes, grandfather, they're fuckin' crooks and criminals! You seen it with your own eyes, they took them right from me own hands! Watch yourself in here grandfather! I can't save you now!"

Educated men deny the news they have cancer even though I break the news to them in a calm, reasonable, empathetic way. But these men aren't smoking crack at the age of eighty and they weren't told by a quack only two weeks ago, "You do not have cancer." I refasten Izzy's right arm as Izzy watches Gord get frog-marched out.

People call me "doctor." I am a doctor. I place my hand on Izzy's chest. "Your heart is not good," I shout, but with a shout that tried to be caring. Is that even possible? "Not good. You could die, Izzy, not good!"

The RCMP arrive, two Mounties with their arms pre-crossed. Mandy must have called 'em. Hospital procedure, she had to do it, but the serge suits don't make Izzy trust us any more. Serge suits do not build rapport. *O sole mio*, Izzy!

"Youse calling the fucking Mounties on me? What kind of fucking hospital is this?" Izzy writhes again on the bed, desperate to be free. He should be as calm and relaxed as possible to reduce the load on his heart. We are killing him, making him more agitated.

Other patients and family members in the department stand at the edge of the curtains marking off their beds from the rest of the room. Izzy is high, fine, tragicomic spectacle. He screams, "My heart is good! My heart is good! Fuck you assholes, my heart is good! I trust my real doctor!"

I double, treble the dose of fentanyl. I increase the drug dose to comatose. "Good as the day I was born!" he sputters out. "Good

good good," he repeats, the words slowing but not stopping. Medical ethics lectures whizz through my mind as I draw up more drug and consider the wisdom of starting propofol:

Autonomy: I know best—you are having a heart attack. You don't understand the disease or the consequences of refusing treatment. I therefore hold you against your will. What is will? Will is strength, weakness, pain and relief, dominance and submission, nurses on your legs and you between theirs. Will is deciding where, when, and how to die.

Beneficence: In my white coat, I am charged with doing good. I must have your well-being in mind. I need to stop your heart from being attacked—something that is good. If you can be at the wedding of a granddaughter and dance, if you can still get a grandson to bring you crispy chicken and try to bust you out of the joint, then, Izzy, I know there's something inside you that's good too. Grief has the strongest of wills, doesn't it, Izzy? No beating grief.

Non-maleficence: You hit my nurse. Do I want to smash your face? Yes. Will I try to heal you instead? Yes. This involves administering medications that could kill you—give you a stroke, make you bleed. Clot-busters, Izzy! But Izzy you've got a bad heart, bad, you're sweaty, in pain, short of breath, and my medications are good, real good, much more likely to help than to harm.

Justice: Izzy, you're eighty years old and addicted to crack cocaine. Opiates too. If I let you leave, it'd be easy, we'd stamp the chart AMA, Izzy, against medical advice, I'd even write *left with a family member*. And you'd die. But just because you're aggressive and mean and despicable doesn't mean I'm not going to try to save you, because your heart is good, Izzy, I believe you, your heart is good.

Izzy is a tinker-toy man with small limbs and saucer hands. He thinks I will kill him. "My heart is good! My heart is GOOOOOOOOOOD! GOOOOOD! GOOOOOOOOD!"

Is Izzy right, is what he's saying medically true? One of the more obvious principles of medical ethics is **Honesty.** Doctors should only tell the truth because it is the only way to get anyone better. I shout in his ear, "Your heart is bad. Your heart is BAD," but Izzy is louder than me, he's had more practice in his life. "GOOOOOOOOOOD!" he yells.

THE ALCOHOLIC PHYSICIAN

Let us also remember to guard that erring member the tongue, and if we must use it, let's use it with kindness and consideration and tolerance. —Dr. Bob Smith

Dr. Smith walks two miles to the hospital every morning. The walk helps work the alcohol out of his blood. Every morning he takes two aspirin. Every morning he knows he'll get drunk that day. Every morning he has rounds, patients to see. He gets up every morning to be a doctor and surgeon.

All the hospital staff know about Dr. Smith's drinking. *Dr. Smith drinks between surgeries! He has a tumbler in his office for sprucing up! He could end up in the infirmary himself!* Though they say these things, his colleagues excuse him because of his skill. Though Dr. Smith walks in the hospital craving alcohol, needing a drink to bathe the nerves and steady the hands, he still walks in the best, most experienced general surgeon on staff.

Due for a polypectomy on the mayor of Akron in an hour, Dr. Smith knows the OR nurses won't let him operate if he shakes too much. Coffee makes shaking worse: more sober, more shake. He stares at his hands, willing them to rest, but the more he concentrates, the more he shakes.

I already know I drink too much, he says to his hands. What he won't admit to himself or anyone else is that he also *doesn't* know he drinks too much. Each day might be his last as a practising doctor. All

Dr. Smith requires is one bad outcome in the context of the rumours about his wildly shaking hands and the hospital director will hang him. Weak and failing, Dr. Smith's routine of staring at himself in the mirror at three a.m. doesn't help. *How did I get here?* he asks himself as he guzzles the rest of the gin straight from the bottle, his eyes closing, his face disappearing from the mirror.

The mayor will be a good case, he swears. The man's small polyp appears in Dr. Smith's mind. The doctor mentally reviews the series of steps he'll take to remove it whole. Dr. Smith believes in process, his spiritual principle as a surgeon is: The Same Things Done In The Same Way Achieve The Same Results. He learned this dictum from Dr. Roger T. Vaughan, the best surgeon Rush Medical College had ever seen.

His hands slow their motion. He promises them this: *I'll get the mayor's cancer out and then I'll walk out of here. I'll never come back*. The image of the verrucous polyp, bloody at the tip, leaves his mind, replaced with the next procedure: the taverns and hotels of downtown Akron. An hour after placing the polyp in a formalin jar, he'll black out. In two hours, or three, he'll move to the dead streets of Scranton, and from there to Biloxi, finally coming to rest in New York. He sees his body convulsing in an alley, then breathing coma-quiet in a state hospital, then lying still in a coffin.

A month ago, Dr. Smith took time off from work after a hard night of carousing that concluded with two black and bloody eyes. He woke in his own bed, next to his wife Anne, with no idea how he'd been hit, where he'd been assaulted, or how he got to his own bed. He first noticed his black eyes when he looked in the mirror the next morning, reaching for alcohol behind the garbage can. Anne screamed when she woke up that morning, Dr. Smith's side of the bed streaked and splotched with red.

Dr. Smith walks with his hands in his pockets so no one sees him shake. He bears down, wills himself to keep walking, thinking of Anne's refrain, Anne who begs him every night to stop drinking.

"What good are you to people when you're killing yourself?" she asks. "What good are you to me?"

"I'll stop," he says. "I'll stop. I promise."

Anne's grace and his own surgical grace are the last things he has left. He feels both kinds of grace leave him with each step, the Akron General looming a quarter mile off in the distance. Depleted, his pace slowing as the hospital comes closer, Dr. Smith finally walks through the thick double doors and down the hall to the surgeon's lounge.

His Excellency Mayor George J. Harter waits in an anteroom, fearing the state of his doctor, needing him just the same. The Mayor knows Dr. Smith is a drunk. Entering the preoperative suite dressed in full surgical garb, Dr. Smith stretches out his right hand. "How are you doing today, George?"

His Excellency says "Fine. Just fine," as he pays close attention to the steadiness of the doctor's hands. Dr. Smith shakes the mayor's soft hand with a firm grip. Dr. Smith is in the hospital now, on hallowed ground, home turf. His hands have to earn another drink, his hands are making promises too.

His Excellency relaxes, his salt-and-pepper slicked-back hair no match for the balding authority of Dr. Smith. The nurses relax too, having watched the men shake hands. Some days the nurses whisper, "I wish Dr. Smith would take a couple snorts before he gets here just to get past the tremor." They didn't need to say that today.

Jeannine, his instrument nurse, hands him a snare in a plastic package. As he holds the snare in his hands, deciding if this was the right size he needs for the procedure, Dr. Smith realizes he's dying.

Sitting in his recliner, Reb, an army anesthetist moonlighting on civvy street, watches Dr. Smith operate. Reb had witnessed Dr. Smith hobble, wobble, and lurch into the operating room for the past month. He watched Dr. Smith operate for marathon hours on the really big cases. *Why do they give the big cases to a drunk*, Reb thought about the surgical group at Akron General. Reb watched Dr. Smith gaze up at the clock as if coming up for air. Dr. Smith's view lifts from red, suctioned cavities as if to wordlessly tell the Lord above, as Jesus did on the cross, "I thirst."

After a surgery a week ago, Red entered the changing area of the surgeon's lounge. He had just come from reassuring a semi-conscious patient that the medications for nausea and pain "were great nowadays, don't worry, we'll fix that right up." Reb untied the greens from his waist, in a hurry to go home to his wife on base and tell her, "Just a few more of these shifts and soon we'll be in the Pyrenees."

That day had been a long one. In the morning, his wife, Judy, said "Anesthesia is not the natural state of marriage. I want a child, Reb. How many times do I have to beg?" As Judy walked away into the bathroom, she said, conclusively, "I want to feel." All that day Reb thought of ways to make her feel, like the Pyrenees trip, and he was still thinking of them when he exited the lounge, walking past Dr. Smith. He saw Dr. Smith holding a bottle at the vertical, swallowing with a surgical precision. Dr. Smith drinks like he operates: concentration obliterates his awareness of the surrounding environment.

During surgery earlier in the day, Reb jostled Dr. Smith out of his reverie of technique once. The patient with a colorectal carcinoma suffered a sudden drop in blood pressure. Startled, Dr. Smith drew back from the body, his hands lifting from the crevasse he'd just created. Dr. Smith stood against the wall, away from the resuscitation. Injections and compressions weren't surgeon's work. Dr. Smith watched Reb try to save a life, blood bubbling up from where Dr. Smith had just cut. If the patient died, Dr. Smith reassured himself with the thought that they'd have been dead anyway if he didn't operate. But he had to tell this to himself while his hands shook in bloody gloves.

Dr. Smith's hands entered the green gown offered by the nurses. "My self-embalming," he says. His hands push into white gloves that stretch tight against his skin. If the gloves tremble like a white flag, everyone in the room would imagine themselves on that table, in the hands of Dr. Smith. And everyone wouldn't do a damn thing about it, except Reb, the new man in Akron.

Reb watches Dr. Smith's hands calmly close around the scalpel; a line is a line is a line. Dr. Smith makes a transverse incision in the abdomen, diving through layers of skin, muscle, peritoneum. The patient doesn't feel a thing, Reb knows his work well. When the mayor wakes up, he'll have a blunted memory of his own body. Dr. Smith's surgical signature will be there, a catgut smile soon to tighten into scar.

How much anesthesia does it take to forget? Reb told the administrator about Dr. Smith's bottle of booze the day after the incident.

A half hour into the procedure, Dr. Smith tells Jeannine, his instrument nurse, "George will be shitting pretty in a day or so." Jeannine first came to the Akron General ten years ago as a young scrub nurse, married a year and considering children. Jeannine tried to fit in with the bitch club nurses who made her work far more than was fair—*because I'm young and pretty and the surgeons still want to fuck me,* she thought. *Jealous bitches.* In the early going the charge nurse made her work with the biggest assholes, the dicks who blamed their nurses when things went wrong. Jeannine ducked as grown men threw instruments at windows, lights, glass casings, and at fire extinguishers. If she was a beat late or a beat before an instrument handover, she'd be lucky to just hear about it and not have to duck the blade coming at her head. But the bitch club, thinking they'd break her, did her a favour. They put her with Dr. Smith.

"I need to prepare you," Charge Bitch said. "Dr. Smith was a good man at first. Educated at Rush, fun at parties, generous with the poor, he didn't throw tantrums in the early days. But he drinks like a fish now and he flies into rages. You'd better learn to duck."

"More than usual?" Jeannine said, trying to look as coquettish as she could.

During her first surgery with Dr. Smith, his hands shook so bad she wondered how the circulation nurse managed to get the gloves on his hands. He looked up at the clock every five minutes. *I've seen this surgery a hundred times before. Maybe I should do it to get it over with,* she thought. Instead of insulting the poor man, she patiently said: "Dr. Smith, we have time, as much time as you need."

From that moment forward, Dr. Smith never raised his voice to her. He nicknamed her "Good Nurse." Jeannine wished he wouldn't call her that. The bitch club hates it, and it makes them hate him more. They're trouble for him too.

Rich, Jeannine's husband, hears about the bitch club daily. "Those gossips and cows let themselves go at least a decade before. They hate what they never were—good looking," she tells him. Rich waits for her to finish. He listens carefully, kneading his hands as she talks. His hand movements look like he's trying to wipe away everything that had happened to her at the hospital.

As she hands the scalpel to Dr. Smith, Jeannine thought back to a week ago: a disheveled Dr. Smith sat on a bench behind the hospital. Transport trucks brought milk, vegetables, and volatiles to the loading area. Jeannine was on her way home to Rich when she heard Dr. Smith sob. His face was in his hands, but he still had his OR gloves on, soaked in blood and streaked in shit.

She felt strange, asking the doctor what was the matter. "Nothing's that bad, is it?" she said. Everyone knew what the matter was, and so no one ever asked. Jeannine touched his shoulder, spooking Dr. Smith as if Reb just told him to step away, that the patient was about to die.

"What? What time is it?" he shouted, standing up and listing into her. Frightened, Jeannine pushed him back onto the bench and hurried away, hearing the crying strike up again.

Dr. Smith asks for a retractor, having already cut deep into the belly and freed the tissue that, if left alone, would surely kill His Excellency. Dr. Smith's hands move with purpose. Jeannine feels grateful to assist such a graceful surgeon. Dr. Smith is so good, so slick, so anticipatory, so automatic, but only when he doesn't have the shakes so bad.

The surgery is a success. Tumour tissue floats in formalin for safekeeping. Dr. Smith holds up the sample bottle with the mayor's cancer to the overhead light. *Do I say goodbye now?* he thinks. He goes to the sink, removes his gloves, and washes his hands as he's done after a thousand procedures like this one. His hands move slowly and smoothly over one another, washing off the soap. He is clean.

Before Dr. Smith leaves the surgery lounge, a call comes. The hospital director asks to see him immediately. Dr. Smith's lanky, paunchy frame straightens with the news. He walks up the hall to the gilt-edged office door that, as the director himself routinely mentioned a dozen times a day, is "always open to staff." Dr. Smith slowly opens the door without a knock and finds the director talking and laughing on the phone. *He has never touched a cancer in men,* Dr. Smith thinks. *Cancer claims all.*

Dr. Smith sits down on the leather couch. The director finishes his call, taking his time. The message is obvious: *You, Smith, are but one of a thousand administrative duties I discharge today.* His phone call nonchalance evaporates. "Dr. Smith," he says gravely. "You drink too much. It affects your work. Our privileges committee has decided you will no longer operate at Akron General."

Dr. Smith says nothing, thinks only of what's in the director's desk drawer, what might be in the cabinets lining the wall.

"You're a talented surgeon. But I personally feel your position is hopeless. The hospital has to act."

Dr. Smith remembers he drank the last of his gin the night before, in front of the mirror. "Excuse me," he says to the director, "do you have any gin?"

Dr. Smith glances at a likely cabinet. Why is the room full, absolutely full, of pictures of the director? The director in Maui, at Machu Picchu, with Mickey Mouse. "No. Look, Smith, I'm firing you for boozing and you beg me for booze?" the director says.

Dr. Smith says, "You can't fire me. Who are you to fire me? You're suspending my privileges. And I'm not begging. I'm asking." He reaches in his back pocket for his wallet as the director, slightly chastened, mentions an asylum in the Carolina foothills. Dr. Smith searches for dollar bills. He has none, making him consider pleading for his privileges back. The words of another Dr. Smith in another director's office come to his mind: *I can change! I'm the best surgeon this damn city had ever seen! I can lick this problem. I'll save so many lives, donors will pour their money in!*

But the thing is, Dr. Smith sees his hands resting on his lap, as calm as can be. His hands tell him at that moment that protestations disappear after the first drink and that blackouts are the true annals of misery. "Can I have twenty dollars, please? I'm all out," Dr. Smith asks.

Expecting a defense, anger, a ploy, a plea, the director says, startled, "I've only got ten dollars on me."

"I'll take it," Dr. Smith says, happy. His hand on the paper, Dr. Smith walks out of the director's office, leaving the door as open as the director pretended it was, returns to the mayor's bed in the recovery room. A good doctor, he checks on his patient one last time.

The nurses tell him that the mayor's recovering nicely—too well. A randy mayor, George has been feebly making for some of the women's asses. Jeannine in particular is his target. Dr. Smith hears the older nurses harry her with nitpicking details designed to get her to go to the mayor's bed as often as possible. The intravenous drips a green liquid. The mayor, pale but a dedicated skirt-chaser until such time as he meets his maker, croaks to Dr. Smith, "Bob, did you get it all?"

"I did, George, I got it all." Dr. Smith feels free. Turning to Jeannine, he says, "Good Nurse, I want another snare for the next procedure." He moves his gaze to the more senior nurses. "Something less creaky and old, though. The last one must have been up on the shelf for twenty or thirty years at least."

Jeannine and the other nurses didn't know he lost his privileges yet. "But I think I did give you a new one," Jeannine says. Baffled, Jeannine does as he says, leaving the mayor for the supply room, determined to find a brand new snare. Dr. Smith smiles, watching her go. The mayor croaks after her, "Nurse, nurse, nurse."

Delirious now, Dr. Smith leaves the Akron General. Doctors line the right side of the hall, all the doctors he's ever known. On the left, all the nurses who have taken orders from him stand. Dr. Smith shuffles past them, thinking of Anne. Is that his wife, there, standing at the end of the line? Yes. Anne sadly swings the hospital's double doors open for her husband. He wants to tell her something, he wants to promise something to her. The doors close behind Dr. Smith. He hears the noise of birds, cars, and ambulances, the sounds of orderlies chatting as they smoke in the shade.

Later that night, before the director kisses his wife and falls asleep, he tells her that he fired Dr. Smith. "He'll go straight to the hotels, won't he," she says. His wife shouldn't know about Dr. Smith, but she does, the director told her about him, his problem. "You did the right thing, dear," she says. Dr. Smith would have agreed, if he had heard.

SITTING

I sit in my chair.[1] I think at the sad, the pitying, the all-around ain't-it-a-shamers, that the chair is electrified as *I* am electrified, that I am electrifying—the chair is my body electric, operating on *batteries*. I move forward and turn by using my right index finger to track on a pad. Lo, I am a mechanical pharaoh, borne aloft by a slave with wheels.

Boring Presenter Dude in the blue serge suit and the bow tie (never trust a man in a bow tie) brays about when to anticoagulate the patient in atrial fibrillation. Conventional practice for over forty years seems like a throwback to medievalism: poison the human body with rat killer to treat a heart beating to its own irregularly irregular drummer. The cardiologist—has to be a cardiologist, the guy loves acronyms way, way too much—drones about when to admit patients with TIAs[2]—what circumstances reflect high risk for reoccurrence in the first forty-eight

---

1 Six wheels, ATX suspension. A model from a popular series, though I won't name the brand. Some things are private. I do have control of my mouth and my lungs, so the "sip-and-puff" power wheelchair control system was an option. But I found the appearance of the system intrusive—when I puffed the chair past a mirror, I thought I looked like a helpless cyborg. So I use my touchpad, though it required a few adjustments early on—I made the chair go too fast, so the scale of my finger motion and resultant chair motion had to be adjusted.

2 TIA: Transient Ischemic Attack, or in the common and incorrect usage, "mini-stroke." I don't know about you, but doctors using acronyms to describe the cessation of blood flow to the brain is ominous, but how much more ominous is the lay usage of "mini" when attached to the hand of god, striking someone down. I call it even.

hours? Study after study is shoved down my eyeballs, Powerpoint slide after slide. This guy wants to put warfarin in the water. This guy is dull as dishwater. Be still my strong, ceaselessly beating heart.

My heart, stalwart in its motionless casing, beats *against* his information onslaught. Since the accident, attention is my greatest asset, but my focus wanes until it's finally snuffed out for good when the cardiologist admits he is currently standing in front of a screen crammed with "TMI,[3] do you think?" Well, yes, I do think, too-small tables do not tickle my fancy. "Sorry guys, this slide is a little busy I know, but the take-home message is . . ." (slide skip slide skip slide skip slide discussion X 5 minutes … slide skip … alight on a slide:) " …yes, this is a little too overkill I know but Giocomantonio et al. did a study called IOWAMO[4] that tried to duplicate the results of WHAMMO[5] but with more intense anticoagulation monitoring of course and of course they found nothing which should be reassuring for you guys because you don't have to change your practise habit of course but maybe I'll stop editorializing for now and just get to the good stuff … slide skip slide skip slide skip… I'm getting even shorter on time, well, I'll just run through quickly what's left and hit the take-homes."

Allotting only a few seconds per slide—*the bastard knows!*—in a race to get through it all, to be worthlessly, revoltingly thorough, all the trees speciated in the forest but no one given an answer to the question *what does the forest mean?* Personal take home: never marry a guy like that. Wish I'd known that sooner, though. My ex-husband was just like that. Bow tie pedantism and all. I suppose I'm being coy. I knew the cardiologist in much the same way I knew my husband.

---

3 TMI: Yes, the heart doctor used this acronym too, and it's just what you'd think it is (too much information).
4 **IOWAMO:** Intensive On-Warfarin and Mortality Outcomes. Or, *I Only Warfarinize And Make Obscurantisms.*
5 **WHAMMO:** Warfarin Home And Multidisciplinary Monitoring of Outpatients. Or, *When Hammering Acronyms, Make Manly Ones.*

Question: why do I still want to be part of the medical fraternity? Answer: What else am I supposed to do? These conferences are the only thing I enjoy doing outside my Occupational Therapized house. Everyone suffers the Is-It-Worth-Its and the Whys, I'm no different despite the electrifying life. Except Brian, maybe. He's different.

Drool rolls down my left cheek. Drool is my passive-aggressive fuck-you riposte to the stiff presenter. *You are so boring, you asshole, you make me senselessly drool.* I could use my index finger and turn the chair 180 degrees, make the back of my chair face Dr. Trivia and his nervous glances at the clock, but the thing is, the dork is a friend of mine. Or he used to be, existing on a time scale pre-accident, like most every other person I know. We even fucked a few times before I got married, long before I ended up in this chair. He had big arms, did a lot of reps at the gym, he attacked the iron, he liked squeezing his women, lifting them, but in the end he preferred them to be on top, in control, pinning his hands down. I liked those arms and hands.

Christ, Dr. Trivia's even taken care of me a few times in the hospital when something goes down my throat the wrong way and I choke or get aspiration pneumonia.[6] Gross, right? Or weird. It's better now that he's fat and bald, not as awkward for me anyway. Imagine if he still looked as good. And anyway, who protests at events like these? Raging Grannies pissed off about Big Menopause? Fifty family doctors gather on Clinical Education Day to listen to local specialists every last weekend in April. A radical group, us. Sweet, sweet Guelph. I come every year, I look forward to coming here every year. I might as well fall over in my chair, fall dead right now, but my heart won't stop.

---

6 The pneumonia of milk, chocolate chips, Frito-Lays, and soup—what goes in the mouth can go down the trachea and end up the lungs. Lungs do not like food. Jimi Hendrix had a large, acute aspiration that was enough to stop him from breathing. I suspect Alan Ladd, hero of the movie *Shane*, died from the same thing. Disabled patients, including the "regularly addicted," live the less glamorous life of chronic aspiration.

My attendant Brian, dean and overseer of my bodily functions, doesn't even pretend to listen. Brian has big ears, but that doesn't mean what you think it means. A ridiculously precise shaver and lover of all things facial, Brian's been with me for ten years, pretty much since the incident. I had female personal care attendants before, but I hated them because they could still walk, they could have a man, they could get pregnant (and one of them *was* pregnant.) I hated myself, so I hated them, and even though I knew I didn't hate them at all, really, I pretended I did hate them because it was easier. But Brian showed up from the agency one day as a replacement and I never wanted anyone else. I mean, how could I ever be jealous of a man?

Devoid of curiosity, uninterested in today's strutting specialists and the questions from the generalist audience, Brian drinks free coffee, scarfs biscuits, and fantasizes about the coming lunch funded by our meagre medical society. Brian chews, swallows, and doodles. Damn the treats and the swill and damn complimentary pens and notepads. My only means of communication is my index finger. I raise it to tell Brian that I want him to be quiet, to stop embarrassing me. *Brian, fuck off with the lip-smacking and pen-scratching!*

Why do I care? Brian's banquet-crasher behaviour suggests that I don't take the conference seriously, but I do take the conference seriously. Listen to the index finger, Brian. Hear me roar! *Wag wag.* One wag for Yes, two wags for No. Three wags for—Take Me Brian, Take Me. But Brian never will. He never has. He flirts with men.

Alerted, Brian stops his munching and pen-scratching. Ahhh. I can focus again. Oh no. Am I supposed to be tickled by the cleverness of researchers who name their trials to make the snappiest, cleverest acronyms? UNBELIEV-ABLE2[7] and STENT-ORIAN[8] might make

---

7 **UNBELIEV-ABLE2**: Use Normalizations. Big Elevations Love Inducing Exsanguination Voluminously. Assess BLEeding 2x/week, or *You Know Brian, Eating Little Items in Enormous Volume—he's ABLE2.*

8 **STENT-ORIAN**: Stent Only Randomized In Aspirin And Nitrates, or *Scarf The ENtire Tray Of Risky, Inedible, Abominable Naan.*

people giggle, especially dorky naked cardiologists, but they don't make me take Mr. Trivia seriously. With ceremony, I wag my finger at all acronym inventors everywhere. *Wag wag.*

I learn more about Dr. Trivia. He's become as vain in mind as he used to be in body, invoking all these trials in exhalational puffs of informational smoke. But he has a good bedside manner when he takes care of me, he talks both clinically and personally. I mean that he knows he's taking care of a doctor, so he treats me properly, like doctor and patient both. I wish a wag of my finger like a magic wand would cause him to come to his senses. The organizing committee better not bring him back next year! At the end of the monotone drone I will instruct Brian to circle the rating numbers on the feedback form, 1/5. For now, though, my finger just points at Dr. Trivia as he massages his computer. My finger is symphonic. My finger contains multitudes. My finger with the vast binaries, yes and no.

Lunchtime! Cheap, crumbly breakfast foods wheel out and finger foods wheel in—forty minutes late. Fuck Dr. Trivia, the know-it-all of nothing much. I feel like I did when I was able to walk, travelling to these kinds of conferences by plane. Every so often I escaped my seat after a long international flight stuck next to a garrulous specialist speaker—take home: don't sit next to doctors on planes—whose conversation concerns p values and intention-to-treats. Brian notices me look at the finger foods. He has always been attentive of me. Take Me Brian Take Me to the Finger Food Table, wag wag wag. He doesn't—three wags are my private motion. There are only two different wags. Fine. I drive to the table myself.

Though a queue forms, space is made for me, the disabled queen. I am put at the front of the line. When I was first getting used to being a disabled person, I wagged my finger if anyone tried to humour me and put me up front. I defiantly took my place at the end of the line. But some people cannot abide this, they insist on ushering me forward, thinking I'm too stupid and moronic to understand the magnitude of their generosity. Now I just smile and drive up to the trough. Why fight a good thing? The generous appear conspicuously generous and I get food faster.

Brian knows what I like, what I like never changes. Wag wag wag. Brian fills a plate with the few foods that loosely adhere to the mechanical diet regimen I've been condemned to consume for the remainder of my days, O woe is me, and he grabs an orange juice I'll sip with a straw. What a happy day, when they let me use the straw that first time. It's not like I can lift the food to my mouth, I wanted to scream at the pretty speech-language pathologist.

"Oh Dr. Gallu, we know you want the straw so bad but we need to be sure you've recovered enough to work the swallowing muscles properly." A young, ebullient thing, and just out of school. What the hell could she tell me in those platform shoes? I wanted the straw and I got the straw. *Ha,* I wanted to say when I used it the first time. *Ha,* I wanted to smirk. I was too hard on her. She ended up marrying a doctor. What a nightmare.

I'm here to participate in conversations and catch up on colleague gossip. I want to hear them bitch because I can't bitch, all I can do is drool and say yes or no with my finger. Men bitched the most and they pretended they were powerful but all they were doing was admitting they had no power. Bitch sessions were the greatest pleasure of my formerly ambulatory days. Most of the people here know me, they've known me for years. Other than get-thee-to-the-front-of-the-food-line, I am spared the usual disabled condescension. No one here speaks to me in singsong—Brian took care of that a long time ago. Everyone knows I've still got the same mind, I just can't move. I sit and listen as circles of conversants swell to allow my bulky presence. I sit and listen as obese gargoyle.

I don't attend symposia to hear the hallowed "doctor" honorific in front of my last name. Brian calls me by my first name, Tracy, and that's the way I like it. (Brian's last name is Latimer. Take me Brian

Latimer Take Me doesn't have the same ring.) The accident amputated most of my life—the doctor part certainly was cut off. Sexuality is impossible. My husband Noel, a neurologist, couldn't love my deficits, financial burden, or chronic urinary tract infections.[9] I can't walk, pick up a feather, or embrace a living thing—specifically, him. If I sound like I'm grieving, then make a fart noise with your mouth. Who can blame the bookish asshole? Who knows what I would have done if he got shot instead?

"Do you want to go over there and see Laura?" Brian asks. Wag. He takes me to a small group of women. I used to practise down the hall from Dr. Laura May. Laura smiles and the circle clumsily widens to accommodate the chair. Laura, I wish, I wish, I wish I was you, the thriving practice, the preserved beauty, arms that can pick up anything.

Mr. Legaire came in late one evening. A drinker, I reported him to the ministry four months ago when he tried to sit on the examining table but missed and hit the floor on his ass. Smelling alcohol on his breath, I asked, "Did you drive to the office?"

On his rear, stunned, he said, "What? Help me up."

I extended my hand. When he was standing again, I asked once more, "Did you drive to the office?"

The suspendered, crotch-discoloured, plaid-shirted Mr. Legaire snorted and said, "So what."

"I have to report this to the ministry," I said.

Legaire's face transformed from a snivelling expression, a request for more "sleeping pills," into a mobile, hellacious rage-face. I weighed just over one hundred pounds back then, pre-accident, but he was six feet tall, a construction worker in his forties, burning through his third marriage. "You're a fucking bitch, I'll fucking kill you," he shouted,

---

9 I often need to be catheterized. This means I get nasty infections. Or, I feel a burning in my loins. I make a "p" scribble with my index and Brian relieves me of my backed-up urine, but as he does so he introduces bacteria into my bladder.

leaning in. He jutted his index finger out and waved it under my nose. "Take my licence bitch and I'll fucking kill you." He slammed the door, stomped out of the clinic, and climbed into his red Chevrolet Silverado. Initially he put the truck into forward gear and came within a few feet of the office wall, just to show me how serious he was, or how drunk he was, I couldn't be sure, but he got the truck into reverse, pulling out of the clinic lot. I watched him weave down Speedvale Road.

A week after that encounter, I received a cordial note from the Ministry of Transportation reassuring me that the "appropriate measures are being taken."[10] A month later, Wendy, my battleaxe secretary, told me she saw Mr. Legaire at the liquor store returning a huge stack of empties in the Silverado. "You reported him, right?" she said.

"Yeah, I reported him—over a month ago," I said.

"I see him sometimes at Rob Roy's too. He drinks pitcher after pitcher of draft. He sits by himself. And how can you miss the red monster truck in front of the bar. I mean, do the police have eyes?"

Though I reported Mr. Legaire, no one could make him stop drinking. No doctor's report could stop him from driving. He did what he wanted to do. He didn't care.

Four months later, I heard yelling coming from the waiting room. "Where is that fucking doctor bitch? Is the bitch doctor back there?" Doctor witch? Witch doctor? Doctor which? Did the voice mean me?

---

10 Section 203 of the Ontario Highway Traffic Act states that "every legally qualified medical practitioner shall report to the Registrar the name, address and clinical condition of every person sixteen years of age or over attending upon a medical practitioner for medical services, who, in the opinion of such medical practitioner is suffering from a condition that may make it dangerous for such person to operate a motor vehicle." I filled out Mr. Legaire's medical condition reporting form in fear, but I always filled out the reporting form in fear, because notifying the ministry of a medical condition is the one instance a doctor can be hated as much as a police officer or a judge. It takes a lot of courage to threaten judges and police officers, but it just takes stupidity to threaten doctors, and stupidity is, both thankfully and regrettably, one condition doctors need not report to the ministry.

Wendy screamed, something like Drunk Skunk. You're drunk? You're a punk? Wendy had never screamed in the years she'd basically told me, her employer, how to run a practice. I plucked Wendy from a retiring doctor, and the guy was great, he told me the best thing I could do, starting out on my own, was to hire someone with a brain who wanted to answer the phone.

"The combination is rare," the old guy said. "Who wants to talk to anybody else?"

The sound of stomping came closer to my office. Wendy shouted, clearly and distinctly, meaning the altercation was moving closer, "I'll call the police!"

Mr. Legaire appeared in the doorway. Dishevelled and swaying, he held a shotgun in his right hand, using it as a cane. He came in, closed the door, and tried to lock the door behind him, fumbling. He gave up. There was no lock.

"Took my licence, eh, bitch?" he slurred. "Took my fucking licence?" Mr. Legaire's face reminded me of when he fell on his ass months ago.

How much had he drunk, how much alcohol gave him the courage to come to my office? I still thought of him as my patient. Things were bad between us, our relationship was not great at the moment, but my job was to make him well, not to make him happy. How young I was then, how naïve! On Thursday evenings, no other doctors work in the office. Thursdays were my night, and tonight was the night.

"You give me back my licence, you bitch of a doctor!"

I opened my mouth. What was supposed to come out was a short, calm sentence to the effect that I don't have that power, that Mr. Legaire's licence was in the hands of the Ministry of Transportation. What came out was a shameless, terrified scream. I screamed Wendy's name.

Mr. Legaire shook his head. "You'll give it back," he said. The shotgun muzzle lifted from the floor, the gun pointing at my face. He told me he was a Korean War veteran back when I first took him on as a patient. *Please, please, please god let the police be nearby, please have made some idiot vandal kid break a window next door or shoplift chocolate from Joel's Mini Mart, please police be called for that, or please be here inspecting a break and enter. Please be here investigating a collision. Please be close, be where you can be in an instant, here, where I need you, right fucking now, save me!*

I heard the phone ring on Wendy's desk. For some reason I imagined Wendy answering the phone, booking my next appointment. I hoped to god she was getting the police. "I'll do anything you want," I said.

Mr. Legaire gestured to my desk. "Sit down," he said. "Write the government that you're a bad doctor, out to get me. Say I'm not an alcoholic, that I never have been. Not once in my life. Tell them the truth."

I took his dictation. "I'll send it to the Ministry right now—I'll fax it while you watch."

He pulled out a bottle of Captain Morgan from his pocket and drank the balance of it down. After that hit, he mumbled. I couldn't make out what he was saying. I took this as verbal assent to move to the fax machine. I punched in the numbers with my index finger. Send.

"You used this fucking machine bitch to take away my licence?" he said, brandishing the shotgun. He shot a shell into it, making the new Epson sparkle, buzz, and wheeze. He struck my face with the gun and shoved me down on my knees. "Hands behind your head, doctor bitch." I moved my hands from my broken left jaw and put them where he wanted them. Where were the sirens?

Wendy's son cut the clinic lawn that afternoon—a whiff of the two-stroke engine was still in the breeze. I felt the gun nuzzle the back of my neck. He said, "Bitch bitch bitch, you never should have taken my licence. Thirty fucking years driving and not even one ticket to my name!"[11]

---

11 On average, an alcoholic will drive drunk 80 times before they are caught. They also lie. The number of statistics generated about the operation of a motor vehicle and alcohol is impressive. Studies assess number of drinks, blood alcohol level, response times, the relative risk of getting into an accident. I'm aware of no studies which assess risk to the reporting physician. A strange paucity of data that requires further study, preferably published without an acronymic title, though the appearance of MADD in the article somewhere is inevitable.

Abject, desperate, thinking I'd die, I told him I could make everything right. I lied at the end, I admit it, I choked out that I could restore his licence. "I have that power, I can do it just like that," I told him, snapping my fingers behind my head.

That was the last thing I ever said to him, to anyone.

I am Borges,[12] am Milton.[13] Brian reads to me obsequiously, talking in voices (don't let him get his hands on Austen, he gets carried away.) He's a good, steady reader. When I have the stamina, he reads to me uninterruptedly for hours. He does lose himself in the story, though. I fall asleep sometimes to wake and hear him mimicking the diction of a New Jersey mobster.

After the shooting, I was in a coma for months. Those who took care of me were blunt. This never ceases to amaze me: just because a person is in a coma doesn't mean they can't *hear*, that they're not *there*. Don't ICU[14] staff know anything? Isn't it their business to know? Nurse Donna, my "primary," said to my husband Noel on day 61: "Tracy can't talk, can't walk, who knows if she ever will. You're a neurologist, so you tell me. Who knows how long she was at the scene, not breathing even. Might have been down as long as twenty

---

12 Borges, like his father, suffered from a hereditary form of blindness called Retinitis Pigmentosa. This incurable disease is like being told the Oulipo will place a constraint upon your sense. Subtract from the sense of a genius and another sense will compensate for the loss. In Borges's case, the sense was thought, writing, labyrinth.

13 So many things could have made John Milton blind, including Retinitis Pigmentosa (though that is, actually, fairly unlikely based on the preserved vision of his mother and father into their old age.) But don't worry, I won't list the differential diagnosis. When I used to do overnight call, I was wary of diagnosing my patients over the phone, without a physical exam. Speculating about glaucoma or retinal detachment or even diabetes in the great man is quite silly. What isn't in dispute is that Milton couldn't see some time during his fourth decade. Not seeing is, for a genius, believing.

14 ICU: incurable unit. Not Intensive Care Unit.

minutes, hey? You know what that means better than me: *significant brain damage.*"[15]

Nurse Donna, you're using your limited medical knowledge against medical me and my medical husband? I willed my fingers to react. Irate fingers, move irately! I thought of the so-called *scene* Donna mentioned. I never thought of it as a scene before. In my comatose dreams, I thought of it where I almost died. I still think of it that way. Only my index finger moved, but it moved like it wanted to poke out Donna's eye. "Look, look there," Noel blurted, God bless him. "Her finger, it's *moving.*"

A few weeks after Finger Move I started to breathe on my own. Weeks after that I had the motor control to communicate with Finger Wags. The rehab specialists speculated about further recovery: physiotherapists and occupational therapists plied me with wishful thinking. The women who worked on me felt like I was some kind of hero, as if I was like a cop almost killed in the line of duty.[16] Despite the early breakthrough of my pointy pointer, I regained no more motor function.

I might be a hero, but I am a disabled hero. The women who worshipped me went away and worked on less hopeless cases and they felt good about incremental progress, but I stayed stuck, suffering

───────

15 Donna, there are a number of top-notch papers you might want to consult before you advocate pulling the plug on your next ICU victim. I recommend the entire body of work of Steven Laureys, out of the University of Liege, who has written more papers on the subject of misdiagnosis of the vegetative state than the number of times you've performed CPR. Particularly interesting is his "Bedside detection of awareness in the vegetative state: a cohort study" that he coauthored with a number of other clinicians. In case your journal search skills aren't up to snuff, Donna, then go to the hospital library and ask the librarian for the Dec. 17, 2011 issue of *The Lancet*. We still get paper copies.

16 As I mentioned before, this area needs research. Statistics are not kept for lethal violence against physicians, and only in the more sensational realms, like abortion, are cases easily found. There is useful published data in the literature but the data is inadequate because it is not prospective or comprehensive. The data I refer to is generated by occasional surveys, such as that of Baukje Miedema in the March 2010 issue of the *Canadian Family Physician*, which should serve as a good advertisement for the CIHR to encourage further research in the area by dangling a big grant.

nightmares in which I see Mr. Legaire hunting down my family, leaving me for last, then making me stick my hands behind my neck and feel the hole he made. The nightmares started in the coma and they haven't stopped in the ten years I've been on this chair.

In coma, I tried to combat bad dreams with good dreams. I tried to think of Noel and me on our wedding day, the wedding dress that really shouldn't have been white, or of my first day practising medicine as a real doctor. I wore a white, white coat, and it deserved to be the whitest white there was. But none of these good memory-dreams was strong enough to prevail. I was forced to learn therapeutic bad dreaming instead, cuing counter-nightmares to take the place of shooting nightmares. I dreamed of Mr. Legaire driving drunk, hitting another car, and killing all those inside—a mauve mommy, a stubbled daddy, a pink little girl, a baby boy with a truck design on the bib still attached to his neck. Mr. Legaire walked away from the dream-accident unharmed, not even looking to check on the other vehicle. Or, I dreamed I was sitting in the passenger seat of his Silverado, a seat belt noosed around my neck. Mr. Legaire muttered *bitch bitch bitch* with each escalating KPH. When he hit the car with the mommy, daddy, little girl, and baby boy, I flew out the windshield as the family was consumed in a petroleum-fuelled inferno. Before I hit the asphalt, I thought: *I tried to do something, I tried to stop this guy, I reported Mr. Legaire to the ministry.* Maybe these contra-dreams were the real reason why I finally moved my finger. Hearing Nurse Donna muse about "flicking the switch for this poor creature" was one thing, but letting Mr. Legaire kill a family was something I didn't let him do. So get the fuck up then, coma self, and spend less time dreaming about feeling your own aerated neck. All heroes have holes in them.[17]

It was a few back-and-forth days for me to get off the vent after the finger-move, though. Donna capitalized when Noel came in again: "Poor thing. No one knows what she knows. Hasn't moved that finger

---

17 Martin Luther King; Abraham Lincoln; to lesser degrees, the doctors who snitch on drunks and addicts; and, equally, everyone else throwing their life preservers to the dead, the life preserver being porous, gaping love.

since that one time. Maybe she was saying goodbye. Now what kind of a life will this be for her," Donna said, trying to kill me again.

Noel didn't say anything, the bastard, which meant he was thinking the same thing. I waved my finger slightly but the two of them didn't see it I guess. It took a lot for me to move the finger, and I was too exhausted to move it when the doctors wanted me to say "yes" and "no" to meaningless questions earlier in the day. Don't doctors have anything better to do in this cocooned unit of suspended animation?

Donna started talking piously about "progress" and "resources" again. Fuck Donna, why don't you just openly kill me, turn the drugs wide open, or the oxygen down low? She bent down to my face and in a sing-song voice said, "Dr. Gallu dear, do you want us to restart your heart if it stops? To breathe for you if you stop breathing?"

Donna, I'm a doctor, you said so yourself, I know what CPR[18] *is*. Outraged, my finger did the calypso. *Yes, yes. Yes yes yes. Yes. Yes.* God bless him, Noel pointed out that my finger seemed to be moving rather a lot, and in a regular rhythm.

As I said, Noel is a doctor. Part of the reason I come to these conferences is to prevent him from coming. The bastard left me a few months before I got shot. When I "came to," as Donna loved to put it, Donna made sure to tell me she knew Noel had been carrying on behind my back for a long time. "*Years*, Dr. Gallu. Years," she whispered. A cliché of marrying a doctor is to be left for the office secretary. Oh well. It could have been Donna. When I gained the strength to communicate my needs more reliably, the ICU staff sometimes asked me if I wanted them to call my husband. Wag wag.

Noel wasn't great in bed but the thing was, I made up for it. I thought he'd always be loyal, the milquetoast. But the same year I got shot, he got his secretary pregnant, and I hated them both speechlessly.

---

18 CPR: Cruel Punishment Ritual. Callous Perpetual Ruse. Complicated Prank Rub. Try this at home. (No, buy an AED...)

Deep in the afternoon, the data on Mr. Trivia's screen vaporizes in my vision. Fact after fact is much less important than the nap I need. At conferences, I nap in my chair. Brian hates my naps in chair, he frets I'll get a sore. Prissy Brian!

At the front of the room, Mr. Trivia looks fat and decrepit, a broken-down version of when he was in his prime. After asking the audience a question and getting no response, he flashes a Herman Cartoon of an Otolaryngologist Conference. The caption reads "So, you guys listening?"

Even Brian laughs at that one. "Doctors don't listen," he snickers at me. We agree.

Ten years ago, I would have raised my hand to answer Mr. Trivia's question. Ten years ago I was in love and I was young, too, with lustrous brown hair and lithe arms, I was what male colleagues called "pretty for a doctor."[19] I wish I had married him. I might not have had an answer for Mr. Trivia then, as now. When he presented at conferences, Noel always worried about the questions he'd face. So did I, so did I. Noel doesn't have to worry about me ever asking him why he left. Mr. Legaire took care of that.

In this room, I am a doctor again. I can no longer practise, I can't perform physical examinations, but I still learn what's wrong with people though, and with my eyes I can still diagnose. I see people on the street and diagnose them in secret. I've diagnosed Brian with two chronic diseases—diabetes mellitus and osteoarthritis.[20] We are

---

19 The first recorded female physician in history is Merit Ptah of the Bronze Age. The bronze beauty's face is part of her tomb in Saqqara, the necropolis of Ancient Egypt. Unfortunately, in the same terracotta picture she holds medical instruments, and I cannot hold a thing. Her coquettish smile must have served as a source of great healing.

20 I've diagnosed Brian with lots more, including, provisionally of course, various malignancies and life-threatening syndromes. But these two are the most reasonable and backed up by evidence. In terms of the osteoarthritis, Brian is slow-moving, rubs his joints, and stretches a lot. As for the diabetes, he has polydipsia and polyuria and he often falls asleep. Plus, he uses a glucometer. I am Sherlock on six wheels.

both growing older, he and I. Brian likes the food too much at these things—Brian, the seismologist of my finger.

I don't have my title on my credit card. I don't insist that Brian or anyone else refer to me as Doctor. This kind of grieving is almost as bad as needing a man.

While taking a pre-lunch, pre-Brian-scarfing nap, I dream I want to show everyone my scar. My hair hides a big keloid that grew to fill the bullet-excavated hole. In wakefulness I long to touch the scar, and in my dream I am able to reach up and feel it. Can I peel the scar back and pull out the buckshot still stuck in my spine? No, the scar is solid, it won't move. Giving up, I sit, completely still, sleeping and dreaming now of all the doctors down on their knees, praying to the all-powerful gods of information and knowledge,[21] the ones with the power to kill.

---

21 The gods of information, as expected by their plurality, are not part of a monotheism. The chieftain god, as Zeus was in Greek mythology, is Sirin, the god of lost information.

GORBLIMEY!

Poetry, crosses, and other birds of folly mix with the blood and pus filling my failing lungs. I thought I'd get dead by bullet or bomb, but instead I marinate in the damp and rain, the victim of pre-existing asthma. The war kills me non-violently.

Poetry is no ounce of cure, words won't cleanse my lungs. I won't survive the night if the field hospital moves, and if it doesn't move, I won't survive either—we'll be overrun by the advancing Germans. All men are dying somehow—in the bed, or holding a gun. I gag on secretions, but what's a little shortness of breath? Ah, to bellow a bawdy song for one and all from the top of my brimmed lungs:

> Don't want my cobblers minced with ball;
> For if I have to lose 'em
> Then let it be with Susan
> Or Meg or Peg or any whore at all,
>
> Gorblimey!

Why not sing? I sang these songs in the bars of France, surprising fellow officers with the uncouth common tunes. Now I sing for myself and other dying men, my mouth forming a terminal O, a pursed lip seal with the sky. Huff, puff, Elizabethan poetry's panoramic, rapturous, breathy O's stopper my lungs, the sound of the O shaking me, gagging me, cinching tight.

O is the poker tell of apostrophe, the first sound poets make when addressing the dead Renaissance masters, the dead Roman orators, the dead generals. I sing O, now,

to nurses,
to doctors,
to the folk of Wimeraux,
to horses,
to dogs,
to the dead.

Small arms fire crackles through the usual artillery noise—the Germans are close.

"Lisette, *run, go.*" O my nurse, so plain in your bluebird uniform but also so alive, so thin and efficient and birdlike, I know you won't. I wasted my strength singing the dirty lyrics. All that comes out of my mouth is wheeze and hack.

Five days ago I patched up poor men falling apart from war. A sewing sawbones, I staunched, excavated, ligated, decompressed, cannulated, irrigated, and salved. Like a lark, I felt above the fray. But I came down with a cough that rattled me until my hands were too weak to operate, and then I couldn't stand, and now I can't sing, not really.

After three days laid out flat on this cloth cot, I confess: I once dreaded bombs because I professionally witnessed the damage done to the human body, the wrecked limbs and open heads. I, the King of England's minion, meet the soldier as the nursery rhyme has it—*all the king's horses and all the king's men can't put Humpty together again.* But I never got hit by a bomb, I never did, I got hit by a fever. I should know by now, dead is dead, method doesn't matter. "Run, Lisette, get out of here."

War sounds move closer. I consider death by bullet, by bayonet. My body breaks of its own accord, sinking from infection. I rasp out,

> I don't want to be shot down;
> I'm really much more willing
> To make myself a killing,
> Living off the pickings of the Ladies of the Town;
> Don't want a bullet up my bumhole,
>
> Gorblimey!

The last private I saved, he thanked me. He lived to thank me because of a simple rule: he didn't bleed enough to die. Here, doctors keep men alive by stopping exsanguination. Tying and turning his vessels, cleaning the wound full of mud, I wondered: could faith fill this hole? The private said *Thank you*—and because he didn't die, he retained enough breath to speak. That was eight days ago, before the fever hit me.

We couldn't spare soldiers to evacuate the private from the front because every able-bodied man had to shoot guns. Now I lie beside the soldier who thanked me short days ago. In the end, I didn't save him—the only way he could have been saved is if he walked out of here, but he was too wounded, and he got the fever too. It's rare for a patient who comes to surgery to walk out of the hospital.

"Lisette, put a gun in my hand if you leave."

"John, there's the morphine –

"No, Lisette, I want to surprise the first Kraut that comes close." God, I wish she'd undress—slip out of the uniform, give me a taste of the bawdy.

If the Germans overrun my field hospital, I'll defend the dying men. Perhaps a bomb will hit the hospital first, in anticipation of McCrae and his necrotic army. I might not get to kill anyone. Perhaps the last brave lark I hear above the hospital will be blown to smithereens. From the direction of the latrine, someone sings:

> On Monday I touched her on the ankle,
> On Tuesday I touched her on the knee;
> On Wednesday such caresses
> As I got inside her dresses,
> On Thursday she was moaning sweetly;
>
> Gorblimey!

Generals die in bed. What kinds of beds? I'm a mere Lieutenant-colonel in a bloody cot, sheets stuck to my skin. I didn't just doctor human flesh, treating men in their sickbeds, I commanded them to fight as an officer in the artillery. Look around—I'm the highest-ranking dying man here. And the war, technically, didn't get me. I have the prestige of killing myself, asthma turning into pneumonia.

If shrapnel embeds anywhere except the bowels, the metal can be removed and the patient may live. But if the metal runs through the guts, then infection claims the soldier. Perhaps I am dying in a usual way, then.

Lisette, come close, touch me, bathe my brow. Run, get the hell out of here. The worst of all possible fates for the dying patient is to fall in love with his nurse. Naturally, the nurse thinks the dying man is delirious. The amused and sad corners of Lisette's mouth will be the last lips I ever see. I do need Lisette for one important thing: her pen, her paper, and her time.

I already wrote Jacqui in Montreal to tell her I love her. The chaplain took it three days ago on his way out of here, shaking his head at my pun, "The writing is on the wall." I wish I had sung to the bastard chaplain this verse:

> I don't want the Colonel's shilling,
> I don't want to be shot down;
> I'm really much more willing
> To make myself a killing,
> Living off the pickings of the Ladies of the Town;

But I thanked him instead.

Now Jacqui is far away, she'll marry well. Did I want to be remembered as a hero when I wrote her? Sick with waves of nausea and haze, I tried to be cheery:

Front
January 28, 1918

My dear, I can't see the sky. I've finally learned the needs of the human body after years of study. The human wishes for everything, endlessly. I cross myself before I operate, but not out of faith. Why should the useless chaplain be the only one to make the sign of the cross?

Touching each body, I think of you, Jacqui: of your laugh, of how we played doctor and nurse. I don't wish you here. I don't want death to touch you in letters and poems, or at all.

I miss you. When the war is over we'll raise a family in our little city of Montreal. I'll give up surgery and return to pathology, live the Canadian life. You'll give me children. I'll name the boys after poets. You'll pick the girl's names. We'll be married, have I ever mentioned that? We'll marry in Guelph at First Presbyterian, Pastor Luke will bless us, will say forever and ever. Every time I cross myself, I say I love you.

John.

Death is in us all. I told Jacqui the truth, the best truth I knew: what I wanted, what I wanted. After writing the letter, I fell asleep to dream of reaching into bloody crevasses of human bodies on operating tables. As I touched the wounded in my dream, I heard snippets of the Hippocratic Oath shouted in a German-accented voice:

I SWEAR BY PANACEA   TO PLEASE NO ONE   MY LIFE AND MY ART

The voice intoned the phrases when I touched the patients and fell silent when I removed my hands.

I visited French graveyards too much. I'd like to see one now. I used to leave the operating theatre between cases and walk to the unit graveyard. Poppies crawled around crosses. Men identified by their names on the crosses exist in the doctor's mind as records of injury: there, a man dead from arteries that couldn't be ligated in time; there, a fellow who died from a post-operative infection, his guts blown up, his smile so happy when he saw his surgeon. After a few minutes of contemplating the poppies, I'd return to the theatre. Blood wiped away, a fresh and living body placed on the table, it was time to wash my hands and amputate an arm or a leg.

Men convalescing in the hospitals of the English countryside sing this song, I hear them in this fever-dream:

> Now the next thing we'll pray for, we'll pray for some cunt.
> And if we only get some it will make us all grunt,
> And if we have one cunt may we also have ten,
> May we have a fucking knockshop, said the soldier, Amen!

> Now the next thing we'll pray for, we'll pray for our Queen,
> To us a bloody old bastard she's been,
> And if she has one son, may she also have ten,
> May she have a bloody regiment, said the soldier, Amen!

The cemetery crosses lean against one another due to the blasts, toppled and broken, resting on beds of poppies. In the unit cemetery, two poor soldiers are condemned to dig six foot slots in the earth, timelessly moving across the field. Even now I hear them dig, their round shovels hitting stones.

War obeys the principle of hemostasis: get control above and below the vessel. A few days before I wrote to Jacqui, I operated on a man with shrapnel close to the femoral artery. I worked against time, removing the pieces while a clamp was placed above and below the artery. To fix the problem, the bleeding has to stop—the surgeon must have control above and below the injured vessel.

Snapping the vascular clamps shut, I knew the soldier would never use the right leg again. But I saved it, he'd still have a leg. He'd live. When I saw him the day after the surgery, he thanked me, still pale from blood loss. "Doc McCrae sir, I'll be going to England now, I imagine! Well, the very best to you now. The men sing your praises, sir, we know if we get sick or injured, you'll be here for us."

The soldier was right. He should transfer to England at a convalescent hospital in the countryside, the saved leg to drag behind him for the rest of his life. But I didn't have the heart to tell him that the transports had stopped. Shelling increased, becoming relentless, allowing nothing to move. He's in the corner now, begging to be taken away. In medical school, I stared at the front of the lecture hall the same way he looks at the tent ceiling.

I'm dying. Everyone in this place wants to dictate a letter. We're filled with last words, but the nurses are too busy and few to be secretaries. I could use my rank and relationship with the nurses to get a letter out, but I can't breathe. If I catch my breath, what I dictate must be short, the length of a poem. Something about men lying in graves as the living above dance with guns. To help with the meter of my poem, I think of this verse:

> I don't want to be a soldier,
> I don't want to go to war;
> I'd rather hang around
> Piccadilly underground,
> Living on the earnings of a high born lady;
> I'd rather stay in England,
> Merry, merry England,
> And roger all my bleeding life away,
>
> Gorblimey!

The only singing the chaplain did was make canticles over the ancient wounds of graves. I heard him in the cemetery when I amputated. Lisette looks like a nun. I won't sing the verse to her, she'll think I am in shock. "Lisette, please, yes. Come here. Something short I want you. To write down. Please. Write this down:

> That's the wrong way to tickle Mary,
> That's the wrong way to kiss!

Don't you know that over here, lad,
They like it best like this!
Hooray pour le Francais!
Farewell, Angleterre!
We didn't know the way to tickle Mary,
But we learned how, over there!

Lisette's hand loosely moves over the page—too quickly, and with her eyes looking at me and not at what she's writing. She smiles; she is humouring me. I will die being humoured. Did I humour men like this? I did, by touching men in the operating room of dreams.

Blood stains Lisette's blue uniform. She has blue eyes like the chaplain's, implacable blue. Responsible for a dozen other patients, Lisette looks to another man. I say, "Lisette. Please. I know more men are coming in. Another man will take this very cot soon. Please. Write this down. I was going to write a poem days ago. Forgot to. I had operated all day and all night. But I'm ready now. Yes. Thank you! In Flanders Fields the poppies blow…"

STAGES OF CHANGE IN A FAMILY DOCTOR'S LIFE

INTERVIEWING

Sean is in the plane, leaving destination three of twelve, thinking: *Why?* Ten thousand dollars to make the whole circuit, so why interview at every school when the only question being asked is *Are you trouble?* It's obvious that Sean will be trouble. Why do they ask him to come anyway?

Sean answered the question truthfully in Halifax, St. John's, and Ottawa, but still has nine more schools to go. Near the end of the last interview, Sean decided to tell the doctors about Joey, a kid he knew from grade seven home room at Harold Peterson Junior High. Joey kept Reuben, an anatomically correct orange figurine with a giant erect penis, on top of his desk. Joey screamed if Mr. Estabrooks tried to take Reuben away. "*My* Reuben," Joey said, as if this were prison and Mr. Estabrooks was fingered to die in the yard.

In the cramped chair, Sean anticipates the questions he'd face in Kingston, his next destination. The story he told about Reuben didn't go over well in Ottawa. Should Sean mention Joey and Reuben again, but then pretend to interview himself, with his left hand making the blah-blah-blah gesture, *And Sean tell me how did that make you feel, having to deal with Reuben's big dick on a daily basis?*

Wasn't it a family doctor's job to listen to the stories of other people? *Interviewing is stupid,* he thinks, as he takes the tray table down from the seat ahead. Sean wishes he had a picture of Joey and

Reuben to show the next "interviewing team," two dumbass doctors with all the PR skill of an oxycontin prescription. Sean knows this wish confirms he *is* trouble for any family medicine residency director.

Like all the other students before they hopped their cross-country planes, Sean prepares in his bathroom mirror, rehearsing stock answers to standard questions. He hates looking at his grotesque, fake face. He wants to stick his fingers in his cheeks and slobber out, *I was born on a pirate ship.*

Sean imagines the Kingston-bound 737 as a flying replica of Reuben's orange penis. But thoughts of Reuben are replaced with rehearsed thoughts of why he wants to become a family doctor and why he wants to live in—**Insert Stop 4/12**—Hello, Cleveland! Er, I mean, Kingston!

Yes, Sean would be trouble for anyone. He daydreams of Reuben moving orangely, agilely, and erectly through a wooded scene, commanding a platoon of green army men. A green army man salutes Reuben, shows his commanding officer a melted green bazooka and says, looking at his boss's unrealistic erection, "We need more firepower sir, yes sir!"

Successful applicants to residency programs pretend to have never hurt a patient. Out the window, a floor of cloud hangs from the plane. Sean remembers *The Shawshank Redemption*, a movie in which Morgan Freeman, playing a murderer serving a life sentence, tells the parole board every year that he is reformed. Every year, parole is denied. But one year Freeman tells the truth: he admits he killed a man, that at the time he was glad he killed the man, and for a long time he was only sorry that he got caught. But now that he's old, he wants to get out of prison and live as a free man for the time he has left. And he wants to stay free—what would be the point of coming back?

What would Dr. Reuben say when asked, "How do you feel about death?" Maybe he'd say, "Patients die the same way." So far, Sean's interviews were conducted in examining rooms with emphysema posters coating the walls and medical textbooks straining the shelves. How much personality should a doctor *display*, let alone *have*? Where are the pictures of family in these rooms? Do the best doctors shed their own personality? Sean's problem was excess of personality. Drifting off to sleep, he dreams of Reuben's orange penis poking through puffy white cloud, threatening to puncture the aircraft.

Reuben picks Sean up at the Kingston Airport in an orange checkered cab. "Where you headed?" Reuben asks.

"I need answers from you, Reuben, *answers*," Sean says, "not questions." Sean shakes his head. "The university, Reuben, and step on it. I need to see if I'm family doctor material."

Jetlagged, Sean waits an hour before he's called to the interview. He tramps through a hallway and sits in a family doctor's examining room. Emphysema posters, check. Twenty-year-old textbooks, check. Critical lack of personality, check.

"My name's Dr. Pilon. I'll be interviewing you today. Have a seat," the grey-haired doctor says as she walks into the room. A single picture of some other female physician shaking the hand of another indeterminate-age physician adorns the office—this isn't Dr. Pilon's office then? "Sean, it says in your letter that you like to fly fish. Could you tie a knot for me, please?" Dr. Pilon hands Sean some line she takes from her pocket. Sean notices she wears an engagement ring with a very large diamond.

"But what kind of knot do you want? There's lots of knots," Sean says.

"Just tie one of the knots you ... use... when you fly fish," the doctor says, uncertain.

"Are we going fishing later? Are you trying to land me?" Sean says, tying a clinch knot. Turning his head this way and that, he says, "Where's Moby? I'm gonna land me a Moby."

"So you *can* fly fish. That's real. Good. We just wanted to know. Everything else in your resume in the 'extracurriculars' is impossible to check. So I believe you." She broke into a big grin. "I believe you, including the... it says here... underlava basket weaving," she says, the grin turning into a smirk.

Family Medicine, here comes Sean.

FIFTH YEAR OF PRACTICE

'Twas the night before Christmas, Telehealth in Toronto fields a call from a drinker of Stolichnaya. Sean knows him well—the tottering Mr. Basque. According to the laws of consumption obeyed by all humans, Mr. Basque drinks more on holidays.

"Do you have to go?" Sean's wife asks.

"I think so," Sean says. He isn't sure. If Mr. Basque dies, no one would care. Based on that logic, Sean says, "He's the kind of guy who needs visiting the most."

Sean's clinic was booked lightly that day because no one wants to see the doctor on Christmas Eve. Unless they have to, and even then, can't it wait until the party's over? Mr. Basque put off calling to the last minute. Sean drives to his patient's trailer in Stanley Park after listening to the Telehealth nurse's tale at nine at night. Vancouver may have the huge public space of the same name, but it has nothing on the small-scale genteel poverty of Erin, Ontario's version of Stanley Park: a small creek winds through trailer homes, dogs run wild and bite the weak and the small. Mr. Basque lives in a narrow cigar box home, a woodstove puffing out smoke signals from the chimney. He has no car in his gravel driveway and walks everywhere he needs to go because Sean reported him to the ministry of transportation five years ago. Mr. Basque never fails to bring this matter up every time Sean leaves the office to visit him in Stanley Park. "You took my license, so it's you, doctor, *you* who should come to see *me*."

The trailer home door swings inward into empty bottles. Dressed in a dirty suit, tie smart but stained, Mr. Basque slurs *Hrrmpo* and waves towards the kitchen table. Empty forty-ouncers sit on the table like they're part of a hopeless game of dominoes. Alcohol put Mr. Basque beyond speech, or so Sean thinks, until Mr. Basque says, "Remember my son? He died from the meningitis on Christmas Eve. I wish there was a doctor who cared half as much about him as you care about my goddamn driving."

Is it right not to believe in someone? Sean doesn't believe in Mr. Basque. They met five years ago for the first time. At the end of that interview, Mr. Basque said, "There's no hope for me." Sean didn't believe him then, but Mr. Basque was right.

After mentioning his son for this, the hundredth time, Mr. Basque turns his back in the chair and sobs. On previous visits to the trailer home, Sean asked Mr. Basque about his family, if he had enough money to live. The bottles on the table are partial answers to those questions. *Does he call me only when the alcohol's gone?* Sean asks himself.

Mr. Basque tries to tell Sean about love. "I love," he said. "I love," slamming the table with his fist. "I love!" he shouts, beating his breast.

The solution to this man's predicament is simple: love's not enough. "You love what?" Sean asks.

"I love. Love I love. I love." Mr. Basque hits the table harder, making the shoulders of the bottles fall into one another. "I fuckin' love."

What's to love? The burnt carpets, small cupboards, and full ashtrays of this trailer? The windows frost over as Sean surveys the scene. Mr. Basque hangs no pictures, stacks no books. Either he moves on from love or he stays with the subject, it is hard to tell: 'But," he stutters. "B-but, bb-but, but but, but."

Sean tries to finish his sentence. "But I love?" Sean says.

"No, no, no, I love, I love, b-but."

Mr. Basque only ever had one child, a boy who died from meningitis. Sean helps Mr. Basque get up from his chair and onto his dirty bed on the opposite side of the wood stove. Mr. Basque falls hard onto the mattress.

Sean thinks of his wife in bed at home. What would Sean tell her of this night? To anything he'd say, she'd say "Not worth it."

But I want to help him. That's worth it.

Sean leaves Mr. Basque snoring loudly, one-hundred-proof drool pooling on the pillow. On the drive back to Guelph, Sean witnesses a whitening Christmas, a few deer hoofing the snow at the wooded borders of a farmer's field. Sled paths of children and the heavy boots of parents stretch further into the forest. The highway wears light white dust.

ON ACCOUNT OF, YOU KNOW, THE HOLOCAUST

At The Manor Home's nursing desk, Sean reads Eliza's latest writings:

> The guards. The guards. The guards serve arsenical coffee laced with cyanide and perked inside of boots. See my number, it's on my arm. Shout to commandant: 87134523.

Sean hears Maureen coo, "Now Eliza what's gotten in to you? You've shredded your napkin. Aren't you going to eat your dinner?"

Sean happens to be reading Eliza's writings as already jotted on napkins. Napkins are Eliza's preferred parchment. He keeps on reading:

> Starve and die. Starve and die. So many of us imprisoned by this commandant Sean. To survive is to witness. The commandant Sean only comes around once; he comes and in his wake Zyklon-B billows. All things die in the commandant's face—even the memory of my Josef.

"Eliza, there's no reason to be upset!" Maureen trills. "My dear, you're so agitated! Do you want that little pill to put under your tongue? Should I call the doctor?" Sean already knows why Eliza's upset, knows Eliza will refuse the sedative. She's not here, she's in Ravensbruck circa 1942. She's there for a few days at a time, until she's not. He continues to read:

> Here, they are good enough to offer you poison for the tongue—poison snowflakes, a cyanide Eucharist. The commandant's face is a Luger. They did experiments on my bones, they took my bones and they didn't give them back. I screamed when they took my bones.

Sean leaves the napkin scrawls at the nursing station and walks down the hall to Eliza's room. Maureen looks terrified; Eliza has a paperweight ready to throw. Sean looks Eliza in the eye from the doorway and tries to reassure her. "Eliza, it's the doctor. Remember me? You're confused and you're scared but we're here to take care of you, we always have been and we always will."

Eliza throws the snow globe at Maureen's head and connects. The globe breaks open, glass cutting the nurse's face. "Ha-ha-ha!" Eliza says, pumping her fist. Sean tries to grab Eliza but the spry old lady dodges the doctor. Eliza runs past the bleeding Maureen but slips on the blood and the water and falls on her right hip. A napkin falls out of Eliza's pocket and soaks up the wet, drowning these words:

> The Germans are trying to hurt me. I see goose-stepping jackboots that become the dainty slippers of pain. Long trench coats become pain's smoking-room gowns. How many pain units can be crammed into one cattle car?

Sean grabs a pillow from Eliza's bed and puts it under her head. Maureen yells, "Help! Call an ambulance!"

Sean says, "Maureen, I'll have a look at the cut. You don't need to call an ambulance."

"Not my face, Sean," Maureen says. "For Eliza. Look at her leg. Her hip's broken, right?"

Probably yes. It looks shortened, externally rotated. But I'd have to examine her, Sean thinks.

Eliza yells, "I don't want to go to the chambers! Don't take me! Pain is good for my bones. My hip isn't broken! *Aufseherin.* Save me!"

Covering the cut on her forehead with one hand, Maureen walks out of the room. Her bottle-blonde hair drips blood. Eliza tries to fight off three male orderlies with three beating limbs, the broken one still and restful.

"Stop fighting us, Eliza! We're trying to get you back into bed!" Maureen yells from down the hall. She's concerned, she hears the men grunt and struggle. Eliza has brittle bones, she could break more than she has. "Eliza, I'm your nurse. I've taken care of you for over a year! You're all right! Your leg might be broken and you broke your snow globe on my face and I'm cut but you're all right!"

Eliza relaxes. "That's right, Eliza, that's the spirit!" Sean says. "Bed *is* good. It's good. We'll get you to bed and then I'll examine you."

Hearing this, Eliza starts to kick and flail again. "Commandant! 87134523. God knows this number. You never look on a face more than twice."

"Let me look at the leg, Eliza," Sean says. "Eliza, let me! I only want to see if it's really broken."

Maureen returns with a towel pressed against her forehead. A red blotch spreads in the centre of the towel. "We should get a painkiller. There's no need for her to be in pain," Sean says. "Maureen, draw up some Demerol, twenty-five milligrams. I'll inject it."

"She thinks we're trying to kill her. If we give her a needle, she'll think that even more," Maureen says.

"I have a secret name in a secret place. I am Eliza. My name means my god is a vow. Commandant can't help me, my number is too great," Eliza says. Then: "OWWWW!"

"I know it hurts. Here you go, Eliza. A little pinch. That's good." As he slips the needle in, Sean looks quickly at her hip. Yes—broken.

"What did you call the commandant's face? Eh, *Aufseherin?* Retired?" Eliza asks Maureen.

"I'm a what, Eliza?" Maureen asks, forgiving the old woman with the broken leg.

Sean talks on the phone to an orthopod. "Mrs. Eliza Brandt, a ninety-three-year-old woman, fell and probably broke the right hip. She's agitated. I've given her something to calm her down. But the pain's bad and I don't want to overdo it and sedate her too much. She was experimented on in Germany. That's her you hear in the background—she's screaming. There go the sheets." Sean puts the phone on his shoulder, says "Maureen, let's get something back on her okay?"

Maureen makes a face. "Wow, Sean, thank you *so much* for your medical expertise, I didn't know patients *weren't supposed* to be naked, in full view of everyone!"

Sean registers he's pissed Maureen off by avoiding the conflict totally. He puts the phone back over his ear. *I'm sorry* he mouths in a few beats at Maureen, whose towel is now sopping with blood. "What's she screaming?"

(*"Aufseherin! Aufseherin!"*)

"Yeah. You can hear that in the background?... She *is* loud! She thinks she's back in the concentration camp. Huh? See if she has pulses and sensation in the right leg? Well. That's hard to do. All right. Fine." Sean has to work a full day at the clinic tomorrow. It's three a.m. He's fifty-six years old. If only his wife were alive, waiting for him in their bed.

"Here he is! Silent like a star. Commandant, examine my flesh. Look at my number! You gave me this number!"

Sean puts his hand over the receiver for a moment. "Eliza, I don't tell people what to do. I just ask people for things. I'm not here to hurt you. I know about your tattoo. We have to fix your leg." Sean lifts the sheet Maureen's been battling to keep on Eliza. "Eliza, I need to see the leg. The tattoo, I know you have it on your arm. I know!" Sean feels the still leg while the free leg tries to smash his face. "Okay! I feel a posterior tibial! Great. Eliza. Did you feel me touch you there?"

"Commandant?" Eliza asks quizzically, reaching back with her unbroken leg. Sean looks up to see her heel smash his chin.

Sean speaks into the receiver again.

"Yeah, sorry, I know you're busy. Sorry about putting you on hold. But this is a bit of a situation. Thanks for your help. Right. Look, I'm really sorry to keep you waiting," Sean says. He can't talk into the phone hands-free, his chin hurts too much.

"Aufseherin! Blonder Engel. Das Tier von Ravensbruck!"

"Great. Thanks for seeing her," Sean said. "Oh. Well, there's no family to call for consent. There's no next-of-kin. On account of, you know. The Holocaust. Yeah—no operation means pneumonia and she dies." The old doctor takes down the stethoscope from his neck, rubs his eyes.

"You are beautiful and calm, commandant," Eliza says.

"Give her an Ativan if she'll take it, Maureen. One milligram."

"Here, Eliza." Maureen says. "The doctor ordered this too. No, don't spit it out Eliza! You need medicine. We're here to keep you comfortable!"

"Stick a needle in my eye."

"I don't think she understands anything, Maureen. She's just throwing out word-salad," Sean says. "I wonder what gives her these deliriums."

Eliza's head rolls on the gurney. "You all look like deathshead. Rape two women a day, mornings and evenings, and then kill the chattel when you're done. You whisper their camp number into their ear before pulling the trigger and shooting them in the ears, their numbers are the last thing the women hear before they die."

Maureen smooths Eliza's hair. "Eliza, please take this. I don't want you to be in any more pain. There's no reason to. No reason to—let me just, there."

"*Danke Aufseherin.*" In a minute, the old woman settles. She's as comfortable as she's ever been, a broken leg, the pain shoved down into unconsciousness.

Sean walks back to his old car and drives home, passing a quiet ambulance on the way. He's got a whole house to himself.

JITTERS

Medical school is a responsibility game. Real responsibility only comes when Mark graduates and enters the land of My-name-is-on-the-chart, meaning: this patient, this *human*, is mine to watch live or die. As a student loafing on the wards, Mark watched others who *were*; and watching real doctors only confirmed he wasn't ready.

Janet, Mark's girlfriend, sleeps through the five a.m. buzzer. *Buzzz buzzz buzzz buzzz. Get. The. Fuck. Up.* Mark needs her to kiss him as if everything will be all right on this, his first day of real responsibility. She sleeps on, hibernating past the sound.

The hospital budgets for winter. A fleet of front-end loaders clears snow from sidewalks. *Snow is the ultimate weather of anxiety*, Mark thinks at his most aphoristic. *Or should it be: Snow is the weather of ultimate anxiety?* Through the locked glass doors, he sees the dark coffee shop meant for daytime folk—open nine to five. He knows the cafeteria deeper inside the hospital will open at six a.m. He wears a white coat the hospital mailed him a week ago, with D-R M-A-R-K A-N-G-O-I-S-S-E embroidered in red on the right upper pocket. Pens, prescription pads, manuals, and reference books fill all the coat pockets as the stigmata of real responsibility.

Getting away without a white coat—that's for medical students or for staff physicians. Residents are like construction workers, they need to wear their gear, but so that other people are safe. Mark's battle-hardened pager is ready to ring, but Mark isn't ready for it to ring, he isn't ready for anything.

A scene plays in his mind: a barrel-chested old man tries to die in a hospital bed. The team requires direction from the team leader. In a few seconds, Mark horrifyingly sees that *he* is in the scene, that *he* is now the leader of the team. The resuscitation must start but Mark, paralyzed by the terror of being team leader, can only croak out, "Whaaaaaaaa—aaaaa—aaat?"

What was the children's game he used to play, walking behind his older brother, throwing his arms out and screaming *Poop* at the top of his lungs? Follow the leader. The last brother standing gets to be the new leader. The daydream rolls a little more: instead of smooth orders from a calm Mark, he sees himself babble *Shit, I'm not ready!* in Ojibway, Aztec, Sumerian, and finally Morse. DASH LONG DASH! he screams. Monitors attached to the dying man sing like the muses, and in his daydream, Mark does the one-hundred-metre dash out of the room and out of the hospital.

It's my first day as a resident, this is normal, Mark thinks. *I'm a sort-of real doctor now. I can't use the excuse of "just a medical student" anymore.* Confidence is something Mark is wistful about on the walk to the hospital. *The confident doctors are the ones who've killed people and know the mistakes not to make again, or the confident doctors are cons, quacks.* Mark fixes on an image of Janet as he left her ten minutes ago, her long black hair covering her back, still sleeping in their bed.

Eighth floor. He's thirty minutes early, the caf's not open. Soon, sullen union staff will man the counters. In the cordoned-off cafeteria, a man wearing a hairnet fills his coffee mug by dipping the mug into a huge vat. Another man wearing a Jolly Roger surgical cap pushes a broom in the corner. Coffee is Mark's aqua vita, his ritual, but the union guys will not let a doctor past the ropes, no exceptions.

On the outside looking in at coffee, Mark's thoughts turn to his obsession, death. *Why does North American culture require doctors to preside over death?* Mark thinks. *Why are hospitals organized, completely, against death? Doctors adopt the role of priest, hovering over dying men and women and following last-rites protocols. Every single misbegotten beat of the heart requires a special ritual. Are doctors the right witnesses?* Mark was a strange medical student. Everyone else wanted to put on the paddles. He wanted to think about the metaphorical implications of shocking a body back to life.

Mark reviews last-rites protocol as he waits for the cafeteria to open, passive-aggressively standing just behind the cordon. Reviewing the steps is comforting. He considers the word epinephrine, shortened at the death-bedside to *epi*. Mark considers the short-form, compares it to hip hop slang. *If you know da code, raise your syringes in the air, shout EPI like ya just don't care!* Long ago the Americans coined the word epinephrine, but Mark much prefers adrenaline, an older, British, word. Adrenaline is the word used in the rest of the world—why is medicine fetishistic about jargon, why must there be at least two names for every important medical condition, pharmaceutical, and clinical sign?

Answer: two names for a single thing increase the chance of forgetting both names. The more names there are for a drug, a treatment, or condition, then the less real it is, the less it can help. In an emergency, the team leader needs a lot of fudge factor.

Alternatives to *epi* depend on the whims of the wayward heart: vasopressin for one deadly arrhythmia, calcium and atropine for another. The protocol drugs are the closest Mark comes to poetry in the hospital. The protocol enacts meter, too, the counting of beats: how many chest compressions to breaths? Answer: the ratio 30:2.

Mark takes a deep breath, 30:2 his new om. He inhales more anxiety. 30:2. *Epi.*

A page detonates overhead: *Doctor STAT to 8012, code blue.* There are many code colours on Mark's protocol sheet: white for violence, red for fire, brown for chemical spill (code brown, Mark joked, when walking past a patient reeking from an enema). Blue is Mark's personal colour, though not his favourite, the colour meant for him and the waiting dead body. In the hospital, firemen run to code reds, and police run to the whites, but blue is Mark's hue.

Mark imagines someone else, a more competent doctor, running to the bedside of the dead. *The protocol is being followed right now*, he thinks, aware of the awesome rite, a protocol placard in his hand. *Should I go to 8012 and peek in?* he thinks. *But I might have to lead the team, and, technically, I'm not officially a code team leader for another hour and ten minutes. In ten minutes, at six a.m., the cafeteria opens. I need a coffee.* The hairnet guy dips his cup into the huge vat again.

At seven a.m., Mark is scheduled to work his first real minute as a real doctor. Starting early is bad luck. When Mark held his degree in his hand at convocation, he didn't feel like a doctor. He kissed Janet robotically—"You're a doctor now!" she said, truly happy for him. He didn't feel a thing, except scared.

Mark wills the cafeteria to open as other people arrive to wait with him, uniforms announcing their role. Commissionaire. Cleaner. Nurse. The cleaner razzes the two Food Services slowpokes, saying "Hey guys, does a few minutes really matter when you're on the clock anyway?" but the slowpokes laugh.

The guy in the surgical cap says, "Good things come to those who wait."

Feeling like an imposter, Mark waits for another doctor to come, whitecoated or not, someone who possesses the knowledge he covets. Mark can't talk about anxiety with his friends because if he talks about it, his friends tell him *Everyone feels this way when they start out.* His friends lie. They are doctors inside, but he isn't. They entered the land of experience long ago, throwing themselves at every clinical opportunity. *Dead and dying bodies, HOORAY!* But Mark was famous as a medical student for avoiding every single code blue he could.

Avoid enough things and you are an imposter, he thinks. *Or should it be: avoid ultimate things and you are an imposter?* A bunch of people run by, pushing a crash cart, heading for trouble.

What the hell am I doing? Mark asks himself as he follows the sprinters. At the end of the dash, a morbidly obese internist leads the code blue. Mark looks at his own slender arms and legs and compares them to the internist's huge billows of dough. "Get me the 3 Mac blade. This woman had head and neck surgery a week ago? A fucking flap? Great," the doctor says to a grim nurse with a clipboard.

"Yeah, you know us, the head and neck floor," the nurse says, screwing up her face. "Same time, same station. I was thinking we'd turn this floor into a secret wing."

The fat man grabs the blade a respiratory tech hands him. He fastens the blade to the laryngoscope. "Well, let me see," he says. "It does feel like same place, same station. Another cancer disaster operated on by Dr. Fleischman, the reclaimer of the doomed. You say *full code* and she's post-op from squamous cell cancer of the throat, Stage III. She never should have had surgery in the first place! Oh, and let's not forget you found her here and the last check was before she fell asleep five hours ago. It all sounds familiar to me."

Clipboard nurse wants to eat Fat Man's head and neck, but instead she just writes the comments down, verbatim, smiling.

Mark looks at the patient with yellowed fingers and corpse appearance. The crash cart monitor shows asystole, the flatline. Fat Man's mad, he knows he's about to perform the ultimate ritual in hopeless circumstances. Fat Man tries to bend the old woman's fingers. "See," he says. "Stiff. This woman is dead. Full code my fat ass." Fat Man looked at the nurse with the clipboard. "You tell Fleischman I said that, too."

"You tell Fleischman I said that, too," she says deadpan, writing furiously.

Fat Man tries to snake the endotracheal tube in but meets resistance. "Hey, this woman can't even move her damn neck! Are you sure she wasn't dead *yesterday*?" The nurses stop compressions. Fat Man gives epi, Oh epi. One mg, another. Fat Man calls the code after seven minutes, unable to get the tube in, the drugs unable to revive the mutilated woman. Finally registering the presence of Mark, the wallflower in the white coat, he says, "I hate the day before the residents come on service," he says. "I could have been sleeping right now. Who the fuck are you?"

"I'm Dr. Angoisse. The...

Doctors are trained to catastrophize, they think of the worst possible outcomes in order to be prepared for those outcomes. Instead of thinking of the worst outcome for a patient, though, he thought of the worst outcome for himself: he'd be alone at code blues with real doctors like Fat Man ten minutes from the hospital by car.

... the new resident for the floor."

Fat Man taps Mark on the forehead. "Hey. C'mon, then. Rounds." Fat Man walks out of the room and into the hall. Mark follows as Fat Man walks-and-talks. "Eighth floor admits the usual: emphysema, regurgitant hearts, pneumonia... that's us, bread and butter, medical patients. We just wasted our time in Fleishman's Future Graveyard, the head and neck cancer horror show. The body falls ill in a set number of ways. For us, it's bad hearts and lungs, but for Fleishman, it's cancer and his Hail Mary approach. Statistically speaking, ten percent of your patients die each month."

Fat Man reaches into a pocket and pulls out a breath mint. "I need to shower. I hate sleeping in here. That's for you and for patients. And it's too bad you didn't help with that dead lady. Would have been a perfect code for you too since she was dead, D-E-A-D, you couldn't have done a damn thing wrong. Okay, let's start rounds." Fat Man grabs the chart carousel and pretends he's a crash-test dummy, slamming the charts against the weak wood of the nursing station. *Boom boom boom.*

Fat Man rolls through the ward like a wrecking ball, bashing the carousel into doors and walls. With his eyebrow raised, he asks Mark, "Isn't a hospital the ultimate smash up derby? Write this shit down, Dr. Angoisse. Every time I tell you to do something, write it down." Fat Man snorts, handing Mark a piece of paper, then miming surprise as he comically searches in his pocket for a pen. "I understand. You don't have *paper*. You need a *pen*." Fat Man pulls a pen from his ass. "A magic trick!" he says. "Very handy, you know." Mark takes the pen and writes down all the Fat Man's orders for the fifty patients of the eighth floor. "You go see the asshole Snide now. He's one of your future corpses, I hope. Do a peritoneal tap on him. All right. Time for my office. Don't bug me—I am in a cone of silence for the next six hours."

Mark writes "abdominocentesis—Snide" on the paper.

Mark enters Mr. Snide's room once Fat Man leaves for his clinic. Snide smoked and drank too much in life, and in his bed, recovering from a Fleischman special, he bragged to his nurses that he'd smoke and drink when he got out of the hospital, too. Fleischman could pick them, it seems. Snide's chest sounds like a death rattle. As Mark tells him to take deep breaths, he expectorates blood-tinged gobs. "So you want to be a doctor, eh?" Mr. Snide asks after horking up red phlegm.

Mark thinks, *I am a doctor.* But he knows the fact is unconvincing even to himself. Mr. Snide knows a confidence problem when he sees one. He says, "Being a doctor is showing up for work and hearing assholes like me complain. That's all anyone ever wants from their doctor—show up and listen. Don't get me wrong, I don't want *you* to *listen*, I'm not *gay*. I'm not *needy*. I just want you to fill that white coat you got on your back and do the shit that gets me out of here." Mr. Snide coughs, inspects the results in the tissue, and nods.

"And what would you listen to if I talked anyway, which I won't. Well, I might tell you about my third wife, the witch who never comes to see me. Or my kids who learned not to come from her." Mark is thinking about how he is but isn't a doctor and loses track of the conversation.

"Who learned what?" Mark asks.

"C'mon lad, keep up with me here," Mr. Snide says.

As patient, Mr. Snide outclasses me. He is more of a real patient than I am a real doctor, Mark thinks. Mark nods and says: "I'm listening. I'm concentrating too though. I'm putting out the tools I need to do the procedure."

"Good," Snide said. "You're getting it! Have reasons not to listen! Be distracted! And have you ever done one of these belly taps before?" Mr. Snide asks.

"A few."

"I'll tell you how well you do by how well I feel, it's a deal. Where was I? For god's sake, don't be confused. I don't care if you make me *better.*" Mr. Snide bends his left hand into a fey gesture, but then balls both hands into fists, coughing until he vomits over his bedsheet. The sheet is now a mosaic of white, green, and red. Snide wipes his chin with his hand. "Doctor, get me something to barf into," he commands.

Mark shoots off in search of a kidney basin. *Maybe the dry supply room?* he thinks. *Where is dry supply?* To help his anxiety, Mark turns his thoughts to the etymology of the word adrenaline: Latin for above (*ad*) and kidney (*renes*). He passes the dry supply room five times until he finally stops, walks slower, pays attention. In the room, dozens of turquoise plastic kidney basins are stacked onto shelves. Bedsheets lean in piles on the countertop. *Why do we have so many nasogastric tube kits?* Mark thinks. *How many kits does one ward need?*

When Mark returns to Mr. Snide's room, a nurse named Annette changes the sheets. Green tributaries flow down Mr. Snide's chin. Snide says, "Here's another lesson. Never do a job that someone else will do for you. Never do a job that I want a pretty nurse to do." Snide's a lecher, making grabby hand gestures at Annette. She ignores him. Mark likes Mr. Snide. As pure experience, Snide makes Mark's anxiety go away.

But Mark can't do what the Fat Man wants. Mr. Snide is too nauseated, so the procedure is postponed until tomorrow. Mark spends the rest of that first day checking labs and chasing down x-ray reports. He waits for the code blue page while calculating if Fat Man has enough adipose tissue to theoretically provide enough energy to run around Earth's equator. Mark considers calling Fat Man about Mr. Snide's nausea but Fat Man had tasked him with dozens of items during rounds, better to have most of those done before bothering Fat Man with the first obstacle.

When the penultimate task is completed, checking an insertion of a nasogastric tube on a Fleischman wreck, Mark hears the overhead page in the bathroom of the radiology department: "CODE BLUE, 8019, CODE BLUE, 8019." Mark's pager does the macarena.

8019 is Snide's room. Mark runs to the stairwell and climbs the eight floors to the ward. The crash cart sits patiently at the bedside. Four nurses lean over Mr. Snide: one at the head, pushing air into the lungs with a bag-valve-mask. Another performs chest compressions. The third tries to get a vein in the left arm. A fourth sticks electrodes on Mr. Snide's chest. When Mark arrives, the women look at Mark with something like maternal conciliation. "Yes, doctor," the one at Mr. Snide's head said. "What do you want to do now?"

Another nurse appears—the one that despised Fat Man. The nurse at Mr. Snide's head says to her, "Hey, Loretta. You chart, okay?"

"Kay," Loretta responds, picking up the clipboard from the cart.

The monitor shows asystole. Mark knows what to do. Epi, epi, epi.

"You're putting the tube in, right?" the nurse at the head says, squeezing the bag.

"Yes, right," Mark says. The nurse at the head guides Mark through every proper part of the protocol, including the order for epinephrine. Mr. Snide remains dead. Fat Man arrives in the room to hear Mark feebly call the code. "Time of death, 4:10 p.m."

"How did the tap go?" the Fat Man asks, nervous.

"I didn't even do it. He started to vomit," Mark says, starting to sway.

"Why the hell didn't you call me?" Fat Man asks, pulling the final trigger on Mark's anxiety. Mark vomits all over Mr. Snide's head.

"I'll call the family. You go home," Fat Man says.

The nurse who helped at the head hands Mark a towelette. "You did fine," she says. "Isn't it a rule or something, do what the nurses tell you?" She winks at him, and Mark's anxiety lifts enough for him to notice that she's young, younger than he is.

Mark did what the Fat Man told him to. The sun just set, the only light in the hospital now is fluorescent. Janitors clean messes. Mark hadn't called Janet for fear of admitting his fear. She's waiting for him now, perhaps with supper ready. She told him the night before to call if he needed help on his first day, if he wanted to hear her voice. All day he wanted to talk with her, but he was afraid of what he'd say.

Mark walks out the hospital's large revolving doors. The snow outside flies as compressed dust whipping into brick. He hears traffic noise and presses the crosswalk button, waiting for traffic to stop.

A K-car stretches the yellow light as a snow plow turns in the intersection. The K-car smashes against the façade of the dense truck. The front end of the car crumples. Mark is far enough from the hospital now to pretend he isn't a doctor. *I need Janet, she's waiting for me at home.* People leave their cars and run towards the crash. "Did you see that?" a man asks as he runs to the trouble. Mark realizes he's still wearing the white coat. To the watching world, he's still a doctor. What if people see him run away?

Fuck. He runs to the car, its horn blaring. The Fat Man slumps over the wheel, a big gash open on his cheek, a broken mandible sticking out of the cut. Mark's anxiety progresses to another level: he imagines how he would present the case of the motor vehicle accident to the Fat Man: "7:07 PM, car vs. truck, driver of car found unconscious at scene, major damage to car, victim was belted." Mark fantasizes about jiggling the internist's big belly, shaking the love handles and chanting, *Bowl full of jelly, bowl full of jelly.*

Mark feels for a pulse past the metal that lunges into the car. Fat Man's legs are crushed and impaled. Releasing the seat belt, Mark tries to pull Fat Man out, taking care of his head and neck. *Fat Man isn't breathing,* he thinks. *His pulse will stop soon.* Long bones jut out from his shins. Fat Man looks like a broken drumstick.

In Mark's bloodstream, the epi released by the gland above his kidneys soars and thuds. Mark yells for someone to call 911 as he yanks Fat Man from the car. Caught, extremely heavy, Mark wonders if Fat Man will make it out before the K-car explodes.

Without a paper in his hand or a protocol in his mind, Mark moves on to the next right thing. *Gotta leave him in the car,* Mark thinks. He loses Fat Man's pulse. *Okay, chest compressions.* He starts squishing Fat Man, breaking a few ribs with his force even though the compressions come against Fat Man's huge tits, even though Fat Man is sitting up. *What would Mr. Snide advise me now?* Mark hears an ambulance approach, making listening harder: Mark's ear over Fat Man's mouth, Mark's mouth locks on Fat Man's mouth, Mark's hands shove against Fat Man's chest. *Should I take a different route home tomorrow?* he asks himself. A paramedic pulls back on his right shoulder, trying to take over. Mark says, "I need a needle, a sixteen-gauge."

"Who are you?" the paramedic says.

"I'm a doctor. I guess." Half-in and half-out of the car, the Fat Man looks undecided somehow. Should I stay or should I go? Paramedics give Mark the needle. Mark pulls Fat Man's jacket and sweater up to the neck, sticking the needle in the second rib space on the midclavicular line. A whoosh of air, and Fat Man finally breathes.

Sometimes during code blues, the team breaks into applause when the dead improbably come back to life. Pedestrians and other motorists clap as firemen pry Fat Man loose. The snow plow driver taps Mark on the shoulder. "Doc, thanks for saving the life of that *stupid fat fucking bastard*! He needs to look where he's going next time."

Tomorrow, Mark will be anxious in the hospital, fearing every pager ring and PA address. Who would replace the Fat Man? Mark turns around and looks at the hospital in the distance. The ambulance races there through the snow and ice. Perhaps Fat Man codes on the way, perhaps the paramedics pump him full of epi, perhaps Fat Man's lung collapses again. *Tomorrow, I'll head to the red crash cart and draw up a syringe of epi, a fantastical ten milligrams, and carry the syringe in my monogrammed pocket. The syringe will have enough juice to kill five men or save ten.*

Feeling unlike a saviour as walks up the apartment building's stairs, he smells Janet's cooking in the apartment building hall. He thinks, *The Greeks put gold coins on the eyes of their dead, right?* Janet kisses him as he enters the door. "How was your first day?" she asks with winning frustration. She wanted Mark to call her.

Mark remembers his friends high-fiving at a bar after running a successful code. "What a save, what a save," they said over and over to one another, getting drunker and drunker, more and more in love with a small, limited power over death. Mr. Snide appears in Mark's dreams that night, saying, "I'm dying, boy. Listen to me." Mark startles awake and finds Janet there, the groove of her waist made for his arm. The rise and fall of her breathing and the pulse from her aorta are like counting sheep, like rainfall, like the drip from an intravenous line. He falls back asleep.

THE MAN IN THE MIRROR

ANESTHESIA MEDIA

They say to follow your heart, to do what one loves, to love what one does. I separate myself from love by loving the practice of anesthesia: colourless, odourless gases delivered in scuffed silver canisters that brush against the philtrums and lips of the ill. I love drawing up millilitres of liquid into syringes, switching off pain, sight, and thought. The people I touch feel nothing. The highest possible compliment given to anesthetists comes when their patients wake up, turn to a nurse, and say, amazed, "I didn't feel a thing." I dedicate my life to anesthesia.

The problem started on my sixth birthday when my father gave me a television. I watched a movie in my bedroom that very day, a Burt Reynolds feature released about a decade after *Smokey and the Bandit*. Reynolds was bankable then. I could figure the timeline out, research a database; you have your phone there, winking into life with the interest of your patients, your husband? We could watch an Internet clip of Reynolds together! Maybe it's better we didn't. Broken men have only their memories to blame. On such terms, anaesthesia is an imperfect love of mine: I remember everything. Unlike the amazed patient emerging from a controlled coma, I feel everything because I remember everything.

As I recall, perhaps confused by watching the film several times since, the Reynolds character pursues a beautiful, smart woman, the kind that also calls to me in my life. Do you know what I mean? Your dress, your shoulder-length red hair, some man must want you. Anyway, while wisely playing hard-to-get, red tells him, "You're a cold fish."

"A cold fish?" he repeats, surprised. At that time, Reynolds was a blockbuster icon of stupidity and sex, of screwing and screwball humour. In the film he seems cast *against* type, displaced. He pursues women out of some old habit gone wrong or kept on for too long, a habit from other hit movies that threaten the current feature. The redheaded woman is from no other place but the slippery, sheer rock face of *You're full of shit*. She won't be climbed.

"Yeah. Cold," she repeats.

She's right: the Reynolds character is somehow insulated from emotion. He has needs and wants but they're as obscure to the woman as to the audience, other than Reynold's circadian, goofy hope for sex. Reynolds remains an affable wiseacre, endearing in his crudity, but he's also a man no one can ever know. Do you think Reynolds acted the part so well *because* he mastered the ability to play the modern equivalent of kings—sexually powerful male celebrities? Now here he was, in an outlier role, far from a golf course or a tractor trailer, landing by bizarre mistake in a motion picture where a woman, *really, plausibly, correctly* wasn't interested in him *for good reason*. In this way I feel Reynolds did the best acting of his career in this film, the one I'm talking about—Reynolds gave an honest performance, the movie star baffled by the rejection of his object of desire.

I was only six years old then. I shouldn't have been watching that movie, but then there were a lot of things I shouldn't have done. That's why we're here. But at six years old, the look of Reynold's face when he was rebuffed imprinted on mine: a cringing face, a face that itself wanted to walk away from its skull. I had a lot to learn.

Videocassette recorders have red buttons that are always the record button. My brain didn't hit the red "record" button—resulting in my perfect memory—until I hit ten years old. You've studied the theory behind memory, right? Much of the research work on memory is based in my own bailiwick, the practice of anesthesia. In times of great stress, difficulty, and pain, the human body protects itself by *not* recording traumatic events. Shit hurts as you go through it but endorphins help a little in the midst of the shit. When the fan's done throwing the crap, if you've done things right, *you simply don't remember what you've gone through.*

Listen, I'm telling you the most important thing you'll ever know as a doctor. How long have you been a resident? A year? Two? Even if you've been practising for thirty years, you might not know this: pain steals the body's camera and script, secreting them in the body, but the body never releases the film. Remember that when you sit a patient down and try to build an artificial rapport in your goal to get them to talk about their past. You're asking the impossible of them. It's not fair.

I'm a different case. The scene at ten years old begins like this: my father and mother sit on opposite couches. Taggy and Joey, two untrained Shelties, destroy anything small and biteable. The Burt Reynolds movie from four years back is rebroadcast on the television. Turning my gaze from my parents, the dogs, and Reynolds' cringing face, I decide that I, too, will be a cold fish.

With my parents squared off on duelling stained couches, I understand that Reynolds, so obviously pitied by the director's gaze, is simply further along in development than me—older, more stoic. He is uncomfortable and strong in a way I admired at the time. Moral of the story: at ten years old, I didn't want to feel anything, anymore, ever. I found a model in Burt Reynolds.

I could watch whatever came in on the airwaves in my room, which was a much better location than the living room, with its dogs, parents, and doom. My favourite cartoon series back then was *The Weekenders* starring a kid named Tino Tonitini. Tino rolls with several kids his age: a black sports star, a nerdy redheaded genius, a brash brunette. These friends negotiate the pitfalls of middle school together. In the episode I remember completely, Tino is scorched by a peripheral friend's trash talk about video game superiority.

What's a young boy to do? Tino decides, rightly, that the logical response is to separate himself from all feeling. Tino, at twelve years old, decides not to feel. His friends treat him sympathetically early on, but they can't help but be purposefully alienated by Tino. Suppress feelings for long enough, and well enough, and the other people in your life will think you're apathetic and selfish when what you actually are is *separate*. They won't understand. Tino wears sunglasses to underscore the cool change in his being. In time, made lonely by his decision and feeling worse, Tino talks to his divorcée mother. Tino's Mom, which is her actual character's name, says something like the line Burt Reynolds received about being a "cold fish" to her wounded little boy: "Without feelings, life would pretty much suck." Tino looks into his frumpy, sad, sexless mother's eyes and forces himself to bear the disappointment of being human. He resolves to have friends again, to love. He takes the sunglasses off, and the audience is supposed to cheer.

But for me the moral of the story is far deeper: the betrayer and the close friends all behave in that episode the same way—they shun him, even though Tino just tries to protect himself. When Tino reaches to take off the glasses in slo-mo, I screamed "No" at the set. When he took off the glasses, I felt cheated, but in a few seconds I felt nothing at all.

In the next *Weekenders* episode, Tino's geographically distant father, Tony Tonitini, comes to spend time with Tino. Tony and Tino's Mom, a few years into their divorce, resemble a pacifist version of my own parents. Both sets of parents gaze at fixed disappointments in the distance when they talk to one another. I see no hatred on Tony's and Tino's Mom's faces, in fact little in the way of expression. Disney isn't trying to teach kids that divorced parents don't have feelings for each another anymore, that it's not the fault of the child, and that it's hopeless to want parents to get back together. No, Disney wants kids to know this moral: Tino's parents know they made a null mistake by getting married. Just like all the other mothers and fathers out there, Tony and Tino's Mom are past the point of caring about anyone. It starts in the home, with the ones they once loved the fiercest. Hate may serve as the flip side of love, but flip that coin enough and the coin loses its face. The Family Channel is to blame for teaching me to never let my face tell anyone how I feel.

You might think that my problem is over-saturation by media at too early an age. Did I watch too much television, too many films? Sure. It's part of the problem, I admit. From the beginning of my life, I subsumed myself to characters on a screen. The screen spoke for me. For a while I felt bad things I wasn't supposed to feel, adult things, complex and terrifying things, until I didn't feel anything at all, until I made my cold fish decision. But memory reminds me the problem is more one of *story*, not of a specific medium, for I succumbed to the unempathizing radiation of the written page first.

On my mother's knee, her face bruised black from a routine attack, I heard *The Ugly Duckling*. I realize now that she and I are strange empaths: her wounds materializing as pain on my body, the transfer of these wounds becoming guilt in her. When she read to me, I reached my hands into her straight red hair, curled the strands around my fingers. The story's simple, I'm sure you know it: the ugly duckling is actually a young swan fostered by a mother duck. The swan is bullied and abused for not being what it can't be. The swan grows to become something more beautiful than what any duck can ever be.

I felt sorry for the swan at first, but this soon turned to rage at the swan's mistreatment. When the swan triumphs, I felt a vindictive glee. The story over, my mother carries me into bed. If I had had canisters and masks to play with back then, I'd have put them on my teddy bears' faces, everyone nodding off together.

Swans are vicious—keep your distance. In the Halifax of my youth, a few years after my mother read *The Ugly Duckling* for the first time, a mass murderer terrorized the Public Gardens. Swans died one after another in the park, their necks surgically severed from their bodies. One swan died at a time (the park always stocked two swans for reasons of companionship); after three deaths, swan vigilantes appointed themselves Guardians of Our Collective Swan Heritage (GOCSH) and formed a posse that patrolled the park at night for signs of the swan serial killer. Two days after the fourth replacement swan was released into the park that cruel summer, GOCSH heard a terrible squawk and shone flashlights upon the sound. They found the serial survivor swan chasing the new guy, who naturally expressed bewilderment about the nature of the disagreement—*They're getting along so well*, GOCSH patrolmen said to one another—and tried to dodge the aggressor's beak. But the aggressor snapped his beak shut on new guy's neck and violently flung the new guy back and forth, snapping his neck like a cornstalk, cutting the stem clean off.

On television the next day, the leader of GOCSH was quoted as saying, "We never knew it was one of our own." The camera zoomed in on the lone, homicidal swan floating in the middle of the main pond. The swan dipped its face in the water, serenely serving as a white tufted centrepiece for the entire city of Halifax, hundreds of people coming to the park each day just to spot the swan. The city shipped out what the *Chronicle-Herald* dubbed the "White Maniac" in its headlines to a lone lake in Cape Breton. Two new replacement swans were brought in to satisfy tourists.

In the Public Gardens, parents to this day encourage children to throw breadcrumbs to the swans, but the breadcrumbs are usually eaten first by the more nimble and numerous ugly ducks. The ecosystem of the park is simple: ducks grow fat from the presence of the swans. Swans stay svelte; ducks grow ever uglier. If kids get close to ducks, the ducks run away. But get close to a swan and the children's necks and hands will be bitten severely.

Moral of the story: beautiful things are vicious and best left alone.

Screens exposed me to the emotional delirium of rape, murder, torture, grief: view enough extreme pain and feelings will become displaced. I learned that pain is given and received, there is a transfer, one cannot be without the other.

Then what is feeling, I ask you? How should anybody, child or adult, actually go about feeling something? Some people would diagnose such a question as pathological. Some would say I am profoundly desensitized. Not true. Anesthesia isn't desensitization, it's *no sensation*. Desensitization is a moral problem, but anesthesia is release.

Was I born a swan? Was I always an anesthetist? My career in feelings ended for good when I watched a man and a woman onscreen break up with one another. My father turned to me as I cried—ah, the woman's visible heartbreak was a burning effigy of feeling, a pyre of despair—and said, "Fuck boy, it's just a show." I felt at that moment like I imagine the swan vigilante leader did when he found the swan's severed neck: *one of our own.*

Another step in appreciating the drama of my real life came when looking at a television screen. Harry Hamlin in *LA Law* tries to save the life of a wrongfully accused rich woman while also resisting the urge to bed her. A retarded man brings Harry his mail; the two men have a conversation about sandwiches.

The contrast between the virile and accomplished Hamlin and the slow, anxious, overwhelmed, and overweight retard made me wonder about the nature of compassion. Hamlin finishes talking to his hot client who speaks to her attorney in a breathy, suggestive whisper-rasp. Hamlin sweats, loosens his collar, appears uncomfortably aroused.

His entire being outwardly says, *After the case, Harry. Just wait until after the case.* Then the retarded man enters Harry's office, performing a simple and brief task: he delivers a letter. Hamlin's task is to prevent the woman from going to jail for the rest of her life. The handicapped man is dressed simply, in a cardigan that throughout the show's many seasons never changes in pattern. Better shaven than the louche Hamlin, the retarded man's hair seems to be tended by the same barber who hacked the hair off Moe from The Three Stooges—or his mother cut it, the show never revealed the gofer's stylist. He speaks hesitantly, with a stutter.

In awe of the busy law office with its bustling traffic in vast, unknowable things, the gofer is in awe of Hamlin too: Hamlin's genuine likeableness, his decency. Hamlin is willing to listen to people, unlike the other alpha-male sharks in the office. But the problem of the scene is simple despite my elaborate set-up: what do you say to the most powerful man in the world if you are retarded? If your job—a job that may have rescued you from some other hell, from your mother, father, or yourself—is to deliver mail, then as a retarded man you deliver the mail while mentioning something innocuous to those who see you. What do you mention? You mention *sandwiches.*

The gofer could have spoken about abuse and love, need and disdain. He could have chatted about how he worked as hard as he could, at the highest level he could, and it would *never* approach a fraction of Hamlin's usefulness. He could have bleated "I'm sad!" He could have talked about feeling lost. For his part, Hamlin could have asked the gofer about his feelings. Those feelings were there for the audience and other cast to see: churning chaos behind the gofer's fearful face. But Hamlin was too aroused by his hot client; he had to open his mail; and according to office standards at McKenzie, Brackman, Chaney, and Kuzak, he had already done quite well by the retarded man. Hamlin talked to him like a human being. Hamlin noticed him.

"I brought baloney and mustard today," the gofer says, as eager as a Michael Jackson was when he was alive for a child, or childhood, or childish things.

"Wow. I made that too," Harry says distractedly. After a few seconds, with nothing else for either of them to say, Harry turning his attention to papers on his desk and the gofer opening and closing his mouth like a dying fish, the camera follows him out the door, on the way to the next office with the next letter. Seconds after that, the camera follows Harry out of his office, on his way to lunch with his client.

Moral of the story: even the most decent of us can only be so good.

My father came in the door at that moment in the program, throwing the door against the wall. The dogs rioted with barks, then whined after a loud noise sounded in the hallway, as if something were being knocked over or kicked. Then a series of thumps. My father lurched. He threw himself on the couch, zipper open, clothes stained. He kicked his legs up onto the coffee table, a table bought from Medjucks, a furniture dealer that used rare wood and hand-treated it with a special finish. The few who came to visit our home all remarked upon the incongruously expensive-looking tables and chairs in the house. He bellowed for me to take off his boots.

Joey dragged himself across the floor to his food bowl. One of his front legs had an open fracture, blood flowing onto the floor. I sat in a small chair at the side of the room. My father had tramped in mud from the fields or from someplace worse. I got up and started to untie the filthy boots, undoing them according to how he tied them, with the double loop around the back and the double throw. I pulled and pulled, the pulling made more difficult by his lack of cooperation. He sat there, too drunk to do this himself, but not drunk enough to leave me alone. This aspect of his character was never numb.

Do you remember the moment in the film version of *Winnie the Pooh* when Pooh visits Rabbit's house and slyly says he's hungry? Pooh then proceeds to eat Rabbit's entire store of honey. After pleasantly eating all the honey, seemingly without malice, Pooh decides to leave. Pooh exits the house through the hole that is the door, but he gets stuck. All his friends try to pull him out, his friends in a line, forming a chain of hands, pulling, singing a song as they pull.

Yet Pooh remains stuck. It's some time before Pooh starves enough so that he can be dislodged. Yet during that time, Pooh is tempted with food by Gopher, and Rabbit has to scare the tempter off. Pooh, even though he is stuck, would happily eat more.

When I first watched this film, the most interesting thing to me was not that Pooh would be a glutton, nor that Rabbit would enable his gluttony. Not that Pooh's friends would try to help, not that Pooh would be tempted as he waited to get free. No, the most interesting thing to me was that Pooh continues to eat the honey in full view of Rabbit's increasing dismay. Pooh eats and eats even though he is, with each greedy slurp, making his friend more and more unhappy.

Writers, animators, and directors should practise the same honesty as that of their creation, Reynolds' beautifully uninterested woman. Harry Hamlin should have either spoken to the gofer about unrequited desire or have treated him harshly—not kept to the purgatory of no-congress. Hamlin should have told the gofer that he had a hot client and wanted to fuck her and that he knew he shouldn't, but instead Hamlin treated viewers with condescending respect—the respect of *sandwiches*. Pooh too should have interrupted his gluttony for a moment, perhaps tipped his head out of the pot with a grin, looked at the viewer, then turned his head to look at Rabbit, then dipped his head back into the pot, to resume stuffing himself.

Moral of the story: be honest about desire, or don't portray it at all.

I pulled the first boot off. My father began to bang the other boot so as to say that I was taking too long, impatient in his stupor. I looked at his face to see if he was looking at me. He was feeling the couch for the dog-maimed remote control, reaching for it so that he could change the channel.

The second boot came off.

I wish I could say now that feeling is like that boot: tightly tied, slowly unknotted, stubborn to come off, and with a freeing jerk, released. But at the time I realized that the boot was covered in dried shit. When I had gripped the heel and the toe, my hands got covered in shit. The television threw a numb blue glow upon my snoring father.

What makes terror terrible, or terror *terror,* is that it doesn't require elaborate refreshment in order to remain an effective tool. All one needs to do is to properly mark a child with terror from the first, when the child is born. Hold the child like it should be hurled to the street or thrown in the snow. Prefer to be anywhere else, place hands around the child's neck, whisper *These are the hands of the world.* From that point forward, parents need not bother to remind the child of how bad life can be, it's unnecessary. There will always be the awareness that life is bad, terror becomes a fourth vital sign.

That the child knows that he can die is not sufficient, it's not enough to be scared. The point of terror is a two-stage negative: first, the child must acknowledge at whose continuous, blessed mercy he serves under; second, the child must realize that this acknowledgement *isn't* a guarantor of safety. It's not terror if the child practises frantic, fruitless respect the way he wears seat belts or helmets.

In my case, I wore the mask of terror as a way to be prepared for death, to literally show to my father I was prepared. Fear is fealty, you see, but never safety. My father beat me every day, in places where no one would see. But it could be worse, and he showed me that himself, with his own body.

Opening the door, I saw my father had come home from a beating with only enough power to knock. He couldn't see, his face was too damaged, his eyes swollen shut, wide blue moons shining out of a torn and punctured alcohol mask. He must have crawled up the steps. How did he get here?

Shirtless from staunching the blood from his mouth or because his shirt was torn from him, and with only a single boot on, he tried to talk but the best he could do was make blood bubbles pop on his lips. I lifted him up, dragged him to the couch and turned the television on. I was seventeen years old at the time—I lifted him up, my *father*. He fell asleep.

I went to the drawer in the kitchen and pulled out a Polaroid camera. I took a picture of his face, the bubbles forming on his lips, red smeared on his cheeks as if he were a blood god rejected by his followers, now made to bleed himself.

The picture is a small piece of anesthesia. I have it still in a drawer in my study. I feel nothing when I look at it, but I still am moved to look at it. Is it a shrine, do you think, for feeling? Or a mausoleum instead? He looked dead.

A few weeks later, when his face recovered, my father and I approached a beaten-down farm along the Saint John River, just a few miles from Grand Lake. Grown up in alders, the farm grew a small house, peeling, old, and with a For Sale sign next to an old Freightliner parked close to the road. Our car turned onto the dirt driveway. A bent man looked out from his front window.

In the fifteen minutes it took us to drive from town, my father drank half the pint. With each draught, he looked up at the top of the car as if he needed divine intervention. He closed his eyes, shook his head, then opened his eyes. His right hand reached out and he took the soda bottle from me, diffusing the rum. The burn relieved, he passed the soda bottle back.

What to say of his face? I had watched it so often, I wondered if the director instructed Frederick March in Dr. Jekyll and Mr. Hyde to make the terrible transformative face or if it was actually March's own idea. What evil was inside March to mint a visual cliché for our time: the actor's face and limbs contort and convulse as the physical symbol of evil incarnate? Once inside, the terrible potion uncovers the imbiber's terrible insides.

My father's face was far from March's melodramatic skin-stretching. Only the briefest of tells showed that something terrible had revealed him: an upward tilt of the head, brief eye closure, a gentle head shake. His face returned quickly to the standard configuration, just looser.

I remember standing in front of the mirror one night after soda duty. We barely made it home. I looked like Pooh did in my imagination, the scene where Pooh winks at the camera. I mimicked the drink of the rum with my hands and mouth, watching my face for minutes, trying to discern a change. Detecting no difference, I tilted the imaginary pint again, drinking more, longer; still no change.

I tried something different: I lifted my head up, closed my eyes, and shook my head. For a few seconds I felt powerful, terrible, terrifying, the mental equivalent of March's physical transformation, as if I could roar through the house, knock over lamps, break windows, go through walls. I didn't need a screen to watch such things, I'd seen them before. But before I rushed out the door, I turned my head to the right and reached out my hand, as if someone were there to pass me a chaser. The feeling of power passed.

Moral of the story: terror is within, but it needs someone to act upon—the basic function of feeling, of receiver and actor. Terror needs a terror source like power needs a power source.

My father knocked on the farmhouse door. A slow-moving man near my father's age opened it. Seeing my father, he wobbled back into the house and took out a single drinking glass. A girl my own age lay on a couch further down the hall, turning her head back to the television after we came in. She had long, curly red hair and a shy smile, stretched out on her back, just like I put people to sleep.

She was watching an episode of the original *Star Trek* series. Bones runs his spinning sensor over a body; it whistles and whirls under Bones' scared voice. "I'm a doctor, Jim, not someone who watches his best friend die." Loud beeps sound from sickbay telemetry. A sound like a tire deflating—Bones injects Captain Kirk, his best friend, with a resuscitative substance—a shot in the arm designed to banish all extraterrestrial disease. The sickbay beeps settle, allowing Bones to add, "I'm a doctor, Jim, not a pallbearer."

The man put a single empty glass on the table and kept a can of soda in front of himself. The cap was still on. He put a bottle of rum in front of my father.

"Aren't you having a swalley, Rick?"

Rick shook his head and pointed to the can. My father screwed off the cap to his own rum bottle and poured into the glass Rick set out. He drank the alcohol down but didn't perform the usual ritual—turning his head to the right side, sticking out his arm for the chaser. He took Rick's soda and swigged. I wasn't the terror object this time. "I don't like the price," my father said.

"I don't like it either, but the bank set it. They are bound and determined to recoup the whole sum," Rick said.

"The bank sells the truck or *you* do?" my father asked, menace trying to do its work, drive down the price, get something for cheap, take the whole world.

Menace did its work. "What am I supposed to do? The bank will let you buy it at their price. If they're not happy with the sale, they'll kick me out," Rick whined, looking at his red-haired daughter.

James T. Kirk is feeling much better, chasing the short-skirted Yeoman Janice, delectable in red polyester. Come to think of it, Yeoman Janice holds a clipboard. Just like you do.

"Drop it by five thousand," my father said, slamming his fist on the table. The Captain Morgan bottle fell over and spilled onto the table.

"I can't!" the man shouted, standing up slowly. He must have been injured in some way, he rubbed his thigh constantly.

The young woman looked over at us again. The sounds of firing phasers; detonating photon torpedoes; shields dropping; fire on the bridge. Bones frantically triages the dying. I wanted the girl to undress. She turned back to the television, Rick standing between her and the screen now.

"Nina, shut off that television," Rick said.

"It's not worth that price," my father roared. "It's not worth that price and I'll buy it from you or the bank when they drop the price, *whoever the fuck*, I'll buy it from *whoever the fuck*, but I won't pay more than it's worth. Talk to the fucking bank and tell them you've got someone willing to pay most of it."

The man spread his arms wide, shaking his head. My father stood, knocking his chair over and swatting the glass to the floor. Then he righted the rum bottle and screwed the cap back on. "Crook. Fuckin' useless cripple. I hope the bank keeps you in crutches."

The redhead stood beside her father, long scissors in her hand. While Star Trek was on, she was cutting cross-stitch fabric. Rick's head was in his hands, her arms on his shoulders, the scissors lowering to her side. She didn't look at me. On fire, the Enterprise escapes on impulse power.

ANESTHESIA TRAINING

Where was I? A few weeks ago, the hospital parking lot was full but attendants still permitted cars to enter. Cars circled the lot like sharks, slowly following pedestrians in case a pedestrian freed up space by escaping in a car. A man in ridiculous leathers was sitting on a scooter, his helmet on his lap. He was too large for the scooter, looking like a hulk about to crush a child's toy. Leaning against him was a beautiful redhead in a short red dress, a woman who holds the man as if he is the answer to the problem of *right now*. They were in love. Close to them, a shark-car waited for the spot. The shark-car sat, lights shining in the middle of the day, confident it would open. The couple remained oblivious: if I had asked the man if he was, at that moment, sitting on a scooter, he would have been jostled out of the focus of *her*. The shark-car became impatient. A window rolled down on the driver's side. The driver shouted, "Hey, you two leaving soon, or you just arriving?"

In answer, the lovers drew one another closer. The shark-car drove away. Once it was gone the redhead got on the back of the scooter, balancing like a freckled porcelain doll upon a wire. Her dress seemed unwise. She affixed herself to the man as they drove away. Ten years ago, a girl was in love with me like that. Her name was Nicole. All the love stories I've seen since that time suggest to me that I had endured the real thing, to be loved. But did I love Nicole? I did. I remember everything, every emotion. Looking back, the problem for us was the filter of my anesthesia.

I remember lying with Nicole in her bed after sneaking into her farmhouse in Grand Lake. I woke up in the middle of the night and wondered *why* I didn't care about her. I liked being in her, I liked talking to her, she was smarter than me. I told myself I was a cold fish, that's just the way I was.

Nicole wanted to go to our high school promenade on a motorcycle. "All girls do," she told me. She wanted me to learn how to ride one so that we could go as a couple on a red rented Harley or, failing that, a Honda. "I want my dress to trail in the wind." Instead, we went to the promenade in a black, beat-up Ford Ranger, cowshit clinging to the mudflaps. Nicole sat in the passenger seat, her face dangerously even. When we danced, she told me wicked things that we would do later that night.

Michael Jackson presided as musical genius that evening. The teenage DJ from grade eleven got drunk and insisted on playing Jackson's "I'll Be There" every third song until someone else who was drunk shouted for "Enter Sandman" in disgust. Music pumped from the speakers at maximum volume—for the students with boyfriends or girlfriends, it didn't matter what played. For the ones who came alone, it mattered too much.

Expecting something wicked, the promenade over, I followed the redhead into the hotel room I had booked earlier that afternoon. She smiled, sweetly told me good night, and promptly pretended to fall asleep. She left me for good in the morning. "You're cold," she said. "I can't get you angry. I wanted you to hold me down and fuck me when I lied to you but you didn't say a word, you didn't even ask for sex. You don't even care."

In the aftermath of Michael Jackson's death, television pundits said that Michael Jackson was crazy. That he was an addict. That he moved from street to hospital-grade drugs in order to escape his grotesque, fame-warped childhood. These pundits contextualized Jackson's strange doings by commenting upon the extracurricular activities of other wayward former child-stars. I have studied every single appearance Jackson made on television and on screen—a pastime of mine since I learned of the circumstances of his death. I've reviewed thousands of hours of footage, following him from precocious runt to crotch-grabbing skeleton to baby-dangling plastic surgery wreck and I have concluded that Jackson was neither crazy nor an addict, as the pundits would have us believe. Having a professional interest in such matters, though perhaps not as great an interest as you, as a psychiatrist, I believe mental illness and addiction are expensive abstractions, words that know nothing about cause. No, the cause of Michael Jackson's death is simpler than all that. *Jackson was in pain.*

Jackson began his career exorcising pain through the catharsis of song. He sang and danced not because we wanted him to, or because his father wanted him to. This is a common, and very stupid, belief. No, Jackson was compelled to get rid of his shit. That the cameras, microphones, and armadas of industry were involved *ruined* this wish for catharsis. Success, or acquiring an audience, made the wish impossible. If Jackson had stayed at home to sing only in the shower, unreachable by Barry Gordy and his Motown minions, keeping close only to Tito's snapping towel, he might have stayed alive long enough to remember the days of singing in the shower with force and skill, feeling as much pain as we are all given—and no more.

But Jackson grew into an anesthesia that sang *to* him. His singing was both his talent and his doom. He tried to anesthetize himself in song but was cannibalized by song instead. Logic says to those in pain that the bigger the drug, the further the feeling. Jackson never looked on pain and realized how absurd it is to want to be free—we can never be free, he didn't understand that. Jackson's terror object was himself. His talent killed him, his song dulled no sensation and became ever sharper.

The best appearance Jackson ever made was a no-show. The video for his song the "Man in the Mirror" features calamities of all kinds: nuclear fallout, civil war, civil disobedience, and dead celebrities. These calamities get a few seconds of screen time each—their effect becomes numbing, as if Mother Theresa's three-second staged hug of an urchin is equivalent to a John Lennon mourner's tears, as if a rocket can wipe out an entire Israeli family but Bob Geldof can make a difference with a rock concert. Jackson's face does not appear in the video. The intention is obvious: this time he's not going to be the pitchman for Pepsi, but rather the curator of sliding-scale atrocities flaring across the screen to a catchy soundtrack.

Yet the "Man in the Mirror" video is, in a paradoxical sense, the longest look Jackson ever had at himself. If he is indeed talking about the man in the mirror, then the man in the mirror can't see anything except dire need. The character that features most in the video is the generic African child, her ribs and face drawn in starvation. This image repeats as often as the chorus to the song.

I've looked at women like the camera looks at these children, trying to tell myself I felt nothing, and believing, just like I tried to tell myself I wasn't in love.

Take Tino's Mom's advice: *Life pretty much sucks, doesn't it?*

Because I didn't get distracted by falling in love, I worked very hard. I excelled at school, got good grades, and entered medical school. There are exactly 109 spots in a calendar year in Canada for doctors who wish to be trained in the art of anesthesia. I qualified for one of them.

Anesthetists are trained for crisis: shit hits the fan, we mop up the shit. On my monitor in the Operating Room, oxygen saturation is usually the last vital sign to drop. The first awry indicator, as Bones well knows, is the pulse. A heart stops, or gallops, or slows. An alarm sounds—a machine bleats that the patient might die. Alarms jostle me out of my red daydreams. It's the same with all anesthetists; we know that all our training has been for the moment of crisis. But before anesthetists at Dalhousie University are permitted to begin their training, we must first suckle from the bosom of the screen. We watch a training video.

Dr. Haupsturm was a German who claimed he knew the amount—"to the millimetre!" he'd bark—of blood in each vein he touched with his kneading index finger. He injected drugs with precision, insisting that by adhering to strict methodology, anesthetists get positive, reproducible results. Haupsturm forced his trainees to recite resuscitation protocols by rote. With each error, he would look at the offending fool with arched eyebrows and shout, "If I knew only as little as you, a dozen patients would be dead every day. I would lose my licence!"

I apologize. I'm remembering this out of order—my memory is impeccable, but not in sequence. Before Dr. Haupsturm softened recruits with pedantic recall exercises, he first sat us down in a vacant OR with chairs arranged three across and two deep. At the front of the room sat a television screen and a video recorder. He made his grating ritual greeting, "So you will all be anesthetists!" and pressed play as the lights went down.

The interior of a cockpit flares to life on the screen. A pilot and copilot chat amiably about a stewardess who's married but also having certain "difficulties." They speak of their *concern* for her, the copilot with no ring on his fourth finger, the pilot sporting a wedding band. A button on a console begins to blink. The button flashes green. The copilot notices first, and asks the pilot if he had checked position. The pilot stops talking about the stewardess and responds, "Of course, of course, I always do that." Annoyed, he adds, "I always do."

The copilot presses the green button. The button stays green. The copilot then systematically checks his instruments. This array of instruments appears encyclopedic in scope, a panoply of buttons, dials, and readouts. He goes about this slowly. "I'd like to show her how to get revenge on a cheating asshole," he says, pointing at his crotch.

The pilot's ring finger stretches on his knee in response.

The stewardess enters the cockpit with a quick swish of red dress across the bottom of the camera's field. She says, "The resupply didn't come in full, we don't have coffee. So we're giving passengers extra alcohol instead."

The red dress disappears from view. The cockpit door snaps shut. The pilot says, "She sounds like she already knows how to keep men happy."

The button stays green. The copilot mentions the button to the pilot again. The pilot pushes the button. The button stays green. The copilot and the pilot wonder why the button is green. The pilot duplicates the methodical procedure just performed by the copilot, but he can't find a reason for the button to be green. The pilot pushes the button again. It remains green.

My, my, such a green button. "A malfunction," the co-pilot says confidently.

I confess, I wanted to reach my hands into the television screen and push the green button too. It seemed to be the natural thing to do. The camera view was undeviating, showing only the pilot and copilot's legs and the instrument panel of the plane.

The last word is "Wait –

The video breaks into fuzz and stops. Dr. Haupsturm switched on the lights. "This flight carried seventy-four persons, including pilot, copilot, and stewardess. It crashed into a lake in northern England twenty years ago. The plane's instruments were frozen; the plane was in a slight dive. The loss of altitude was gradual. The pilots focused on the green light as the plane was on a trajectory to hit the water of Lake Windermere. If the men had just looked out the window of the cockpit, if they had noticed that they had left the clouds, they would have realized that the green light was not the only indicator that something was wrong.

"So you will all be anesthetists!" he said, his smile wide enough to swallow the screen whole. I wanted him to enter the screen instead, to be absorbed by it. "Think about the nature of monitoring, my future anesthetists. What needs to be monitored, what doesn't? Think about what you are told by monitors and what you are not. *The patient is the real monitor.* If you are an anesthetist, you will *feel* when things will go wrong. You will anticipate them." Stagily, showily, ridiculously, Haupsturm dropped his voice and said: "You will *be* the green light!"

Pain is the first totalizing sense we possess, a much simpler, yet more encompassing, state than love. Pain is the first signal of insult to the organism and thereafter all methods of adaptation and learning are to avoid pain. Consider these few cases: (1) a man who winces with angina pectoris, breathing hard, drenchingly diaphoretic, crying out in the sun as he leaves his car and flags down help; (2) a political dissident from Michael Jackson's "Man In The Mirror" video touching his bleeding face as an authentication of the pain of not being free, followed by an image of the dissident grey and dead; (3) a pregnant woman raped by soldiers in view of her children, the nerves of the woman's fetus and the nerves of her sons and daughters absorbing the damage.

Hmmm. The director's camera cannot see a fetus. Perhaps this is what love must do—but it's no match for the bodily knowledge of pain, the raped woman's insides crying out into our eyes.

A few months later, Dr. Haupsturm separated from his icily perfect wife. Brenda was often away due to her work as a stewardess. Dr. Haupsturm planned to scan the pages of *Der Spiegel* but instead read over breakfast about certain positions, residues, redolent rooms, pleasure trinkets, and insults about his own anatomical inadequacies—Brenda mistakenly left open a chat window on the Haupsturm home computer. The new man in her life had a big, big dick. Most injurious to the good doctor were Brenda's insults about his "sexual methodology," which he had always found satisfactory but which she described as the "sickening same."

The anesthesia residents made a lot of jokes about red lights in the first weeks after hearing about Dr. Haupsturm's pain, but the jokes stopped when it became clear that Dr. Haupsturm was no longer in control of his feelings. No one wants to watch a man's angling down and excruciating, predictable impact—audiences cringe in the face of actual pain. The camera itself wishes to look away because the camera is terrified, an instrument of pain itself, appropriated by pain.

I had just started waking up a man from an easy and quick transurethral resection of the prostate. He was quite young, really, only in his late forties. I used the methodology Dr. Haupsturm insisted on—reducing the drugs, removing the tube, assisting respiration with the bag-valve-mask.

Dr. Haupsturm sat on a metal stool in the corner, chatting up Rhonda, a scrub nurse with hospital burka sexuality: she wore large, ill-fitting greens, a surgical cap contained her hair, and her face was half-covered by a mask. Her eyes moved, methodically, over Dr. Haupsturm's fit body. An alarm sounded: the patient's oxygen level was decreasing. I alerted Dr. Haupsturm, but he absently told me, "Bag the patient up."

I put the oxygen on full, repositioning the mask over the patient's mouth and nose: chin tilt, jaw thrust. I squeezed the bag but didn't meet proper resistance—the patient's chest didn't rise and fall, air squeezed out around the mask. I reapplied the mask and repeated the task. Same result.

The pilots kept pushing the green light, push push push, they didn't change their course of action, push push push. I pushed the panic button, push push push. I, a cold fish, was terrified. "Dr. Haupsturm, this patient is difficult to bag!" I said.

He looked at the monitor, at me, back at the monitor. "Can't you even bag a patient? Are you an anesthetist? You fail at the most basic of tasks!" he barked, then turned back to Rhonda, looking down and down at her indeterminately large breasts. I pushed and pushed at the air, my hands around the bag. Air flew around my hands.

Haupsturm stomped over and began to shout in my face *Bag! Bag! Bag!* The patient turned blue. First his fingers, then his hands, then his face. The monitor broke apart with sound. A deeper blue, darker, the deeper bluer sea.

Haupsturm ripped the apparatus from my hands, repositioned the mask, and arrogantly shoved air at the patient, looking me in the eyes all the while, cursing my incompetence. Air reproducibly flew around the mask and *not* into the patient's lungs. The monitor sang like drugs and pain sung to Michael Jackson.

I pushed Haupsturm aside and inserted a rescue tube into the patient, a blue man, his head blue, lips blue, tongue blue, palate blue, esophagus blue, larynx blue, outsides and insides blue. In a few seconds, he was pink again. The monitor went from red to green. Green, as you know, is good.

Blue Man woke with a headache, vomiting violently in the recovery room. Drugs didn't help. In subsequent days he complained of incapacitating headaches that broke his mind open after he took a few steps. If he continued walking, his eyes revolved in his head and he fell over, retching.

Blue Man never improved, wearing an odd, blank expression for the rest of his days in the hospital and, I expect, his life. He responded to questions with a time delay as if he were radioing a plane. That day in the OR Haupsturm told me and everyone in the room to never say a word to anyone.

Moral of the story: pain is more competent than any doctor.

The guilt from my silence interfered with my sleep. I didn't know it was guilt at the time, but it was guilt. I couldn't forget the colour of Blue Man. After seeing the cue of the colour blue in dreams, Blue Man would come to me to tell me odd and ominous stories about famous physicians. One night Blue Man appeared as I dreamed I was looking into a swimming pool. He said, "Did you know that Robert Louis Stevenson was an alcoholic? Stevenson wrote *The Strange Case of Dr. Jekyll and Mr. Hyde* to explain himself to himself. Instead of stopping drinking, Stevenson made carousing into something he could put on his resume, something he could deposit in his bank account."

I never spoke in these dreams—only Blue Man spoke. As I recount these dreams to you now, I realize I should have asked Blue Man mid-dream about the strange case of Michael Jackson. How did Jackson fit into Blue Man's series of lessons?

The Blue Man dreams only got worse. The next night Blue Man came, summoned by dreaming of Bones in sickbay, Bones' blue medical officer shirt. Blue Man said:

BLUE MAN'S SOLILOQUY

"At least once a lifetime, Dr. Sigmund Freud appears to a dreamer. Doctors your age are taught that Freud is a relic of psychology. You reduce him to the status of cocaine addict fixated on anuses. Students like you are made to believe that Freud is a sick gargoyle crouched upon the Turret of Dreams.

Every night since the night you painted me blue, I dream of a beautiful red-haired medical student lying upon an operating table. Asleep, she could be a cursed beauty in need of a kiss, or she could be about to have a uterine tumour removed. She could have anything wrong with her. Her chest rises and falls underneath a johnny shirt. In my dream, Freud enters the Dream Room wearing a monocle. He walks slowly, with a strange rhythm, taking two steps forward, then one back, then a few steps back, but a few more forward, singing a medley of "Deutschland über Alles," "Dream a Little Dream," and "Man in The Mirror." Every so often he sneezes, rubbing his bleeding nose.

When he reaches the table, he leers and makes a circle with his index and forefinger, using index and thumb of both hands to simulate copulation. He mock-fondles the woman's breasts, his hands hovering and snapping above the big mounds, his head turned to the heavens as if in ecstasy. He removes his monocle, replaces it, removes it, and addresses an audience of cameras: "Oedipus is a kind of blind!" Next, Freud grabs a sheet and cuts holes in it. He pretends to be a ghost, kicking his legs under the sheet as if he is a jackbooted dancer. OOOOooo, OOOOooooooOOOOOO the Freud dream-ghost moans. Freud kneels on the ground and whispers for what seems like hours into the redhead's ear. He sticks his arm out from under the sheet, making it visible. Through his eye-holes, Freud looks at his huge gold watch. He stands, sways, and speaks in a campfire-story shriek, "I AM YOUR UNCONSCIOUS. OOOOoooOOOOO. I AM YOUR UNCONSCIOUS! OOooooOOOOOooo!" The redhead wakes and insists Freud return the sheet to her.

"I am indiscreet," she squeaks.

"You are a hysteric," he responds in a stentorian voice, gallantly returning the sheet. She sits up on the table and places the sheet upon herself, looking through the eyeholes at Freud. She grabs Freud's arm and looks at his watch. They slowly nod their heads in sync and then dance a lively Viennese waltz.

Everyone knows Freud was a cocaine addict and quack but did you know when he started out he was a primary researcher, investigating nerves in lower animals? Merck gave him cocaine, "an alkaloid with strange properties" to investigate. He wrote the very first paper on its use as an anesthetic but abandoned actual trials because of a developing love of a redhead. One of his friends, Koller, an ophthalmologist, finished the work and became the so-called Father of Anesthesia. What do you think I'm telling you?

Blue Man leaves, carrying a copy of Stevenson's *Strange Case* in his left hand and a bag-valve-mask in his right. On his way out the Dream Room door, he looks to the right, closes his eyes, and shakes his head. His hand reaches out to the side. He returns to his natural colour. I never dream of him again.

Moral of the story: I should have told Blue Man what happened to him when I had the chance. But he always knew.

EMPATHY TRAINING

In medical school I studied patients with antisocial personality disorder. They lack empathy, freeing them to kill. Dr. Robert Hare did foundational work at the Kingston penitentiary, discovering that so-called "empathy training"—encouraging antisocial inmates to read literature, watch movies and plays, talk to actual victims—actually makes the prognosis for anti-social personality disorder *worse*. Despite the good intentions of therapists, the wolves look at prey that remain prey and say to themselves, *How better to rape-torture-murder you, my dear.* One memorable killer related to the researcher how, after the empathy training sessions, he'd train himself with a mirror, mimicking expressions of the women he killed so as to see how it "felt." Training became sexually exciting to him, his expression in the mirror that of Pooh eating all the honey and grinning with glee.

I don't have an antisocial personality. I feel things. I do, I still do. I felt terror when Blue Man turned blue, blue on the table with the mask and the gas, terror at his blue in the dream. I know that now. But I tried not to feel it at all, which means I tried not to recognize it. Psychopathy was something I studied because it seemed to be real anesthesia, true anesthesia, and being true, it was something one was born with, not something learned, empathy also being bred.

TRUE ANESTHESIA

A breathing mask is an incredible thing. Attached to the mask, a canister. In the canister, a volatile gas. What would it have been like to be one of the doctors at Massachusetts General's ether dome in 1846, putting the very first patient in history to sleep, viewed by the public! Excitement, fear, terror... and *waiting*.

The art of anesthesia's been improved many times since then. One gas for this kind of surgery, another gas for that. My personal and professional preference is sevoflurane. Sevo isn't caustic, so one can breathe it without coughing. A few short breaths at a good flow rate and one will lose consciousness quickly. I apply the mask to my patients' faces, they fall asleep, and then I insert intravenous needles and a breathing tube. They literally feel no pain, no pain at all, until they wake up and emerge from their dreams into the aftermath of the surgeon's deliberate, curative infliction of pain. I can't take away what he's done, but it's a memory in them, something they never felt at the time and yet their body reminds them the surgery occurred.

With the sevo, my patients' eyes roll back, their breathing deepens, slows, and stops if the gas is coming too fast. At this moment, I see on their faces the look I perfect on myself. The patients practise how to look like me: blank, dead, expressionless.

When a surgery is over and the room has been cleaned, the table broken, the utility emptied, the patient resting safely in the recovery room, I put the mask to my face. Such a quick means of anesthesia; sevo's a clean drug; no one needs to know. I lose consciousness and become unable to hold the mask to my face, causing me to wake up; then I put the mask to my face again. Nurses don't count sevo like they do opiates. I balance like a porcelain doll on a wire.

KOLLER'S SCREEN TEST

The laparoscope enables surgeons to see inside the human body without a large incision. Once upon a time, surgeons cut men wide open via a hack and slash method, working deeper and deeper until the piece that had to be removed was exposed, the surgeon part archaeologist, part dowser, part butcher. Once a surgeon exposes the area he needs, finally seeing what he needs to see, he reaches his hands in to feel and touch the diseased part to know how extensively it has gone wrong. He maps it with his hands as certain surgical approaches and techniques come to him in his mind.

The laparoscopic method takes much less time and causes much less damage. Nowadays the laparoscopic surgeon cuts Winkin, Blinkin, and Nod into the abdomen, three small holes that allow a good surgeon to "sail off on a river of crystal light into a sea of dew." The laparoscope attempts to see what can be seen, trains a spotlight on the nature of the problem. The camera shows bowel, spleen, liver. To operate the mechanism is like trying to grasp a drinking glass with one's foot. With enough practice it's easy, but it will always be easier for a surgeon to look into a swath of deep cut and pull out the terrible part. The camera can only show what it sees according to its limited view—it misses things.

I believe laparoscopes have feelings. Laparoscopes are weary, having seen everything that can go wrong in the human body. They get impatient after not moving to the necessary area quickly enough. They feel like invaders into the human interior, but also like a looking-glass, the healthy body a beautiful Wonderland. Laparoscopes are like all other cameras. All things feel if they see.

The non-human dramatic actor shown by the laparoscope's gaze is the multipurpose arm. Without the laparoscope, the retractor/snare/cautery arm would be blind; without the arm, the laparoscope can only see, tissue can't be grasped or burned.

Biff, a young surgeon with small kids, likes to turn the laparoscope and the arm into characters from children's television programming. This is a big hit with the nurses that are moms. One day the laparoscope is Kermit the Frog, the snare Miss Piggy, and the gangrenous appendix The Great Gonzo. Another day the laparoscope is Iggle Piggle, the snare Makka Pakka, and the gall bladder Upsy Daisy's Bed. The surgeon speaks in grunts, squeaks, and silly voices.

Watching videotapes of operations as seen by the laparoscope, it's easy to be convinced that surgery is effortless, that it's just the sticking of a camera into the body and zapping the offending part. The illusion is that the surgery is hands-free. The camera casts a sharp eye on life, on death. The cautery arm cuts out doubt and disease as swashbuckler, as magic sewing needle.

After a hysterectomy a few days ago, I took the blood-covered laparoscope and cleaned it in saline. I turned on the camera and the television, placing the scope in front of my face. On the television screen, a face like my father's appeared, only calmer. I moved the camera as close to my right eye as I could without actual contact. I looked deep into the television screen that displayed the interior of my illumined eye, revealing an infinite feedback loop of feeling. Venous pulsations; static arteries; a haloed disc, no wound except for an abyss. Did Karl Koller, ophthalmologist and Father of Anesthesia, ever see himself like this? I returned to my stool and took a long suck of sevo. As I drifted off, my lack of breath the only brake, I wondered about the nerves involved in respiration, about the brain's respiratory centre in the medulla oblongata. Carbon dioxide, oxygen, and the offloading of gas: thought stops, my diaphragm paralyzes, then moves again when the gas dissipates and I wake. Do I dream?

When I wake, I check to see if someone has noticed, if someone has seen me stealing.

THE MONITORS GO RED

Ready to put the mask to my face again, I heard a commotion down the hall. Shouted orders; the sounds of a crash cart ricocheting off a stretcher; a stern voice alternating *hurry* and *faster* with *fuck* and *Jesus*. I turned the sevo valve off, put the mask back where it belonged, dangling from a happy green monitor.

The OR doors burst open and she was there, the redhead from the parking lot with the dress designed to billow, the dress of unreachable youth. Her hair was thickened by caked-on blood; her right leg had opened up and was splinted to keep bones and nerves in alignment, to keep blood flowing to her foot. Her eyes were closed. Packaged blood ran full bore into her arms. My old mentor, Dr. Haupsturm, pushed her in.

I am trained for situations like this. I watched the trauma team suffer the terror that that this young woman would die. As trauma team leader, Dr. Haupsturm sweated and shouted orders on the fly to frantic underlings. Dr. Haupsturm revised his orders a beat later. Should the girl die, the team members would blame Haupsturm for not being decisive enough. Feeling as calm as a camera at the back of the OR, distanced from the drama, I realized they would be correct in blaming Dr. Haupsturm. This girl could probably be saved.

"Where's her boyfriend?" I asked Dr. Haupsturm, who didn't hear. He shouted at a nurse to hurry the fuck up with the cross-matched blood. I don't think anyone knew I was even there.

Two surgeons entered, an attending and a resident. Dr. Haupsturm suddenly went from being the most powerful man in the room to the least. Nurses still have a role but now Dr. Haupsturm is subordinate to the surgeons, he couldn't do what they could do with their saving hands. The saviours discussed body parts, techniques, triage. The surgeons thought Dr. Haupsturm excitable and useless, a glorified escort. So did I, everyone did. Since his divorce was finalized last year, his fortune halved, then quartered by his lawyers. The whole hospital called him "Scoop'n'go" behind his back.

The terrifying thing about surgeons is their confidence. According to a surgeon, if the patient dies, it was because there was nothing they could do. But if the patient lives, it was because they, the surgeon, had made a glorious save. Blame falls, always, on the anesthetist.

Broken, the redhead remained beautiful, the red hair curling over and around her ears, the blood an accessory to her natural flare.

In the film *Malice*, the red-haired female lead, Nicole Kidman, gets an operation from a god-complexed Alec Baldwin. Kidman intentionally overdoses on a drug that torches her ovaries; Baldwin is the surgeon who performs an emergency bilateral oophorectomy. In cahoots with the redhead, Baldwin takes the reproductive capacity from Kidman so that she can defraud an insurance company. Patient and doctor hope to become very rich. In one memorable scene, a hairy-backed Baldwin takes a long pull from a bottle of bourbon in bed. He and Kidman have just been fucking, and in the earlier scene Baldwin had come. His bourbon tips back to the vertical. Kidman's character is the kind of woman who excoriates everyone around her, the fire on her head fetishized shamelessly by the camera: alternately long and flowing, or tied in a ponytail, or brushing against Baldwin's black and wavy chest. Kidman takes the bottle from Baldwin and juts a carnal look at the camera, telling Baldwin, "Save drinking for later. You still have more to do." Baldwin mounts her and yanks her hair.

Moral of the story: love may not always square with the ideal. Just see the way he looks at her.

The surgeons scrubbed outside the OR. Dr. Haupsturm looked lost. One of the orders he made five minutes ago but reversed three times might have been necessary, might have saved this girl's life. Rhonda cries in the corner because Dr. Haupsturm accused her of not administering the drug he insisted it was her duty to have given five minutes ago. Everyone knew Scoop'n'go needed a scapegoat. Who knew if the tranexamic acid was supposed to go in or not?

The float and assist nurses stared at the redhead on the table, then at Rhonda. Float looked at me. "Jesus. You're there? Dr. Koller?"

I stood. "I have control now. Thank you for bringing her to me," I said confidently to Dr. Haupsturm. He gratefully left, complaining about door-to-OR time all the way, trying to blame the nurses for being slow. If I were dreaming of Blue Man right now, Blue Man would tell me that dreams are life's door-to-OR time.

The redhead was dying, but she could be saved. If there is pain when one is unconscious, I have never felt it. It takes love to imagine such a thing, to detect the deep love underlying the depths of anesthesia.

As I resuscitated her, the team complained about the trauma team leader. Float said, "Boot to his ass time, shitty Scoop n' Go, Dr. Poop Scoop, fuck him."

In a whisper, Assist said: "If only he fucked Rhonda as good as he screamed at her."

Rhonda cried, squeezing a blood bag, shoving red cells into the dying girl.

Pointing at me, Float said, "Look. If Super Scoopy Doopey did resuscitations as good as Sandman here, then this girl would have a chance. But Scoop'n'go gets scaredio—nothing's worse than a fraidy-cat doctor. I swear. Don't be in a goddamn car crash in this city when he's on for trauma call."

Dr. Haupsturm lost his kids and most of his money when his wife took up with a well-endowed co-pilot who made a lot of Heathrow runs. I saw Haupsturm in pain—the buttons he pushed were all wrong, were the same button. He didn't change a thing in his life.

The redhead's orifices sprouted tubes. Fluids ran in and out, nothing left to do for me but watch. The surgeons finished at the sink and entered the OR, their hairy arms slightly green from antiseptic soap. They shared a regal air. One of them saluted me as the scrub nurse gloved him. The redhead might die but still he recklessly put his right hand close to his surgical cap—if the asshole touched it, the nurses would make him wash his hands again.

All the king's horses and all the king's men put the girl together again. I sat on my stool, listening to sonics: rhythmic beeps, the cautery's sizzle, the whoosh of mixed oxygen pushed into the woman's lungs.

Looking at an X-ray on a box, Alec Baldwin shouts: "We have to operate or this woman will die! *She has necrotic ovaries!*" The camera moves from an anesthetized Kidman, to the X-ray, back to Baldwin's wide eyes. "*Necrosis!*" he bellows.

Finished, the surgeons left the room. Rhonda remained to help me wheel the redhead to the recovery area. Rhonda's breasts seemed somehow bigger; I noticed a prominence underneath. Pregnant? "Just finish your shift with counts." I said. "Take it easy."

Rhonda said, "But the nurses need report. I have to stay."

I said, "Can't I just flash them my winning smile?"

Rhonda smiled. I haven't smiled, not once, in this hospital. She looked at the redhead one last time and left.

George Clooney fucks a lot of nurses as a primetime MD on the network show *ER*. Immersing himself in the lives of his women, he conducts his affairs in series and parallel. His genius as a Casanova lies in never mixing lovers up. He possesses an uncanny ability to juggle names, scents, appointments, and sexual preferences. Clooney is an obvious lion. More interesting is Clooney's colleague Anthony Edwards, a balding beta male, a doctor who forms monogamous, lasting relationships. But in one episode, Clooney, due to some cosmic accident, is without a woman, happily devoting himself to being a doctor of children, of being the bearer of news to mothers and fathers, of calling the protectors of children when he suspects abuse. Edwards, on the other hand, blunders his way through juggling relationships with three women. He cares about all of these women, but he keeps forgetting their names and he fails to respect the cad's code: keep paramours apart from one another at all times.

In an inevitable convergence, all three women encounter Edwards in the Emergency Department. One woman is a gorgeous nurse in greens from a different floor in the hospital; one is a pant-suited public relations executive, also comely. And another is a former patient, someone he had resuscitated a year ago. She too was Clooney grade, intentionally out of Edwards' league. In the scene, the blonde finds Edwards first and wonders why he's behaving so nervously. She peeks around the corner to where Edwards is obviously trying not to look. Edwards tries not to catch the eye of the brunette nurse from another floor, but the brunette pleasantly tries to make eye contact with Edwards as she chats with a hulking paramedic. The two women look at one another, then at Edwards. Edwards looks away, only to now see the redhead rushing in to see him. She smiles, about to tell him something never uttered because she sees the two frowning women and the guilt on Edwards' face. All three women angrily leave the emergency department, passing the pediatrics area as they go. They see Clooney dreamily listening to the lungs of a child with pneumonia. He smiles at each one as they pass.

Moral of the story: be what you are.

The girl, broken porcelain, was glued together. Did I feel love? No— just a numb echo of Nicole, something I missed. As I watched the redhead's chest rise and fall, I wondered about need. Do we need to be put together again, or do the pieces themselves have that need? Old books of fairy tales teach that children will be carved to pieces. Humpty Dumpty was a silly fellow, someone who'd risk his life on a whim. You could tell by his smile in illustrations: he looked like the gofer who wanted to discuss sandwiches. But Humpty Dumpty looked, pre-fall, like he felt no pain. Therefore pain was what Humpty Dumpty needed. He needed to fall. Only then could he be glued whole.

I used to wonder why Humpty fell. If he jumped, or if it was an accident. In time I developed a theory: he was *pushed*. Like a detective, I tried to figure out who pushed him, if it was Red Riding Hood or the Little Piggy Who Had None. Could it have been Mother Goose herself? But the answer was contained right there in the story of Humpty Dumpty: *all the king's horses and all the king's men*. They did it, they snuck up behind Humpty as he sat on the wall, they pushed him like air rushing out of a mask. Then they ran to him when he was broken on the ground, surprise on their faces. Yet what they felt was relief, because now they were of use.

All children can relate to Humpty Dumpty, their parents are the royalty that brings them to life and breaks them anew. My parents broke me and broke me until the pieces soldered together and sang into anesthesia.

My redhead would wake to gallant cavalry and dim fluorescence, to the sound of cranky monitors in the next bed, to a respirator pushing the tide of the world into her. The king's horses and the king's men would breathe for her. She would have just one thought: *where is he, my one, my man*? Then: *he is not here.*

He is a piece of her memory. He is in pieces. The nurses said he's dead.

What else do I remember? Let me see. After wrapping the mask around my face, I turned the valve to full flow and lay down next to the redhead. My reasoning was: if I sat on the stool, I might fall forward and the mask could dislodge at impact—I would wake up before it was over. I looked at the billowing, crusted flame of her. I watched and watched. The king's horses, the king's men, they would soon come. They would push.

But I woke to cavalry, I ended up across from the redheaded girl in the ICU. I became a Blue Man with a constant headache. I remember being in love, I lay down next to a beautiful memory. It was what I had always wanted to do. What are you going to do with me?

HOW TO DRINK, FAIL,
AND BE MYSTIFIED
BY WOMEN

JD ACCIDENTAL

Nothing happens in dining rooms. Mothers serve meals they slave over, or meals they reheat, or defrost and microwave. Fathers sit at the table, ready to throw a bowl, to be in love, to be anywhere else.

The mother and father are gone. Promise was sold to them as a gold band too many years ago. They looked at one another and wondered where and who they were, *exactly*. They knew the answers to both questions, *kind of*.

Our swimmer is swimming. His rumpled shirt was pressed before work but had battled through the day, existing now as an off-white relic of some other life. His worn pants slide on shoes that bear the slime of backyard lawns and engine exhaust. Our swimmer looks down. It all has to do with a woman.

A back door opens onto a stairwell. Our swimmer goes down nine stairs to find a kid playing a game called JD Accidental. On the screen an orange K-car gluttonously runs over a woman. The K-car backs up over the woman as her baby squalls in a shopping cart. The car moves back and forth, thoroughly crushing her guts. The game cues the same scream with each change of direction of the car from forward to backward motion: the same *Aiie*, unchanging in volume. This scream is triggered over the background screams of the shopping cart baby. Our swimmer notices that it's a little girl playing the game. Perhaps six years old, she sits in a plush pink Disney Princess chair. Alone in front of the screen, her hands on the controller, she asks: "Do you want to play?"

Our swimmer knows where the mother and father are. They're in the dining room—where nothing happens. The little girl asks our swimmer, "Do you have a car?"

"Yes. I do," our swimmer says.

"What do you do in it?"

Our swimmer raises his voice to talk over the medley of rhythmic screaming. "I drive in it."

"Oh," she says, concentrating again on the game.

Next door a group of boys hunt and kill one another. Everyone hides in JD Accidental until someone new to the game gets bored with being a sniper. The bored roamer always gets fragged, how many times do the message boards have to warn newbies: DON'T ROAM. YOU WILL BE BLOWN AWAY. Our swimmer watches a pockmarked kid eviscerate another kid with nodular acne by means of bayonet. HAND TO HAND KILL BONUS, the screen flashes. But another friend laughs and explodes the bonused killer with a bazooka. One more friend finds the level's super-upgrade and cashes it in for a tank.

"Hahahaha!" he laughs. "I mush you, you are all mush," he says, rolling over everyone in sight with the tank. He crushes the bodies of his friends with his immense treads, lingering with the crush, moving back and forth, eliciting an *Aiie* with each squish. Tank Driver declares, "I win. Last joint's mine. Fair and square." Tank Driver grabs the prize and pulls out a lighter. Before bringing out the flame, he looks at our swimmer and asks, "You play?" Tank Driver wants to give the controller to our swimmer to prevent his surviving friends from activating the level self-destruct while he smokes the joint. Self-destruct the level and the tank's destroyed too in JD Accidental.

"No. I don't play." Our swimmer hears an explosion upstairs—a wine cup detonating against a wall, wallpaper splash like bloodstain. Then the music of an overturned cabinet, the sound effects of a father ripping everything out of the fridge onto the floor. The pockmarked boy who lives here hangs his head. His friends look away. Our swimmer takes the controller and pretends not to press the self-destruct button.

Next door, a toddler in a tow-truck T-shirt and diaper plays JD Accidental on a green Leapster. The game involves a flower: push the big silver button at the bottom of the console, Leapster makes it rain. Watching the toddler is a father with a gin bottle in his right hand. The little boy delights in making the sky thunder. The boy's father sways in his seat, his face opaque, a darkened screen. The father regards our swimmer and slurs, "I should be upstairs."

Our swimmer says, "I know. In the dining room."

The little boy puts down the green game with only one button. He climbs on top of his father to pinch his father's neck. Squeeze, pull. The father shouts, *Aiie!* The boy says to our swimmer, "Mommy!"

Next door, a group of girls plays JD Accidental. On the screen, a "new girl" character who just moved to the high school tries to make friends. Hot bullies score points by ignoring new girl, but this is a low-scoring strategy, so the hot bullies spread slut and lesbian rumours about new girl, but this too is a low-scoring strategy, so the hot bullies swarm new girl and gang-push her. New girl begins to scream, *Aiie*, but this remains a low-scoring strategy. The hot bullies kick at new girl's head, bashing her face against the brick of the school. This remains a low-scoring strategy. The hot bullies kill new girl, pulling her hair as they pluck out her eyes. With each violent act, new girl makes the same scream: *Aiie*. High score is reserved for necrophilia, but before dead new girl can be defiled, the hottest bully turns to our swimmer and says, "She started it."

As the bonus round screen flashes, our swimmer says, "I know."

Next door, our swimmer discovers a basement empty except for a widescreen. On the screen, the JD Accidental logo flashes, black block letters outlined in white. Rectangles start to move up and down as part of the programmed demonstration of the game. A ball hits a rectangle and is sent to the other side of the screen where a different rectangle moves to meet it. Our swimmer thinks, *Beauty is a perpetual motion machine.* Ball speed increases until the ball streaks back and forth across the screen, light-speed, until the ball gets past the left rectangle. The right rectangle wins. Our swimmer revises his definition of beauty accordingly: *Beauty defeats itself by winning.*

Two doors down, tins of tomatoes, peas, and corn sit on the wooden shelves of a bomb shelter. Planks stretch across stacks of bricks. Two brothers take turns playing JD Accidental. The big boss is hard to kill, bathing them in a wide-swath death ray when the brothers come close to defeating it. The brothers are angry, having come so tantalizingly close so many times only to wither from the death ray. When one brother dies, he takes his controller in both hands and tries to split it in half. After thirty seconds of intense flexing and facial contortion, he collapses on the couch, the controller unharmed, and says to our swimmer, "It's not fair."

Our swimmer says, "I know."

The other brother continues to play, sings *Bonus Life* as JD Accidental makes MIDI music to the tune of Twinkle Twinkle Little Star. This means the killed brother can re-enter the game, his living brother will resurrect him with the bonus life. This also means that the living brother will die in the game soon and try to split his controller in half.

Next door is the Human Individual Metamorphosis Church. Inside, our swimmer is surprised to find a crypt. Aren't crypts a Catholic or Orthodox practice? Beside the crypt are rows of split and chipped pews heavily defaced by sacrilegious adolescents with blades. *Hearts and arrows, TLF, JD Accidental.* Lighted by a widescreen television, the room seems like a good place of worship for dead congregants. A face with proptotic eyes looks out from the screen, interspersing misquoted biblical verses amidst brimstone predictions. The spectral face insists that the end times have been calculated by tabulating "the very words of Jesus our Lord" and then dividing them by the degrees Fahrenheit of the Lake of Fire's surface. The screen face states the end of the world will come in 2012—last year. 2012 flashes on the screen over the crypt man's eyes. The date grows, erupting into fire and soon burning down to ash. The walls of the crypt bear a name, date, and epitaph: JD Accidental, Dec. 25 1933—April 6 2012, *Truly, I say to you, today you will be with me in paradise.* Our swimmer realizes the purpose of the crypt: it was built to hold the man who predicts the end of the world. Crypt Man died last year of the wrong prophecy, he foretold only his own death. Ready for the interment of hundreds of bodies, the crypt holds but one.

Our swimmer sees that the screen responds to touch, that he can press a button and hear exegesis, or hear a hymn sung by the sepulchral, proptotic prophet. He presses another button and sees the shimmering Lake of Fire, men and women marching into it while screaming *Aiie* monotonously. Our swimmer watches the men and women try to swim like him in the Lake of Fire, their arms burning to bone and then even the bone incinerating. Our swimmer says to them as they scream and burn, "I know."

Next door, a school basement looks like a hoarder's den. Every computer the school had ever purchased is stacked shoulder-high, creating a maze our swimmer must get through as part of the game. Cords snake around monitors and keyboards, external disk drives are crushed under face-down monitors. Our swimmer negotiates a small passageway though the stacks of different desktop models. Our swimmer wishes that the screens would come to life: *what screensavers would show,* he asks himself. He remembers the screensaver from his home computer, a restless geometric object that folds on itself, morphing from distinct shapes (parallelogram, diamond) into shapes with no name, shapes with a thousand angles, shapes in perpetual motion.

Our swimmer remembers attending the parent-teacher interview about his son the week before. He wore a suit to the interview, a carryover from meeting an app start-up CEO earlier that day. The teacher, a woman who resembled the hottest bully on JD Accidental, smiled at our swimmer, then turned to our swimmer's son and frowned. She looked back to our swimmer and said, "Your son is very capable." Her nail polish was teal. *Did she ever break a nail, a sweat, a man?* our swimmer thought.

Our swimmer said, "Capable of what?"

The hot teacher bully, who had never worked at the school before the age of computers, looked at her pupil and said, "He's capable of anything. But all he talks about is JD Accidental."

Our swimmer said, "I know."

Our swimmer stops remembering. He finds the exit. As he opens the door to leave the school basement, the computer monitors come to life, every screen displaying the JD Accidental logo.

Next door, he enters an empty and unfinished basement he's sure he's seen before. The fuse box lacks a cover. Upstairs, he hears a husband and wife having dinner. He also hears the background noise of a television reporter announcing that, *for the first time in history, video game sales have surpassed motion picture grosses. This is because of the phenomenal popularity of a single blockbuster, JD Accidental.* Man and wife discuss the stock market. He argues for greater investment; she feels it's too dangerous a time.

"We can't. We don't have the money to lose. If we *spend* all this, and it is *spending* what you propose, it isn't *investing*, it's *gambling*,

142

it's *wasteful*. We won't be able to keep our daughter at the *school*, we won't be able to keep the *house*, we won't be able to *eat*. You lost all our money last time, I had to ask my parents for a bailout. And they *hate* you! And they wouldn't give the money to me *unless* I told them *why*! And they already knew *why*! Because they knew what would happen. You lost it all! And they made me say it *anyway*! My father insisted the money be given in cash this time, to me personally, so that he could see *me* accept it face to face! So *no*. No you can't."

The husband says, "But this is a sure thing. It's JD Accidental."

Our swimmer wonders if marriage counsellors are like lifeguards: is sputtering and gasping for air a necessary stage of development in relationships? Is throwing a flotation device a saving measure, or rather the prolongation of a good, proper drowning?

Next door, he finds an underground stage. In the ceiling, cameras record two men jumping and bending in front of a giant screen. On each side of the stage is a mosh pit. On one side, the fans of Team Jimmy scream *Aiie*; on the other, Team Randall's fans scream *Aiie*. Each side cheers when their hero makes the other hero bleed or starve in JD Accidental. An emcee moves between the two teams, interviewing kids to develop a conflict narrative. Team Jimmy hates Team Randall because of schoolyard braggadocio about a new girl that Jimmy liked but Randall's girlfriend killed. Team Randall hates Team Jimmy because Randall really wanted new girl and could never have her, he could never have the good, only the beautiful, the bad.

The emcee booms into the microphone, "Our swimmer, who do you think will be the champ? Who will prevail? Who wants it? Who needs it? Who has what it takes? Who will be the one to wear the belt of triumph, who shoves the video gun in the mouth of the other and pulls the video trigger with real satisfaction and release?"

Breathless, the emcee appears as if he'll construct a top rope to ring the stage, just to fly off it. A ceiling camera zooms in on his mouth.

Before our swimmer can comment as analyst, the mosh crowds try to claim our swimmer as their own. Kids from both sides lift him up on their shoulders and pull him back and forth, back and forth, trying to get him into their territory. Randall and Jimmy jump, bend, and focus on the giant screen, unaware that our swimmer buffets behind them. Our swimmer's clothes rip, he loses his shoes, his hair is pulled, his ears bend back. He feels like a coffin carried by a crowd in a city accustomed to bombing, snipers, and the human dilemma of what to believe.

To save himself, he beats the children, striking their faces. The children trample one another in retreat. Our swimmer hears screams but he can't tell if they come from the pulsing stereo system (dead troll? dead demon? dead Jimmy? dead Randall?) or if they are real children crying out in pain. *Aiie*, the same *Aiie*.

Wading into the crowd, the emcee tries to get a final quote from our swimmer. Our swimmer grabs the microphone from the emcee and uses it as a club, whacking the emcee in the mouth. Our swimmer brandishes the microphone at the wild children.

A poster on the wall bills the Randall vs. Jimmy event as a cage match, even though it occurs on stage. Someone Must Win, Someone Must Lose. Our swimmer runs up the stairs to the main floor. He finds himself in a dining room on the edge of the city. On the table, a roast is carved into slices. He hears a voice that he thinks he knows and another that he doesn't, his own and not his own. Where is his wife? Through the floor he feels a strong reverberation: triumph, cheers, *Aiie*, the sound of children streaming through the backyard grass.

A SERVICE TO HIS READERS

Books line Nowlin's shelves. He tilts his head back to get them all in view. To him, the books are tools. Another man has a tool shelf or wall to display socket wrenches and clippers. For example, a cabinetmaker built Nowlin's cedar bookshelves with tools. But on Nowlin's shelves, the only tools he knows how to use stand straight, alphabetized, ready.

Some of the books are his own but Nowlin purposely scatters those titles amongst the works of writers he admires. Flush with the fresh joy of creation, Nowlin sometimes closes his eyes and spins around in his study. He reaches for a book high or low depending on his mood. Often the book he touches is the presiding spirit of the writing Nowlin just finished. Rarely he'll touch one of his own books, and when that occurs, Nowlin won't write the rest of that day, preferring to feel old, trying to forget he'd written better, much better, before.

He could take his own books down, of course. Put them in the basement, or shove them in a closet. But Nowlin believes his books improved by rubbing shoulders with writers like Milosz, Jeffers, and Mishima.

The gin cabinet is bare. Nowlin drank too much last night. The student editor from the *Fiddlehead* interviewed him about his "origins." *Origins means O, I need more rye and gin,* Nowlin thinks.

Questions about the past are unsettling, even if they are answered untruthfully, even if the questioner is a young woman of bedraggled, low-cut impurity. At a moment of great inner hilarity, Nowlin maintained during the *Fiddlehead* interview that he was descended from a Congolese king and that the king had had many illegitimate children, including an albino moron. The king banished the albino moron and his albino-producing mother to the snow-white country of Canada. Fresh off the boat at Pier 21 in Halifax, Nowlin's mother headed for Stanley, Nova Scotia. Before she left the Congo, the king told her in bed that he had a colony there. She could be a servant in the mansions of lordly potato pickers and nouveau riche backwoods mechanics. These Stanley mansions employed untold numbers of Congolese—the king thought of it as his "new world." Nowlin said that some of the king's enemies believe that by sending the albino moron away, the king was trying to get rid of a ghost, a possessed member of his line that would fill the black population with white venom. But he, the king's son, knew the truth…

The student interrupted. "Couldn't your Dad just have gotten a white woman pregnant—and that's why you're white? You're really white, you know."

"Perhaps," Nowlin admitted. "There were rumours of an affair between Queen Victoriana of Aldara, ice queen of territories annexed by the warlike Finns, and the King of the Congo. It's been whispered that my real mother and father met in the drawing room of Grace Kelly, princess to the stars."

The student uncrossed her legs very, very slowly. She wore a jean skirt and a sweater with the University of New Brunswick block-letter logo straining against her chest. "Where do you get your poetry?" the student asked.

"I don't know where it comes from. Maybe a childhood trauma involving my mother and a potato picker?" Nowlin swelled, became stentorian. "No—to *write* one *must* drink the wine… of astonishment!" Nowlin took a big draught of wine straight from the bottle. He bent forward: "Actually, I get my inspiration from money. Necessity. Et cetera." Nowlin threw up his arms as if he were summoning the heavens to rain. "Oh money money money, Oh money money!" he chanted. "Now what was your name again dear?"

"Jan," she said.

"Right," Nowlin said. "Jan, my books are *tools*," he said, pointing at his shelves...

Jan recorded his decelerating monologue. Nowlin had lived in Fredericton for twenty years. During that time, he'd published a dozen books. Frederictonians threw a party in his honour when he won what he impishly called The National Award of Some Importance. Many people were proud of him—his literary friends, his family—but also people who weren't inclined to read poetry, among them the premier of the province, Richard Chappeau. This latter group, especially, wept at his lines.

But he seemed to be telling the truth underneath the silliness. Despite accolades and admiration, Nowlin always felt dirt poor. He never forgot what it was like to be hungry in the backwater kingdom. He never forgot what it was like to have his mother Mare, the real-life ice queen, leave him with Judd, the in-actual-fact potato picker.

Jan realized that Nowlin wouldn't tell her a useful, true thing. When Nowlin finished expounding about the value of a fully-stocked toolbox, Jan said, "Mr. Nowlin, you seem quite interested in my chest."

"What?" Nowlin said, embarrassed.

"Are your parents still alive?" Jan asked, pretending that she was repeating herself.

Tricky girl! Nowlin feared this question more than any other. It meant that he had to think of his parents outside of invention. Nowlin read the Bible five times through as a child before the potato picker let him walk to the library to take out books. When asked a question like this one, Nowlin felt he *had* to tell the truth. But he would rather have his poetry withdrawn, all of it unpublished at a stroke, than answer this question.

The truth: Nowlin knows the potato picker closely, loving him down to the last drop of shared blood. And yet Nowlin got away from Judd as soon as he could. Nowlin still receives misspelled letters from his father, the last letter ending *Proud of you boy the very best!*

Nowlin left the imaginary faux-Congolese kingdom behind long ago. He was independent now. Nowlin thought of Judd with a pen at the family kitchen table, the table where the ice queen gave birth to the boy she gave up, the ice queen writhing on her back, Judd in the corner watching a midwife make maneuvers. Then Nowlin thought of his father sitting at the same table, writing him that last letter. Nowlin knew that neither father or son could do any better than each other, that their lives couldn't have turned out any other way. The same thing happened to them both, after all. They were both left. The ice queen did the leaving. He had to protect his parents, including his queen. He had to protect himself.

What to say to the book-sultry Jan? Confess that Judd had taught him nothing except how to drink, how to fail, and how to be mystified by women? That the ice queen left him when he was just three years old, Nowlin asking his father every day afterwards where Mare had gone?

Judd told his son, "Mare went away." Judd should have said "Mare left us for good," but instead Judd told his boy "'Mare went away." Naturally, the boy wanted to know when she would be back, hoping each night when he went to sleep she'd be back in the kitchen the next morning. When Nowlin turned four years old, his father having ruined Nowlin's corn meal cake on the fire, the boy stopped asking. Though the cake was burnt and flat, Nowlin ate every piece. He associated the texture and taste of the black crust forever with his mother Mare.

Nowlin heard the real story one night when the potato picker got self-pityingly drunk. Judd needed someone to talk to when he got drunk, and that person was Nowlin. "Mare left us for some other man, a rich slick from Halifax. He drove a big blue car and one day she drove away in it with him. He picked her up here but he wouldn't get out of the car. Mare kissed you on the forehead, said "Remember me, Scampy." Do you recall? You watched her go away, you didn't understand she was gone for good." Judd threw an ashtray at the window. The ashtray broke through the glass and snow whistled in. As she walked away she said, "I'm going, Scamp." The next day, Judd looked ashamed. Father and son never spoke of the ice queen again. Judd covered the broken window with tarp and tape.

Nowlin decided to say something to Jan. "My father was assassinated by rebel soldiers plotting to wrest control of the Congolese diamond industry." Nowlin put his tongue between his teeth, searching for bits of hard crust. Wishing as hard as he could about his mother, he said: "My mother is alive and well just outside Stanley, Nova Scotia." This was the first time he had ever spoken of Mare in over thirty years. Astonished by what he said, astonished by the bitter truth of the resolute fact, he took a long, long pull from his bottle of wine. In a few minutes, he passed out in the chair, emitting oblong snores.

Nowlin's wife, Claudia, knocks at the study door. Startled, he gathers his papers and sweeps them into the desk drawer. Claudia slowly opens the door. "Are you coming to bed soon?" she asks. "It's two o'clock. You need to sleep."

She's right. Last night, the *Fiddlehead* interview concluded with Nowlin passing out in a chair. Tonight, he's writing a poem about his father—a dangerous business. Besides, the gin's gone. His handwriting is ruinous and he can't hold onto the images he needs for poetry. Nowlin says to his wife what he always does at this time of night: "Let me finish this poem, dear, I won't be long." He didn't say what he always thought when he saw her appear at the threshold, the white nightgown rustling against the doorway: *I'm writing a love poem for you, Claudia, these poems are all love poems, they're all for you.*

Mare left, so Nowlin spends his life craving love. In turn he loves his wife the best he can. He never shows Claudia his work—he wants the poems to be an incredible secret. Nowlin thinks the love poems untrue because they don't capture her as she is. The poem he's writing is a simple one. He prefers writing simple poems that people remember because the feeling in them, being memorable, captures love with greater fidelity than any photograph, meaning that his poems constitute the matter of memory.

"That's what you always say. You should just come now," his wife says, wearily closing the door of the study to climb up the stairs to bed. Nowlin hears her slow steps. He had no more gin. *Maybe I should go,* he thinks.

But then he remembers Jan, the earnest graduate student who had said she wanted to capture Nowlin as he is, in his own element. Nowlin sympathized with her then and even more now. That's what he wants to do with his own writing, to capture things.

At eleven a.m., Nowlin has an appointment to see the doctor. Nowlin fears doctors. The tradition in the potato picker's family is to visit the doctor only when a man can't walk. Nowlin told Jan the tradition of the Congolese: "A real man is carried to the doctor, you see." But at eleven a.m. he must walk to the doctor's office on King Street, just across from King's Place. Like a poem he intimates the shape of before he has time to write it down, Nowlin knows what the doctor will order him to do. "Lose weight," the genial fitness freak will say.

Nowlin is obese. *Ideal Weight would make a good title for a poem*, Nowlin thinks. "Stop drinking," the teetotaling prohibitionist will say. The last time Nowlin was in the doctor's office, he was mutely drunk and weighed over 300 pounds. He fell off the examining room table when the doctor asked him to disrobe. Nothing had changed since then.

I'll stop drinking he resolves to himself. But this thought comes only after a few drinks, and then usually when there's nothing left to drink. One summer morning a few months ago Nowlin woke up and found a whole bookshelf empty. Embers glowed in the fireplace. This holocaust claimed first editions of Mishima.

Claudia wants him to stop drinking too. He promises her this in his head a thousand times, but never aloud. He can't stop drinking, so he writes love poems in compensation, poems that she will never read. The amount of leaving happening in the great writer's brain is vast and constant.

"Do you remember your first published poem?" Jan asked him during the interview. On hearing the infernal question, Nowlin wanted to tour the midwestern United States and search for every copy of the Fall 1952 *Argonaut* he could get his hands on. In it, Nowlin's first published poem, "The Doe-Eyed Deer," appears. Written in quatrains of ABAB rhyme scheme and just three stanzas long, the poem lives up to its title through thematic devotion to a doe in a field.

Argonaut

422 Sirin Street
Lansing, Michigan. March 12, 1950
Mr. Henry Weekes, Editor.

Dear Mr. Nowlin,

We at the Argonaut would very much like to publish "The Doe-Eyed Deer." I read the poem on a dreary day when our submissions seemed unworth the postage, really. In fact, after reading your poem, I gazed out the window of the Argonaut offices, my bungalow, and though I didn't see any deer, I believed I could, and moreover I saw the spirit of your poem in the green field: the grass about to be dewed, dusk about to erase any trace of evening, calling man and beast to sleep. You've got talent, Mr. Nowlin. We pay on publication with a single copy of The Argonaut mailed to your

door in Canada, and unless you object, we will use the following
for your bio (cribbed from your cover letter): "Mr. Aldin Nowlin is
an Andrew Marvell devotee living in Hartland, New Brunswick."

Yours,

Nowlin fantasized about packing the yellowed copies of the *Argonaut* in the trunk of his blue Cordoba and taking them back with him to Fredericton, where he'd burn every copy in his fireplace. "My first poem is lost in the mists of time, my dear. I sent it to a man in the Congo, you see. The politics there were quite unstable at the time. The poem was smuggled with blood diamonds to a literary journal based in Senegal where a distant cousin of mine, related on the Semibonogobongo side, was an editor. I never got a copy in my hands because the editor was an enemy of the Senegal king who was my father's cousin. The journal was shut down and all the copies of the issue were burnt."

Jan doggedly asked something else. "Which of your poems do you think will best stand the test of time?"

"Nothing stands in the end," Nowlin slurred out. "Everything is *carried*. But if I had to pick just one poem … it'd be 'The Martian-Eyed Martian,' a poem about a Martian with a single eye that blinks once for truth and twice for beauty. It's a rip-off of Keats. Not bad in my opinion, though that's up to others to judge."

Jan blinked. "The Martian-Eyed Martian?" she said.

"Oh yes," Nowlin said. "Contrary to popular opinion, Martians are actually purple—I said so in my poem. How did it go? I think the lines went something like this, "The purple galaxy swirling around the eye/ will never die. The truth of beauty will be espied." Something like that. Stirring stuff. I meant it to be a satirical commentary on the Congolese political situation. The poem's purple Martians symbolize the simple Congolese peasant and the eye represents the aesthetics of violence."

Jan looked abandoned in the service of literature. *If only I had lost weight,* Nowlin thinks. *If only I had stopped drinking. If only I was thirty years younger.*

"Mr. Nowlin, it would be a service to your readers to point out the poems closest to you, the ones you feel the most," Jan beseeched.

Jan was in the service of poetry. Saying the names of anything private caused Nowlin pain—he felt like he was showing the draft pages of poems from his desk to a stranger. Nowlin couldn't tell Jan about the poems for his wife, but these were his favourites. He couldn't say that every poem he had ever written was for his wife. Instead, he said, "I feel every one of my poems because they are me."

Nowlin thought of the doctor again. Once his doctor told him, "You poets do the real work of healing. All I do is patchwork." The doctor pulled out a copy of Nowlin's *I'm a Stranger Here Myself* from his desk drawer. "Do you mind signing this? I'm going to sign this prescription for you! It's a good trade."

Nowlin inscribed *Don't be a Stranger, Dr. Neilson*! even though Nowlin hated doctors. They police infirmity. Doctors possess a power he's powerless against. A poem a day couldn't keep the doctor away.

"Can you share any anecdotes about the Maritime Literary Community?" Jan asked in desperation. Nowlin told a true story about Milton Acorn in line for lunch at a poetry conference in Bouctouche, NB. At the buffet meal, a horrible odour wafted from Acorn. Once the nose identified the smell, the eyes had to reconcile the appearance of Acorn: stains front and back near all orifices. Ignoring a metal scoop, Acorn reached dirty hands into the potato casserole and cupped out a heap, slopping casserole onto his plate.

Everyone in line watched Milton without an objection. Nowlin was in line about ten people back. "I made a mental note right then not to eat the casserole," he said drolly. An elderly couple in line in front of Nowlin said, "That's Aldin Nowlin up there. He's a great poet."

Thrilled with this anecdote, finally given something, Jan said, "Yes. Yes he is."

Nowlin approaches poetry reluctantly. Each time he sit downs at his writing desk, Nowlin believes a poem will come despite the significant odds. Once he sits down, poetry is dragged out of him. Nowlin professes no theory about his writing, but he does try to answer a central question each time out: *Does love inform poetry, or does poetry inform me of love?*

The poem in front of him wasn't working.

> There is something impossible to do.
> I would tell you a secret; yes, that's it!

He blames himself. He could go to bed and placate Claudia, but he knows he won't fall asleep, he needs more alcohol for that. *How long has it been since I've walked to Odell Park?* he thinks.

Dying elm trees alternate with dented streetlights on the laneway to Odell Park. Nowlin hopes a semi-domesticated deer will come close to the fence and feed from the grass in his hand. A Cordoba passes by, a blue glint in the half-light. The driver rolls down his window and says, "Hey fat fucker, get offa the road!"

"A critic!" Nowlin thinks.

Too late—Odell Park is locked. Nowlin should have known. He had been in this city for a long time and enjoyed drinking wine in the park on summer days. For a few weeks last summer, Nowlin shocked his friends by walking with Claudia through the park for exercise— her idea, but Nowlin suspects Doctor Neilson got to her somehow. Leaves rustle against the gate. Deer sleep a vigil beyond the gate, he can't see them. Nowlin lights a cigarette.

Neilson the cancer crusader lectured Nowlin about that vice too. "I smell the smoke on you when you come in the examining room.

Your fingers are yellow. Your whiskers are yellow. Are your insides yellow?" *Smile.*

To Nowlin, the ideal doctor can only be found at funerals wearing a black suit. Dr. Neilson is slim, white-coated, and weirdly happy. He displays pictures of himself on his office wall, images of himself running across the finish lines of marathons.

I'm a sprinter, Nowlin thinks. *I sprint through poetry.*

Dr. Neilson preaches lifestyle modification, lifestyle modification. As if Nowlin has something so grand as a lifestyle! Books line the shelves of the doctor's office just like they do in Nowlin's office, and only a few of them are medical. The doctor's books include Boswell's *Life of Johnson*, a King James Bible, and an eclectic list of poetry titles.

A year ago the doctor bought all Nowlin's books and put them on his front shelf, a shelf resting just a few feet above the doctor's head. Doctor Neilson told Nowlin, "I want to you live, Nowlin. Write me more books! When I read your poetry, I feel more alive." The doctor flexed his left bicep. "Poetry," he panted.

When the doctor said that, Nowlin thought of tools, a socket wrench spinning on the umbilicus. But the doctor's wish wasn't enough—Nowlin left the doctor's office that day and kept right on dying.

Nowlin walks home from Odell Park. More cars pass—no one else has useful editorial feedback. Claudia isn't waiting at the door. He only half-expected her to be standing there. She works at the day care with dozens of children. Nowlin has three hours before he has to be at Dr. Neilson's office for his yearly physical and annual confession of sins. Will his overenthusiastic doctor say, just like last year, "Nowlin, people get better when they start taking care of themselves."

Smoking in a singed armchair, he wonders how people get better. *The problem,* Nowlin thinks, *is I feel a lack of gin more than a lack of health.* Nowlin knows he'll stop at the corner store at the bottom of College Hill and buy a few more packs of cigarettes on the way to the doctor's office and smoke a few going there. Cigarettes are easy to conceal. Nowlin knows he'll stop at the liquor store on the way back—gin bottles are harder to hide from Neilson's Teetotalitarianism.

Nowlin fingers the burns in the arms of the chair. He registers the desktop's black burns. This is the desk where his poems come. Nowlin looks at the shelf above his head—different than the doctor's. Instead of books or a picture of himself, a photograph of his father's face guards Nowlin's precious things. In the picture, Judd looks like he doesn't trust the photographer or doesn't want to be photographed. Nowlin finally falls asleep by thinking of his father. Nowlin hadn't dreamed a poem in years.

He wakes fifteen minutes before his appointment with Neilson; just enough time if he doesn't change clothes. A new brown-ringed hole had opened up in his right pantleg. He retraces the route he walked the night before. Dr. Neilson's office is just past the park.

How about I write a poem for the doctor? he thinks. I could sign it for him! The poem will be about being carried to the doctor and about what the patient carries to the doctor. Nowlin passes the corner store even though he's winded. No time to stop. Shortness of breath makes him imagine sitting in Dr. Neilson's chair, underneath all the books. He imagines Dr. Neilson sitting across from him in the patient's traditional spot. In the daydream, Nowlin advises "Doctor, our job is to point out the obvious."

On King Street, Nowlin hears the laughter of children. They hold chips and chocolate bars in their hands, waving the candy at a deer in the street. *A deer must have escaped from Odell Park*, he thinks. The white-tailed deer lifts its head and walks in front of Dr. Neilson's office, nuzzling the irises underneath the windowsill. The antlers on the male stick up on a broad central axis, smaller tines extending farther upward. The buck is healthy and strong, thick from years of food taken from children's hands, hands that feed Odell deer year-round. Reaching in his pockets for food, Nowlin realizes that he must thank his doctor somehow, perhaps in that poem.

MEANT

I.

Dr. Remora faces the sprouting fictions, standing at the front of the class. The fictions are everywhere; the fictions are out to get her. The fictions always behave this way, recalcitrant and evil, until, on a whim, the fictions soothe her, sing to her, and tell her that they, as fictions, are meant for her.

A balding fiction slumps in a chair. This fiction is sullen, squat, and lumpy. He refuses to admit there is a reason to believe in anything other than the imagination rendered in plausible detail. Realist Fiction waits to pounce on Dr. Remora, but Romance Fiction distracts him.

Romance Fiction wears a smiley face T-shirt with a tongue sticking out of the yellow face. Those who know Romance Fiction intimately, as Realist Fiction once did, knows she's punctured in intimate places. As Realist Fiction fantasizes about her once more, he puns: *a wholly happy ending.*

Why didn't it work out between those two? Dr. Remora asks herself. They seem made for each other: Realist Fiction tough on the outside and soft inside, Romance Fiction soft on the outside but hard inside. Adjusting the most proximal of her piercings, Romance Fiction looks at Dr. Remora expectantly, eager-to-please. Dr. Remora will try to give Romance Fiction what she wants: the means to write like her ex-boyfriend looks. Romance Fiction beams.

Dr. Remora continues to take attendance. In the front row are two fictions, Gay and Lesbian Fiction, that compete bitterly with one another. Their beef is: who's right about "out." Whose sanctimonious identity-emanations crush the other fiction's argumentarium? Both fictions have equivalently irrelevant grievances. Trouble when sitting together, they are impossible to separate, gleefully exchanging an inexhaustible store of insults about camp and gaze. Their opposition is perpetual, blissful, and though antagonistic, mutually enriching.

Before Dr. Remora finishes taking attendance, Experimental Fiction raises her hand. A hand-raise by Ex-Fic is always a tense moment in Dr. Remora's class. When Ex-Fic asks a question, all the other fictions react with feigned shock. *How can Ex-Fic be so audacious?* Yet next class, every fiction (with the noted exception of Realist Fiction) mimics Ex-Fic's challenge. Ex-Fic's reviled but at the same time she's haute couture: if she attends Dr. Remora's class dressing as a goth, next week the other fictions come dressed for a funeral. One step ahead, Ex-Fic arrives in hot pink. Passé, the fictions remove their sleeves, hoping their flesh tones come as close to the current culture as possible. The following week, according to schedule, the fictions dress like a mommylit maternity ward—but Ex-Fic's invisible, or dressed like Wonder Woman. Yet that week, the fictions are coy about their shared colour and insist their particular shade of pink is distinctive. The hopeless fictions try to convince everyone that there are *patterns* in their pink outfits that only the educated, discerning, *cool* eye can detect. Dr. Remora tries not to laugh as her fictions furtively shoot glances at one another in order to spot special pink patterns.

"Yes, Ex-Fic?"

"Dr. Remora, instead of asking us to write something in a certain way, how about we all write whatever we want and see what happens?"

"Don't you do that anyway, Ex-Fic?" she responds. The class laughs. "When have you ever given me what I ask for?" More laughter. "But then, just what I want at the same time. Fictions, I want all of you to write something that *means*. I want you to write whatever you want to write about, on any subject at all, but it has to be the most important thing to you in the world. You have five minutes. Begin."

The fictions glare at Ex-Fic before starting to type. Ex-Fic smiles, her fingers moving fluidly over her laptop. Dr. Remora figures Ex-Fic will pull one of her stunts, declare that whatever she wrote about that particular moment was the most important thing she could write about. She'd write about the inner lives of drainpipes. What else? And the writing would be amongst the most moving pieces the class generates.

Though the fictions insist on minute distinctions amongst themselves, Dr. Remora knows the fictions are part of a grand and single tradition that she shepherds, a tradition known as Good Writing. But as Dr. Remora watches the fictions work, she sees them disintegrate, collapse.

Realist Fiction's brittle rhetoric melts into a quivering, vaguely resentful pool. Ex-Fic goes up in a puff of smoke, leaving behind only the words *chemistry set* and *random bilge*. Happy Fiction evaporates, leaving behind the words *metal* and *naughty*. Nicknamed "Speculum" by Dr. Remora, Science Fiction breaks into a warped series of words. Once moving along at impulse power, he fragments into a messy asteroid belt of words. The other fictions (Historical, Adventure, Mystery, Plotless, and Non-) gather into a threatening wave of ink. Dr. Remora throws her arms in front of her face but stands her ground behind the lectern, holding back the tide. If only Lesbian Fiction could see her now—a strange, modern Moses.

The word *revolt* charges to the front of the classroom. Revolt climbs on top of Dr. Remora's lectern and waves its terminal *t* suggestively. Revolt put the *t* back in its pocket and wordsurfs to the back of the class, where the black wave is highest, only to move to back to the lectern and show its dirty *r*.

In minutes, the jumbled words melt down further into component letters, forming an entropic alphabetic sea. Letters form like-minded communities: I and U exist in gated enclaves where Realist Fiction used to sit. E keeps making its damn noise, *eeeeeee*, piercing Dr. Remora's brain. Only X is smart enough to disappear. *Ex-Fic?* Dr. Remora thinks. *My turn to copy you this time. I need to get out of here.* Dr. Remora's pupils disappoint her. "*What I know in life is dependent on meaning!*" she shouts in a deep, serious voice at the black tide. Still withstanding the uncommunicative storm of language, Dr. Remora stops shouting. She asks herself, *But what have I ever known?*

II.

The day before her standoff, Dr. Remora watches cable news. Bombs, dismemberment, rape, improvised death: Dr. Remora instantly knows she'll write a novel about a war she has nothing to do with, and soon. She'll compose a book that weaves fractured genealogies into a *meaningful* narrative.

Back-to-back episodes of Wolf Blitzer speak to Dr. Remora's soul. *God, these people are dying, what does it mean?* she thinks. Dr. Remora gets in her Volvo and drives to work with the feeling of a book coming on, in danger of being late for class. She speeds down the Don Valley Parkway mid-fart about the plight of postcolonial society and its world of revolting metal, its children doomed to repeat the errors of televisioned gestation. Her cell phone plays the introductory bars of Roaring Lion's "Caroline." One time, two times, three times: *We do to others what has been done to us,* she thinks. *Only one person ever calls me on that thing. I'll let Roaring Lion ring, ring, ring.* A strident, staccato honk from the car ahead cuts through Roaring Lion's looping refrain, startling Dr. Remora. *Just someone cutting someone else off,* she thinks. For some reason she remembers Realist Fiction's break-up with Romance Fiction.

Traffic slows. Squatted behind a sky-blocking tractor trailer, ahead of a black smart car, and boxed in on one side by a white stretch limousine and a rusted-out silver Chevette on the other, Dr.

Remora debates about whether to wait until Roaring Lion stops roaring. The car radio exhorts motorists to focus on rear brake lights, absentmindedness being "the major cause of delays and deaths on the highway." The female radio sidekick chips in, "But not necessarily in that order." Chortle, chortle goes the male host's voice, with a joke as afterthought: "No sleep 'till Brooklyn!"

The phone stops. It rings again. Roaring Lion is such a smooth calypso dude. Dr. Remora picks up the phone and checks the number. It's *her*.

"What, you?" Dr. Remora says.

"Yes. It's me. You got anyone else callin' you on that phone now?"

"Why? Am I supposed to answer your questions? Including *that* question?"

"I don't know. I thought it was over, but –"

"It *is* over."

"I don't want it to be over!"

"*I* said goodbye a long time ago. You know why, you cheater!"

Dr. Remora hangs up. The car radio mentions recent poll results heading into the municipal election, coliform counts in Toronto tap water, garbage piling up in parks, the construction of new universities "to address the critical lack of infrastructure," an international crime syndicate "here on our shores," hospitals decorated by Dior, the proposed renaming of the 401 into Mayor Ford's Maw. The sidekick tee-hees. "Tee-hee, tee-hee. Mayor's maw. Tee-hee." The male host chortles. Encouraged, the sidekick adds, "Mayor's Maw, that highway of homicidal street racers and alcoholic-addicts. Tee-hee hee."

Roaring Lion roars again. Dr. Remora pauses, forcing her posture into a position that looks final, serious, meaningful, a position that looks likely to win the last word. As if Speculum was trying to cadge a better mark. As before, she snaps the phone open and speaks first:

"I don't need to hear from you."

"I *want* to hear from you. I miss you so much. I want to call you on this phone, all the time. I want to call you on this phone when we're in bed. You can answer it or not... maybe I'm too busy to call in bed with you..."

"You are deluded. Your fiction is yourself! How do you justify what you did to me? You are lying right now!"

"I'm not lying."

...

"Hey! I'm not lying. I want to be with you. Take me back. I'll come to you, it will be good, so good again. I can make it good again."

Traffic starts to move. Dr. Remora will be late. It's been nine months since she has heard her lover's voice, nine months of resorting to the easy fictions of popular calypso singers. Whenever she hears the words "I love you" uttered by a man, woman, or child, on a screen or from a stereo, she weeps, rapt. Sentiment has her. Dr. Remora roars into the phone,

"Once upon a time. Do you hear? *Once. Upon. A. Time.*"

Dr. Remora hangs up. On the radio, she hears an infernal love song. She imagines the integrated noise of a hundred thousand simultaneous love songs played on the highway car radios now, all songs of protest and breasts beaten for love. It wrecks her to hear this common, communal song. Dr. Remora wonders if this is the purpose of her lover's call, to be reminded that all songs and stories start once upon a time.

She parks the car in the faculty lot. Kids stream past. An East Indian with gold chains shouts to an Italian with the same gold chains, "Yo, Marcus! You use the bathroom on the second floor? Fuck, it's gross. That's you, isn't it, the shit on the seat and the shit paper all over the fucking stall." Caressing cell phones, a phalanx of girls who walk in the other direction of the scatological boys laugh. Marcus responds, "No, Adit. You've been in the girl's bathroom again, haven't you?" Adit smashes Marcus in the arm with his fist, their gold chains jangling. The girls roll their eyes at the *disgusting* boys.

Dr. Remora hurries through the Jackman Humanities Building entrance, past beautiful bottle blondes and immaculate girl-next-doors. *Is there an inexhaustible supply of beauty?* she asks herself. Then she remembers the cable news, the arms separated from shoulder sockets. Dr. Remora rushes up the stairs to her classroom, her phone ringing, ringing, ringing. O Roaring Lion, where did *you* sleep last night? Dr. Remora violently turns the ringer off.

Wheezing, she apologizes to the waiting fictions. "Sorry I'm late." Realist Fiction sneers, tapping his watch. Ex-Fic looks asleep, her head reclined back, drool slipping from the left side of her mouth. Dr. Remora's hands reach for her briefcase.

Not here. I have no notes. Do I give the Meaning in Fiction lecture from memory? How was I supposed to begin? I forget. Give a definition of the word "declaim?" De-claim. We declaim the other in order to preserve the other. To preserve. Pre-serve. I'm supposed to start like this, I think . . .

Having a mental breakdown, she begins her address by asking, "How do stories mean?"

Lies are the most meaningful things, she thinks.

"I mean that there is meaning in stories that surpasses what happens in the story."

What is meant by saying "I love you" and what does it mean to hear those words? What could it mean to hear them again?

"What happens in the story is secondary to how the story is told. My fictions, do you care what happens in a story? Do you read stories like you live, addicted to the things you want?"

Provoke them.

"Stories transcend teller and reader. Stories are timeless. Stories begin. Stories happen once in a particular way and never again. Stories happen to the teller just as they happen to the reader. Both are complicit in the telling, both witnesses to the story."

The cell phone isn't switched off after all. *Tell me where you been last night, Caroline.* Realist Fiction glares at her, thinking: *everyone must follow the rules.* Romance Fiction smiles. Gay and Lesbian Fiction smirk. Ex-Fic remains asleep. Dr. Remora's pupils have their stories, stories starting with questions, questions deciding how stories mean. The same song, the song she too loves.

"Raise your hands if you have any questions! What are your questions?"

I wish this were a lie: no matter what the affair means, it will continue to mean.

Ex-Fic startles awake. A trickle of words falls from Dr. Remora's index finger. The flow starts from her shoulder and rushes down her arm. Dr. Remora feels undiminished by this loss. They are not her words, but her lover's lies. Yet these words *are* her words too, for they are saved on her cell phone. Dr. Remora reads them over and over, every day. Dr. Remora reads the words enough to reclaim them. Nine months ago, her lover used Dr. Remora's phone and forgot to delete a message from the sent messages folder:

> Using Remmy's phone. So mssg self-destruct! U so good, bb. So mmm. Meet me 2night. Remmy at some reading, so boring.

"Why must stories mean? What do you mean when you say stories must mean?" Happy Fiction asks.

Dr. Remora's words fall from her hands, a deluge. *Such a question!* she thinks. *Realist Fiction is so, so angry. Did he tell Romance Fiction that he loved her, and did she not know what that meant? Or didn't she care?*

Dr. Remora's phone keeps ringing. She pulls it out of her pocket. The fictions, darlings all, wait to hear what she will say. She slowly flips open the phone and lets this statement answer Romance Fiction *and* her lover, "I mean to mean."

Ex-Fic raises her hand.

III.

As Dr. Remora drives home, she wonders: *is depression a narrative? Does suffering have a beginning and an end?* When she remembers that she had once been happy, very happy, she cries again.

On the radio a man plucks a banjo and asks where his lover had been last night. Why—had he read his lover's text message like Dr. Remora had read her lover's message? Nine months ago, Dr. Remora scanned her inbox for Romance Fiction's phone number. Romance Fiction needed help with her thesis. She intended to tell Romance Fiction, "Write what you know." But she pressed the wrong button, opening the sent messages file. The top message was written in words that weren't her own, addressed to a number she did not know. To bb.

Dr. Remora passes billboards advertising sanitary products, flying by signs that entice motorists to turn off the highway for fast food restaurant conglomerates. At every exit: gas, coffee, ubiquity, and forever. In her head are words for a story that needs a happy ending. The story writes itself in many ways. On the many drives home from the University of Toronto, Dr. Remora had written it a hundred times, but now she knows the words by heart. The happy ending goes like this:

Dr. Remora opens her phone and deletes the text message that had ruined her life. After a few minutes of staring out the front window, choosing to approach a landscape that rushes past, she receives a text message:

I can't live like this. I made a mistake. Please answer. I need you.

The phone dims and goes black. When Dr. Remora was young with stories to write and life to mine, she wrote fast, and it was always shit. Dr. Remora writes slowly now, deliberately. She never loses faith that if a message is delivered in a beautiful way, the truth can change minds—even her own. Persuasion is not a fiction. She remembers lying in bed with her lover, both of them slack, sated on each other's flesh.

How many texts like this had come since the break-up? None, no texts for nine months. Dr. Remora fantasized about a text coming every day. Dr. Remora fell asleep every night imagining her lover standing outside the bedroom window, strumming a banjo, confessing in song where she'd been that night. Her lover is more real than tears. Though not a poet, her lover knows about need.

Authority deserts fiction when it becomes true. When fiction is true, it becomes tedious, boring, and checkable. Dr. Remora wants to be loved, and love is a fiction. Dr. Remora remembers class that day, the day she discovered the text, Realist Fiction in love with Romance Fiction and unwilling to show her what is real, Romance Fiction wanting to be swept away. Into the phone, Dr. Remora types

The End

but deletes it. Then she writes:

I love you.

PRAWN

The import-export business is what I tell people I *used* to do. I took orders from brokers in Indochina, moving foodstuffs in and out of the region. I used to do import-export in a cubicle, one guy in a small nest of cubicles, each cubicle guy assigned to a part of the globe. Territory size depended on how big the action was, of course: one guy got Beijing all to himself, another guy got the rest of China. You see what I mean? The MALADY-ANGUS office was a stone claw clinging to dingy Gottingen Street. We overlooked the Halifax Port Authority, our big second-floor window permitting a pastime of mine: watching boats and tankers enter and exit the harbour, importing and exporting themselves. After a Morris Performance Report, I went up the stairs and looked out the window, planning to commandeer Theodore Tugboat. What to do with Theodore? Ram the police boat until it sinks, then take Theodore wide open and give the children aboard more thrills and spills. *Ramming speed!* I'd get the kids to cheer. *Ramming speed!*

I've lived in Halifax my whole fucking life.

The people I used to deal with on the phone from ol' Indochine wanted to get rid of their stuff today, immediately, *right fucking now*. Whatever they needed, they needed yesterday, as if I'm to blame for turnips not turning up, magically, on pallets in a warehouse before a call is even made.

Morris used to be my boss and he needed me to make money in the same timeframe as the clients: yesterday. Morris let me know, every. fucking. day. that I wasn't strong enough for this business even though I had been doing it for twenty years and he had only been at MALADY-ANGUS for three. Every time Morris sneered at my numbers, I wanted to say, "I've been here more yesterdays than you, Morris." But he would have just taken notes for my Performance Report at the end of the day. "Dougie's not making sense," he might write. "If he can't talk to me, then how can he communicate effectively with our clients who use English as a second language?" BEEEP—the PR faxed to head office in Montreal.

I took work home with me in those days. The quota was a killer—I had to clear ten thousand dollars a day. A calendar chart was pasted near the main door. When an associate came in or went out of the cubicle area, he saw his name and his tick boxes. A tick went next to your name if you made quota, and quota depended upon area. Hong Kong guy needed to secure a hundred thousand, the highest quota in the office. Bastard did it by eleven a.m. most days.

MALADY-ANGUS didn't use the calendar chart when I first started there. It was Morris's idea—he called it "inspiration." My days were either tick or non-tick. When Tammy, my wife, used to care about me, she'd ask what kind of day it had been. On made-quota days my tongue clicked against my soft palate. I'd put my arms around her waist and sing *sugar sugar, oh money money*. Tammy doesn't care anymore, though. Like I used to do MALADY-ANGUS, I'm something she used to do.

Morris picked on me, trying to wring more dollars out of the other company men by harassing and shaming me in front of co-workers. *Howmuchyagot,Dougie?* he'd chant over the electronic hum of computers and the conversational rattle on phones. *Howmuchyagot,Dougie?* Phones would hang up. Even though the men were also the target of the spectacle, I was spectacle. Entertainment!

"Two hundred dollars, Morris," I'd stammer out, or some other equally pathetic sum. Morris smirked a communicable office smirk. It was unfair: other guys had bigger deals to make based on geography, population density, wealth distribution. My bailiwick of Indochine was small fry, only tiny orders. Other guys dealt in larger pieces. Because Morris didn't like me, he gave me the worthless piece, the one that needed scrounging. I used to work Tokyo, one city, just like the Hong Kong piece—my quota was fifty thousand, I made it easily by the end of the day. Morris reassigned me to an "area" that does less business for MALADY-ANGUS in a week than Tokyo does in a single day.

Morris, that fuck, took Tokyo for himself. He gets his quota in the first hour or so of the morning, and then stands in front of the tick calendar with his erasable marker, rubbing his chin with great concentration. And if I make a really big sale, if someone important is travelling through Indochine and the potentate wants something rushed out or in, something expensive, large, or numerous, then I get one tick, that's all—one fucking tick! If I do a deal for a hundred grand, then Morris's stupid system gives me one day's reprieve, I meet my quota for the goddamn day and the next day it's the grind again, Morris with his *Howmuchyagot, Dougie* smile. I'm back where I started, scrambling for a single tick.

Most days I scraped together the ten thousand despite staring at the phone in desperation and thinking of things like commandeering Theodore Tugboat. Morris made Performance Reviews every day, but he also conducted them monthly, making me stand next to the tick calendar and read his collated commentary about my punctuality, efficiency, and collegiality from the daily PRs. Morris meant to break me. The "collegiality" section of his PRs was where he had the most fun. He said awful things about me, but the fact is most days I made quota, I squeaked past the line, and so I earned the opportunity to continue to stand in front of the tick calendar every month. What almost broke me was less Morris himself and more his effect: I used to stare at my cubicle phone or obsessively check commodity prices on the computer screen. I began to chase after absolutely nothing, marathon after marathon in my mind.

Who am I kidding. Morris did break me.

When I say "import-export" to people who ask what I did before retirement, people think I was in the mob and now I'm in the Witness Protection Program. They take my full measure, noting the defeat that clings to the rim of my baseball cap, to the bristles of my ratty moustache, to my Tammy-darkened corneas. My eyes have never seen drugs or the severed heads of horses. I've never run guns! There's no Italian mob in Halifax, no mobs at all. Just lots and lots of idiots. Like Morris. Is government a mafia? You know the MALADY-ANGUS building on Gottingen? It's still there. They're still rearranging deck chairs, all around the world. That's what we called our work—rearranging the deck chairs. We figured trade was one big sinking ship.

Tammy works at the BunsMaster bakery. She and I live together on a parcel of land that, technically, is in the bakery's hands. But twenty years ago we signed a locked lease so the loafers can't get rid of us. The smell of baking bread is in the air, all the time—even when Tammy's union went on strike. Bread smell is the place itself, clinging to the brick, the tin chimneys, the trees and grass, even the snow. Management thought about expanding BunsMaster a few years ago, wanting to knock down our house and build three more ovens. They gave Tammy trouble every day, but she had the union, and management was afraid of the union. They still are.

Morris was never afraid of me.

I wake up, smell bread; I go to bed, smell bread. I never smell bread in my dreams. At the office, I used to earn my daily bread. Some days here by myself, I wish I was back at MALADY-ANGUS.

Tammy's bread union goes on strike every five years—you could tick a box, it's so regular. Strikes last four to six weeks, the point when union brothers and sisters lose enough wages so that the company can rationalize a wage increase. The union encourages grievances to keep management on its toes. Lucky for them, Tammy has eyes of grievance. When Tammy comes home at night she recites epic poetry about how she made the BunsMaster boss look like a fool. She's a secretary, and secretaries can embarrass their bosses like no other employee. Tammy still works and I don't—that's why I say I *used* to do import-export. Tammy's still working. That's my problem now.

Tammy does exactly what her contract sets out for her to do and no more. She brags about *not* doing things, about how she's scared her boss so much that she's not asked to do much of anything at all. In fact, the union leaders ask her to do more than the BunsMaster people do. Union leaders send her to kibbutz with other bread brothers and sisters across the country who have "management problems." The workers, they work it all out with one another. Tammy calls herself "a labour activist." She's a secretary though! The game plan is simple: ritual strikes every five years over money but publicly stress the "working conditions" demands and, especially, *dig in*. Tammy is the one that shows the weak how to dig in, not budge.

One day at MALADY-ANGUS I waited for the phone to ring—it *had* to ring. A man in Myanmar, a rich regime general, demanded a huge supply of sugary cereal for his spoiled six-year-old son and his son's school. Specifically, he wanted a hundred thousand boxes of Kellogg's Corn Puffs. I arranged transportation, the actual niche knack to my job, otherwise Kellogg's could make the sale directly. A hundred thousand boxes of corn puffs meant a big tick—twenty thousand bucks for MALADY-ANGUS in a single transaction. All I needed was confirmation from my rickety network of shippers. I promised Myanmar man that transportation was available: "Trucks, men, and the gods smile," I said in purposely broken English. While staring at the phone for an answer from my idiot shippers, I imagined a hundred thousand boxes of golden, glistening Corn Puffs stacked on pallets and wrapped in a glorious red bow.

To please the general, I needed my shippers to confirm. I needed five or six toothless assholes to say, "Yes, I can pick up the puffs from the port at Rangoon and take them to Bago and hand them over to the guy who will hand them to the guy who will hand them to the guy who will go to the general's pagoda in Mandalay." But if a link in the chain was broken, then the shipment wouldn't work, and MALADY-ANGUS would be on the hook for the failed deal. My go-to shipper in Rangoon, Maung, the first link of the chain, was an alcoholic. I didn't have a lot of other choices that were in the good graces of the generals. It seemed strange: the General wanted corn puffs, but I needed to use the black market to get the corn puffs to him. *Bureaucracy*, I thought then. *What if I told the general to just threaten Maung, or at least to wake Maung up so he'll answer his damn phone?*

Morris asked, "*Howmuchyagot, Dougie*? Don't you have work to do?"

Morris watched me for the next hour and asked me the same thing again. He watched me dial and stare at the phone some more. If I told the general to threaten the shipper, then Maung might end up dead and I'd lose the whole country. Everything goes through Rangoon. Or Maung would cooperate but the general would laugh later to smooth things over and tell him that "the Canadian" demanded violent threats. I'd lose the country the same way, or Maung would fuck me on a big deal not involving a general.

Howmuchyagot, Dougie penetrated my skull. I had dialled the phone for three hours straight. Maung, Maung, Maung. Morris stood over me, his head over my head, his hands waving. In those three hours, grain prices collapsed, Asian Tigers yawned, and Morris ticked off every box for the day except mine. Today was my wedding anniversary, I forgot to get Tammy a present. For what would be the final time, Morris brayed *Howmuchyagot, Dougie?*

The stench of fresh baked bread is as persistent as the smell of formaldehyde. Just like pickling juice, bread smell permeates the clothes. Morticians and bakers are a lot alike. What did Morris say, in his private life, when he described his occupation to those who asked?

"What do you do, Morris?" inquires a bepearled socialite patting at her plunging neckline, a party swirling around the two future consenting adults.

"Import-export" he says to her in a gravelly voice. Morris, man of mystery and danger, dude of underhanded dealings, midnight rendezvous, and dirty ports.

But Mary, Morris's actual wife, is fat. *She scarfs truffles by the seashore, the truffles she scarfs are imported, I'm sure.*

Morris scurried when Mr. Prawn, the owner of MALADY-ANGUS, dropped by the office. Morris learned his management style from Mr. Prawn, who didn't come to Gottingen to scare *us*. Mr. Prawn came to scare *Morris*. When Mr. Prawn was sighted, company men slowed to half-speed. We took outrageous breaks so Mr. Prawn could witness brazen laziness and sloth. Morris glared at the loafing men, fuming behind Mr. Prawn's back, only to smile when Mr. Prawn turned to face him.

Shortly after Mr. Prawn arrived in the building, I usually climbed the stairs to the second floor and looked out at the water. I often imagined Mary, Morris's truffle scarfer, shepherding children onto Theodore Tugboat.

Morris and Mr. Prawn stared, a lot, at the tick calendar. I wished I'd joined the other men who made trouble for Morris, which might have helped to make Morris think twice about ridiculing me. Mr. Prawn came to scare Morris because of human nature: Morris, a natural enforcer, needed to be enforced himself. Mr. Prawn imported Morris into the company three years ago to export terror to employees. Mr. Prawn imported himself to Gottingen once a month to terrorize Morris.

I couldn't take pleasure in Morris's toadying. When Mr. Prawn and Morris stared at the tick calendar, all I could think of was Mr. Prawn mounting Morris's back. Mr. Prawn became a praying mantis, forcing Morris to crawl to every cubicle in the office and tick his own name off on a calendar.

Why do I humanize Morris? Why couldn't I be more like Tammy and growl back at him *Howmuchyawant* or *Howmuchdoesyourwifeweigh?* I always seemed to be looking up to see Morris screaming, *Howmuchyagot, Dougie, howmuchyagot!*

Ramming speed. The sound of Morris's chant captured in my fist, I took a swing while still in the swivel chair and missed his head. But I stood quick and hit Morris's chin with my head. I shoved the stunned Morris out of the way and stomped to the tick calendar. For a full ten seconds, I stared at the calendar, my hand rubbing my chin in feigned great deliberation. Morris staggered towards me. I grabbed the marker from his hand and ticked all the boxes for every employee for the rest of that month. It took me a minute to make all the ticks, and the length of time made the guys laugh harder as the minute played out. But something was wrong—they didn't make gleeful Mr. Prawn-Morris laughter. They made the familiar Morris-Dougie noise. When I was finished with the tick calendar, I walked out. Never came back. Now when people ask me what I do, I say: "Nothing." It's more accurate than "import-export" ever was.

Only twenty-three years old, the same year Morris was hired as manager of MALADY-ANGUS, my daughter Jenny died in a car crash. It wasn't drugs or drink behind the crash, which is what comes to mind of course. Her car hit a bridge abutment. When the toxicology screen came back clean, the coroner thought it might have been suicide based on the lack of traffic, the time of day, the speed. But there was no note. She was a happy girl. She had a boyfriend, she was going to school.

Her sisters were devastated: Eveline, the eldest, a fitness instructor, stopped talking to me altogether. I don't know why. Maybe she blames me. The youngest, Claudine, married within the month and gave up her secretary job to take care of her new husband's two young children. Claudine still talks to me but she won't talk about Eveline—she tells me to drop it, as if I can drop my daughter. They sure can drop me, though. Claudine makes it easier, more fair, because another thing we can't talk about is Jenny.

Though I am the father of three daughters, my life has only one daughter in it. In the living room, three pictures of my girls hang on the wall: Eveline's is on top, Claudine's is on the bottom. Being the middle child, Jenny's portrait is, naturally, between her sisters'. After the crash, I argued every day for a month with Tammy to take Jenny's picture down, like a tick box strategy, like a labour activist strategy. *Dig in.* This is the only thing I can remember fighting about with Tammy, I gave in about all the rest. But Tammy said she needed a reminder of Jenny, that her girl lived. Tammy still grieves Jenny and she does it daily. Like her daughters, she won't talk about Jenny with me. Who knows what they say when they get together. I'm not to blame. I loved the girl.

Since I quit, I grieve Jenny by not being able to talk about her while having to avoid her face on my living room wall every day of my life. I never told the guys at work when my daughter died. I've never wanted sympathy. Morris certainly wouldn't have given a shit. Yet even though I wanted to take her picture down from my living room wall, for the three years before I left MALADY-ANGUS I kept a picture of the three girls together on my desk, Eveline pushing Claudine on a swing as Jenny smiled as I took the photograph. A summer vacation, I think; rocky beach, perhaps the Eastern Shore?

I don't know why I kept the picture there. It was something to look at other than the phone, but I didn't look much. I liked having the three girls together in the frame, it's how I felt about them as a father. With the three of them in the picture, I could choose to not look at the picture, to focus on other things. Grief for me is looking away. Jenny was twenty-three when she died, but for me she is also somehow seven years old forever, her age in the picture on my desk at MALADY-ANGUS. I want my daughter to be alive again, you see. All this is very simple. I don't want to see pictures of Jenny by herself but it's good to see my girls alive, it means we're all alive.

Memory is an import-export business too. When Tammy shouts at me for being a deadbeat, for quitting my job, for being lazy, I stop looking away and I force myself to look at the picture of Jenny on the wall instead, the smell of bread suddenly cloying, total.

Some evenings I see Tammy look up at Jenny's picture and then look back at the television. To me, this means she and I don't see the same thing, or that we don't see it the same way. Jenny was on her way to Dartmouth when she died, about to take the McKay Bridge. No one knows why she was headed for Dartmouth at eleven p.m., it's on the other side of the harbour. She might have gone to Dartmouth every night for all we know. But that's where she was going, she was taking the exit for the bridge, except she launched over the curb and into a huge concrete car-crumpler.

Grief made me quit my job, not a midlife crisis due to a bad marriage or even harassment by my boss. I don't blame Tammy for my actions and I don't blame Jenny. I don't blame Morris, who had no pictures on his desk and who always looked embarrassed when his immense wife Mary visited him at MALADY-ANGUS. No, I blame myself instead. I just didn't have the courage to keep on. I smashed my head into Morris's head not because I hated him, but because I had to get the hell out of there.

When Tammy asks why I quit my job, which she loves to do, I can't stammer out an answer. This infuriates her because she makes bosses answer to her, so she feels she can make a weakling, dependent husband answer to her. "Dougie, you don't make enough money to leave dirty dishes around," she needles. I ignore her. "You go back there and get your job back," she orders, escalating the attack.

But it's been three years since I left. I don't even know if Morris is still there, standing near the tick calendar with Mr. Prawn. "You're not my boss, Tammy, you're my wife," I respond. She still doesn't know what to say to that.

Are we in love? I think so. We still embrace when, on the very rare occasion, we talk about Jenny. Holding Tammy is as close as I can get to Jenny. We don't talk about Jenny until she bursts out of us. Most of the time on the couch, Tammy looks up at our middle daughter's picture and then looks away. I never, ever look, unless Tammy's on me about laziness and weakness. What I do now during the weekdays is I remove Jenny's picture when Tammy walks the fifty metres to BunsMaster, and I replace it before Tammy walks the fifty metres back. It's my job.

THE SADIE CLAUSE

FREIGHT

At the side of the 401, the Freightliner sat in gravel. Dad needed to tarp the top of the load, climbing up the ladder as it started to rain. The tarping should have been done hours ago, but it had been a long night of driving, he tried to make time, and the cost was sleep.

When behind schedule, sleep is for the doctored logbook, duly recorded. The logbook wouldn't protect him if DOT enforcement checked his bloodshot eyes and saw the restless hum. Sleeping for Dad was like waiting for what would never come, though he needed sleep now he was caught up, the Freightliner stopped at the roadside. The bennies were breaking. Dad came down from the stimulant high.

"I'm not afraid of work," he said to me a thousand times when I was small, so he got up there even though he needed sleep. He tried to get the tarp to wrap the load. If the tarp wasn't taut the wind would whip underneath the plastic and rip it up like a fingernail, snapping the rubber bungee cords pretending to keep a lid on the trailer. To passing motorists, the Freightliner would look like a stunt vehicle, the tarp parachute dragging behind. Dad had no replacement for the tarp, so if it broke the load would get wet. The customer wouldn't pay.

The bennie effect subsided to a supra-coffee level of vigilance. He felt ready to sleep, nested in the future of the load, he had his rest road rhythm. Legal weight for once, he stopped thinking about the tarp, unfurled and now close to wrapping the top of the load tight. The unloaders and their lazy schedules occupied his thoughts instead. Unloaders could make him wait hours, and they'd make him wait more if he showed them he didn't like to wait. If Dad got angry, the unloaders knew what to do: smirk-talk about being short staffed, five loads in before you, we want you to wait, fuck you, we can make you wait. Dad hated to wait more than anything.

Almost done, he wrestled the last corner of tarp in the wind. Even when mild, the wind could grip the tarp and throw it high. Dad pulled a cord clasp on to a metal rung. The cord snapped with most of his weight on the end of the cord. Momentum carrying him forward, he grasped at the side of the trailer, but all he had in his hands was glistening tarp and severed cord. Twenty feet up, the wind blew past his ears and his face. Head first, he saw the edge of the tarp wave, one of those last, final things.

Mom told me on the phone, "Your father's in the ICU at St. Michael's Hospital in Toronto. They say he's unconscious. From a head injury. The police found him next to his truck."

"Is he dying?"

"They're not sure. They had no idea how long he'd been there. I'm not going. But I thought you should know."

I know why she isn't going, so I don't ask. I'd just caught my tenth baby as a medical student on a dingy obstetrics ward in Saint John. With three weeks to go on rotation, Toronto seems impossible: Dad always said that when he'd die, he'd die, it would be quick, without lingering. I always thought: *that is the best thing, no one would visit you. But they'd sure as hell turn up at your funeral, alternately victorious, annoyed, baffled, or impressed.*

"Can he talk?" I asked.

"No. He's worse than that, he's in a coma."

"How did they know to call you?"

"He had my address in his wallet. They found pills in his pocket, that was embarrassing. The police wanted to know if he had a drug problem! Hah!" Mom lowered her voice to the tone of a crime drama voice-over actor: "We're asking to rule out the possibility of foul play." She said "foul play" like she was the Wicked Witch of the West.

At the root of questioning is love. Love finds its basis in trauma and mystery. What happened to my father? How do I feel about it? What am I supposed to feel? Questions can also be anesthetizing. Locked into question mode, the history-taking of the doctor-as-son, it's safer to just gather information. The riskier thing is to consider what to do. So, what to do?

I ask Mom, "What do the police think happened?"

"They think he fell from the top of his truck."

The Freightliner—that yawning, plated-grated, silvered, hillbillified bling-thing he loved to abuse until he could buy a new one to beat dead into the highway, the truck that shines on our driveway in between cross-country runs like rhinestones on wheels. Mom, my brother, and I always thought the truck would kill him, both of them at the bottom of a ditch or a river. We also considered a fiery death. We never thought he would *fall*. We even bet on the road that would get him: I picked the 401 because he used it the most, but my brother picked Route 2 because it was a two-lane deathtrap, sinuous and steep. Dad hated to wait, he passed slowpokes on Route 2 recklessly. Mom initially refused to play, but eventually she grew wistful and picked Route 66 Chicago Way. "Because I was in the truck with him there, years ago," she said.

Dad was always overloaded on Chicago Way. He had to be, overweight was unofficial Chom-Fleet company policy. Dad drove past the weigh stations even though they had the comfy familiarity of a local road in places, even though he wasn't on an anonymous megaroute. He was easy to spot, running overloaded time after time was crazy. And when you factor in his speeding, all of this only made sense when on amphetamines. The manner of death is to be unable to brake or turn in time, the weight of our lives relentlessly carrying us forward. No, I never thought my father would have to wait before he died. Death always seemed to be waiting for him.

After thanking her for the details, I hang up on Mom before I say whether I'll go. Medical training provides me with this incredible image: a thick tube in the blood god's mouth, a thin tube in his nose, several coloured catheters in his left arm, a clear catheter in his bladder, a black automated cuff on his right arm. I walk straight into the neonatal intensive care unit and find the attending as he inserts a catheter into the top of a little alien's corrugated head. "My Dad's dying. I have to go to Toronto."

"Boy, go and get me the sledge." Dad's ultimate command: get this, get that, get it *now*. I ran to the garage, but it was a mess. Wood ranks had listed and keeled over. Paint cans full of oil and gasoline were piled in the back, puddles of flammable liquid bathed the bases of the cans. Ripped truck tarpaulins were strewn across the floor and walls.

No sledge, but my panic anticipated that lack, beginning as soon as the command came. Now panic rooted down, becoming more insistent than Dad's command. My adrenalized state made me look in each place again, but panic made me feel vast time passing. Panic made me suffer the impossible choice: if I spent more time looking, I might find the sledge, but it might be wiser to just admit that I couldn't find it, to run as fast and as hard to him as I could, out of breath, starting off by announcing that I knew he was waiting, but...

I kept looking, and he came. "Where is the sledge, boy?"

Any answer other than *Right here in my hand* wastes his time. The sledge was not in my hand. "I don't know, Daddy," I said.

He walked in and found the sledge in a second. The sledge leaned in plain view against a wall. He picked up the sledge, raised it over his head, and swung it down at me. The sound of the sledge hitting the wall beside my ear was the sound of my death, the next steps he took towards me were the steps of my death, and the words he said amplified this death: "You meant to do this, boy. You do it on fucking *purpose*."

I have never driven the 401 before in my life, though I read Alistair MacLeod writing in the voice of a Nova Scotian dentist who says that the 401 is straight, true, and delivers one safe. Yet I have my own ideas about the road. This is my father's road. Straight, no. True, no. Safe, never.

The 401 is impersonal, rendering Ontario a causeway, a conduit. My initial worry about turns and exits turns out to be baseless: the road is a simple straight line. Driving the road to the dying man, I think of epitaphs—as eldest son, I'll be the one to order his stone. A good epitaph for Dad: *401*. Am I grieving? The 401 isn't conducive to emotion. Rest stops ensure that you can stay on the straight line forever.

I leave the Saint John Regional Hospital at five a.m. Four hours before that, I'd assisted a C-section on a woman whose baby looked like it might die before it could even take a breath, before we could get the baby out. *Boy, get the baby* I could hear my father say in my head. The surgeon and I hurried to scrub up, we raced to cut the woman open. We didn't stop to cauterize bleeders. We went straight for the child, hoping it would cry. As the hours on the road pass, I think of that baby on the warmer. Vigorous, in no need of resuscitation, that baby went back to its mother's breast. It didn't need an ICU. What was our hurry for? I should have placed the baby on the mother's chest myself. Instead, the nurses took the baby up and gave it to her.

Did my father bleed after the fall? Did he need surgery? If he needed surgery, could the surgeons find the source of bleeding? Did Dad realize he might die on the way down? If he did look down, then the last thing he might have ever seen was the road.

St. Michael's is dark, ringed by bare inner city parking lots. I try to convince a Sikh attendant that I'm visiting my dying father. "I've come all the way from New Brunswick," I say. "Can you forget the fee?"

He laughs. "Number one, you came here further than India? Number two, we're right next to a hospital. Who do you think parks here?"

"But the day's almost over. It's ten o'clock at night. How about a discount on the flat fee?"

"Number three, people in hospital can die at any time."

I hand him the money and walk through the empty lot on heavily bubble-gummed asphalt to the hospital's blue foyer where the sacrifices of the previously-Catholic administrators are extolled.

Having worked in hospitals for a few years, I have a sense of where things are. The ICU is located next to the Radiology suite, in turn tucked next to the Emergency Department that's always, always, always built next to the road. The ground floor mentality of hospitals is: keep trouble close. St. Michael's downcast face and his upraised arms make the stone statue look as if countenance and arms make different measurements. Derelicts shoot past the entrance into an alleyway beside the hospital. St. Michael's arms reach towards a hospital map. The ICU is located, against my typecasting, on the fifth floor.

Outside the unit, an abused phone hangs from the wall. The glass phone mount is broken, the phone scuffed and dented, a red sign above shouting: **CALL BEFORE ENTERING THE ICU.** Underneath the capitalized instructions, the sign has an image of the archangel Michael peering intently at the floor, the logo of this place.

The ICU doors open into a low-wattage room containing twelve corpses tucked in for the night. Corpse-catheters drain embalming fluid. Generations of a family gather near an old lady corpse mummified from extreme age. The living cry, the dead rest. The other ICU corpses are without families. A lone nurse sits at the foot of each bed. My father lies flat on his back at the back of the room. Puffy, motionless, Dad has a large, bloody drain exiting his skull. His face resembles an abraded purple flower, the stem of the flower an endotracheal tube secured to his head with surgical tape and cord. He looks small in the bed, but the other corpses seem small in their beds too. The beds are seas. Dad's right arm is encased in a cast from

knuckle to shoulder, the noise of his dead breathing contributing to
the jackpot telemetry noise of the ICU.

I look for a man, but this is a corpse. I say to the male nurse, "I'm
Will's son."

In layman's terms, the nurse tells me what's wrong: blood in Dad's
head causes pressure on his brain that so far is relieved by the burr hole
in his skull, Dad's breathing done for him by machine. "I'm sorry for the
sight of all the tubes coming out of his body," the nurse says, looking at a
clipboard, ticking off vitals, "but the tubes are necessary to keep him alive."

"I'm studying to be a doctor," I say, looking at my father. "I'm
in medical school."

"Oh yeah? Congratulations," he says, not looking up. "So if Mr.
Stevenson's heart stops beating, do you want us to perform CPR?"

My theory about the number of things doctors stick into the human
body goes like this: the odds of survival are inversely proportional to
the number of things stuck in the patient. I look at the name tag of
the nurse with the logo of the downcast angel: MICHAEL, the tag
says. The angel and the nurse are both Michael.

"Yes," I say, knowing that's not what Dad wants at all.

Growing up, Dad pointed at the ceiling when I asked a stupid question,
or when he didn't know the answer to my question, which by definition
meant that the question was stupid. "Where's Mom?" Ceiling. "Can
you help me with the quadratic formula?" Ceiling. "Why is the truck
parked crooked in the driveway?" Ceiling.

The ceiling never failed to be the ceiling, to have nothing there.
I would look up as if the answer were there, and he'd look up too,
staring as long as I stared. When I looked back down, he turned to the
television screen. The ceiling was a place that lacked all the answers
I would ever need.

One night the Freightliner blocked the evening sky. Dad was
coming down, he greased the truck undercarriage as pre-sleep ritual.

All questions could now be referred to the ceiling. Mom cooked supper in the kitchen, big baked potatoes, wet squash, sodden meatloaf. The table was intricately set. If Dad asked "Where's the butter?" because it wasn't there, then he pointed to the ceiling before throwing the table's contents off with a yank of the cloth. One can point to something but never really reach it. One can know exactly where it is and yet never get there. I remember that night even though it was a good night, the butter was on the table along with the salt and pepper. Dad ate, always a good sign, and he fell asleep in front of the television. From the right angle, he looked like the Freightliner's hood ornament.

Christ rose after three days, but Dad takes seven. I sit at the bedside in a metal chair Michael brings me. I'm the only family member who comes. I wait for deterioration or improvement, a change, but all he does is lie there. Michael presses his pen against my father's fingernails. *No response to pain,* Michael murmurs to himself as he writes in the chart. *No purposeful movement.* The only sign of life is the artificial rise and fall of his chest obeying the will of the respirator.

Out the window, a man and a woman cut through the parking lot. The woman hectors the man. Reading her lips, I think she screams "Yes, yes you did." The man shakes his head, shouting "No, no I didn't." A coffee cup wheels down the street gutter. A pizza delivery guy knocks on the door of a walk-up. The Sikh man shakes his head in his booth, disgusted with the drama of the couple and their binary argument, affirmative, negative.

Babies are delivering back in Saint John, I think. Babies have big heads, squirmy bodies, and querulous cries. If I don't go home soon, I'll lose the rotation and have to start over again. My attending said, "Take all the time you need," but the attending isn't the Undergraduate Dean.

Dad stirs, his casted arm moving slightly. "Michael, Will's arm moved," I say as if Lazarus' son saw his father rise from the tomb.

Michael didn't see anything. "You stare long enough and you see something, it happens," Michael says, checking vitals on another corpse for a nurse on break. But then Dad's arm moves again, unmistakeably, and his eyes open. How much strength did it take for Christ to get up again, Pharisee bullies screaming over his body, *Stay down you god asshole, just stay down.*

Dad's eyes swivel to gaze at me. He looks down at his left hand, the one without the cast, and points at the ceiling. He can't speak because the tube is in his throat. But he can point. As usual, I don't understand. He points higher with the old anger contorting his face, I can see it. Anger swirls around his swollen mouth.

Stepping out of the old sledge panic, it comes to me: Dad wants *out*. He tarped his truck, fell to the earth, arrived at St. Michael's, has been operated on, but he has no idea of any of that. His finger in the air isn't pointing up at God. He wants to be *gone*, to *leave*.

Visiting hours are over and I've tried Michael's hospitality long enough. He calls the intensivist to reassess. I should call my mother and advise her Dad's awake. I know she will ask if he said anything to me or to anyone. She will have her own roster of questions, and they will all be pointing to something.

WILL

What do I remember about my grandmother? I remember how Sadie died. Formidably: her diamond brooch positioned on her neck, the low church Reverend Brunswick presiding, eldest daughter Margaret and eldest son Will present and accounted for. Sadie's death-outfit involved accessorizing with big dangly earrings, foundation layered on her face like cake icing. She died ensconced, as she lived.

Only eight years old, unaware of the ways of morticians, I couldn't know when I looked in the coffin that the mortician got the details right *because Sadie already did the work for him*. Why trust a man with make-up? She died as an Avon fiasco, a fatality of overdone composure, her serenity collapsing in flesh-tone layers. I had always known her to be this way.

Families grieve according to how they are prepared for grief. The funeral director lowered Sadie's open casket to the level of the ground. Like me, the other grandchildren were little wailers. George, an older cousin of mine, started our group bawling. We knew something was being spent, a conspicuous expenditure of pain. I formed hot, monkey-see-monkey-do tears that blurred Sadie's pumpkin-face. Did Sadie command us to cry? If anything is permanent, it was Sadie's dominance, her pre-eminence in our minds and lives, her power over and past death. To see her quelled and dead was to think, apocalyptically, of freedom: what to do now?

Reverend Brunswick spoke aloud Genesis 3:19. "In the sweat of thy face shalt thou eat bread, till thou return unto the ground; for out of it wast thou taken: for dust thou art, and unto dust shalt thou return." The Reverend tried to be holy and respectful, but the adults at the funeral thought this way: *I worked the most. I sweated heaviest. I earned the most bread. It's my dust.*

Closer to the dust, we grandchildren cried as choral function. What would Sadie have wanted? She would have wanted us to feel really, really sad and really, really guilty. Margaret and Will turned the earth, competing for the shovel, throwing dirt piled for the purpose. Wailing grandchildren were shepherded into cars, shouted at to hold their tears. We complied. Soon it would be time to watch television.

On the drive home I felt marbles digging into my thigh, my pants pocket pulled tight in the too-small suit bought for last year's rep hockey games. The marbles, just one-ers and two-ers, were all I had left after a gambling disaster at school. I thought I could win Sean Hastings' swirled, pale marbles but I spent my Galaxies and Universes until I was left with only the marbles at the bottom of my Crown Royal bag. *What were they going to do with her?* I thought. *Sadie couldn't be buried in wintertime. Do they keep her in the church basement?* The church had a single plot pre-dug before the frost, and then all the funeral ceremonies happened with the same plot, the bodies stored somewhere until they could be reinterred in the spring.

The crying started before Sadie died, of course. We cried in living rooms, cars, and, if the stakes were high enough, even in the United Church pews. Our crying was an act of ghoulish cosmesis—we never had Sadie in life. She never let us, she never wanted to be possessed. We cried because we had to scale a mountain of grief, and the sound made sure everyone could see us climb.

Sadie went crazy in the end, offering to buy her grandchildren multiplex cinemas. She even called me once to ask if I'd like to have a swimming pool in the backyard. Sadie didn't take her medication at the best of times and in the three months before her death, she didn't take her pills at all. I hung up on Sadie ranting about chlorine, her speech spilling out of the phone and filling the living room where I sat, the words racing though the air, past sense. In their speed, her words said: *Chase me, catch me if you can.*

Sadie was my crazy babysitter. Singing show tunes while stirring Kraft Dinner noodles, Sadie never mixed the cheese properly—her specialty was leaving noodles bare. Cheese addicts could get a hit from the clumps left in the pale pasta. "What's that you're playing?" she sang out. In my hand, a pocket-sized electronic piano made doorbell sounds. "Music!" she tittered. "That's the music in you! This family needs more music in it." She said the words in a continuous instant and flew back into the kitchen, where she began to imitate the bagpipes, but that was too, too funny for her to keep up, and she fell into laughter. I mangled Chopsticks on the miniscule keys. She stopped laughing and adopted a serious voice. "The young one is currently playing work he has undertaken to improve Bach's sonatas." *Hee hee hee hee hee.*

My father, Sadie's eldest son, came in the farmhouse then. "The music's in you, boy. Will, do you hear this?" Sadie forced me to play more Chopsticks with the toy. Not waiting for my father's response, she ran back into the kitchen, emitting *hee hee hee.*

"Sadie, take your fucking medication," he said. When she was high, she'd never remember how he treated her. But when she was low, she remembered everything. I put the piano in my pocket where it made tinny notes when I bent down to practise marbles in the back yard.

Long before she died, before she lost her marbles for good, our titanic crying began. Sadie's adult children grieved through accessories. Margaret wanted the farmhouse. My father wanted the Wasson farm. When the big items were divvied, smaller items took on a magnified importance, became the real treaty items. Do you know how much grown men and women will fight over a painting or a cup? They will fight as if the cracked and chipped cup has the power to soothe loss forevermore.

The process worked like this: everyone united against the sibling who won a bid. If the all-against one front couldn't wrest the item away from the winner, the melee began again, the losers assuming a collective victimized air to strengthen their claim to everything else inside the house. Furniture, instruments, bowls, and dishes cued ritual crying until only the forks and spoons were left. And then they weren't left.

Why? Sadie's last will and testament was, of course, incomplete. Everyone knew crazy Sadie wouldn't do a will before she died. A trustee dispensed her spoils in the end—though nothing remained in the house, Sadie had substantial investments and sums in accounts. My father and his brothers and sisters disputed who would "assist" Sadie in the drafting of the will, but Sadie was too crazy to get even the liquor lawyer to agree to a draft. Ultimately my father and his brothers and sisters stole what they wanted right out from under Sadie's nose, right in front of her. Dad delivered boxes of Kraft Dinner on her kitchen table but he left her farmhouse with boxes of paintings, train sets, and gold.

Sadie watched them take, and she was far enough gone that she thanked her children for their thieving without malice or sarcasm or hurt. "Take it. Go ahead. I should have given it to you long ago."

Sadie's children never got along because Sadie set them against one another. By making her children compete with one another, she made them her natural allies. Sadie practised the art of discordance: growing up, each child got loot, but the loot was never the same and could be wildly variable in value. Individual gifts were dispensed as part of a cycle of giving that might reverse with the next round. Unfortunately for Sadie, the children learned resentment from their mother and it took deep enough that in the end, when she was really sick, no enemy would shelter Sadie.

Maybe Sadie did think she deserved her kids carting off her possessions. Maybe she finally saw the truth when she was mad. Or maybe she tried to make things better the only way she knew how. Alone and crazy, she stayed in the old farmhouse with nothing to eat except Dad's Kraft Dinner and no companionship except that of her children ripping off heirlooms. Until she went into the hospital, that is. Admission to the palliative bed in the Oromocto hospital changed the game—family shenanigans became public, and Sadie loved to perform for a crowd. She returned to her old self, a little bit.

Renovated ten years ago into a humble modernity, the farmhouse re-sided with vinyl, the yellow power symbol sat on two hundred acres of land irrigated by an intricate crick system. As the grail of family contest, whoever won the house *won*. Living in the farmhouse meant one owned everything that happened inside, that the winner possessed the power of history. During the final hospital days, bids were made according to an abacus of devotion: *I spent the most time visiting her! I brought Sadie food! I drove the Reverend to the hospital to pray for her!*

What did I think? Someone was dying, but obscurely. I didn't understand, I couldn't know. I saw beautiful and petty things appear in my home. I only had an audience with Sadie once, Sadie's sons and daughters used the grandchildren as pawns. The lie was that I was being protected, but the truth was that I was being used.

Dad sent me in, shut the door behind me.

"Now, boy, here you are! Well. Get me that water from over there, would you, on the windowsill? Thank you. And I need the newspaper. It's over there, on the chair. Yes. Could you raise the bed for me? Do you mind? Well, you just push that up button there. Yes. And I think I need that extra pillow that fell over the side of the bed. Oh, now under my head. Thanks so much. Okay."

Sadie's johnny shirt was stained with drool. Her bedsheet had the remnants of lunch on it, yellow and red bits and sauce. She had lost forty pounds, her skin flappy and sallow. "Boy, is there anything you want to know? These are last words, I think."

"Last words?" I repeated. She was dying, but I still thought this was performance. I thought Sadie still had the music in her, was still calling the tune.

"I've got cancer," she said. "Of the breast. It spread all over. I guess I should have got the check-up but I knew Dr. Ronson would ask if I was taking my medication and I didn't want to answer him. He always seemed to know when I wasn't. They're giving me the lithium in here, though. I suppose it helps."

My father banged into the door with his crib board, knocking it open. Huge and hulking, as much a door as the one he came through, he said, "Okay Sadie, I've got the board and the deck of cards. Boy, walk home."

Sadie looked sad. That's all she'd get. I said, "Cancer?"

My father was angry. "Sadie, you told him that? He's not eight years old yet. He doesn't understand. You've ruined him."

I walked out the door, away from the shouting, and took the stairs down to the main level. I walked four kilometres to our bungalow with grey vinyl siding and looked under my bed. Check: marble collection still there.

One day I came with Dad when he took crazy Sadie the Kraft Dinner at the farmhouse. The box he brought was huge but it only had a six-pack of KD inside, the KD knocking around within the larger box. Will knocked on the door as he opened it and strode inside, overturning his cardboard box on the kitchen table. The KD fell out.

Sadie stepped out of her bedroom wearing a stained pink nightgown. Her orange hair was pulled into curlers. Without her dentures in, she smiled warmly and said, "Will. You brought your son. Are you teaching him how to be a man now?"

Dad walked past her, raising his arms to the roof. He pushed a panel up and pulled down a ladder. I noticed the living room was picked pretty clean—someone even took the old woman's baby grand piano? That would have required a truck and movers. Her television was gone too.

Sadie knew where and how to hit her children. She knew what hurt them and sometimes she told them what they couldn't survive, couldn't ever forget, the words following them forever after. I heard her say this to my father one day after church: "Will, you always knew I feared for you most. Running away from home so early. Made you see the mental doctor to see if they could straighten you out. That boy there, he's going to turn out just like you. He'll steal from you, Will. He'll be just like you, Will. And you know what that's like!" How long ago was that? A year before she died, I think, after a memorial service for my dead grandfather that Margaret and my father sponsored. We were going to take Sadie on a Sunday drive but she said that to Dad and we didn't, we never drove her anywhere again.

Was Sadie her true, mad self the day of the Kraft Dinner delivery? Any of her sons or daughters who wanted the house needed only to live with her those last two months—such a residency would have made them the instant frontrunner in the farmhouse derby. No one had the courage to do it, though. She could speak the truth, talk about love. Her kids didn't know the language, they didn't understand. They wanted a witch, and so they locked her away so that they didn't have to see anything different.

"I want you to be good to that boy, Will. You take what you need to do that. You take care of him. You show him what's right." Sadie had been so troublesome a character in life, a listener might stutter on the possible irony of her instruction—teach the son to be a good man as his father steals from his grandmother? But Sadie looked at my father with such hunger, you knew she was trying to atone.

The difference between this sick Sadie and previous sick Sadies is that this Sadie didn't just tell you what you wouldn't want to hear, she also told you exactly what you needed to hear. My father kept muttering about a brooch up there but after stomping around for five minutes he threw some old photo albums down through the hole in the ceiling. When he got back down on the main level, Sadie had one of her wedding pictures in her hand. "I didn't look too bad," she said to herself. "It was a long time ago."

Sadie's last discordant gift to her children was what she never gave: every single object she owned was squabbled over or stolen, but she smiled as the argument occurred, she gave it her blessing, she hoped some good would come out of it.

That night before Sadie died, my father complained on the couch about Margaret who thought she was "entitled to the whole show." I didn't care about what my father seemed to care about. I wanted Bonkers, Galaxies, and Cosmic Swirls—things Sadie would give me when we picked her up at the Fredericton airport, home from exotic trips to San Francisco, Copenhagen, and Rome. Sadie was my main supplier. No matter where she flew to as part of some midnight whim, she brought back marbles. When Sadie handed me a sack of marbles from Johannesburg, she said, "Sorry, boy. I couldn't find any Galaxies over there but I found ya some darkies! Haw haw."

She made me her ally through marbles, conditioning me to think that she might have a bag of them hidden on her at any time. As Dad talked entitlement, I wondered whether Sadie would will me marbles. I needed sparkly, flecked ones—how could I send her word? There was no way to ask my father, who only cared about the farmhouse, the power of history, having the title deed for anything that happened before and everything that happened afterward. So I asked Dad something else instead. "Why did you take the pictures from Sadie, Dad?"

"So Margaret wouldn't get them, asshole. Take a cup, who gives a fuck. I took the past. It makes for good trades later."

My father was a hard man, but even he bawled about how much a footstool meant in his heart of hearts—he remembered using it as a boy to listen to the radio, his father with his hand on his shoulder. Dad pretended to be tough. He would trade the albums for the footstool, I knew it, and mix into the trade another item or two so Margaret wouldn't know how much Dad wanted the stool. I nodded when he finished talking and resumed thinking about marbles.

And then she was dead. The day Sadie died, an older kid sharked me and my friends, cleaning us out, but the older kid started to play with a younger kid we didn't know. I told the boy, "Don't play, he's just after your marbles. He's a big kid. He'll take everything you got."

The kid from the junior high in his Air Jordans and Garbage Patch Kids T-shirt said to the young boy, "Look, he's a whiny baby. I'll make it fair. I'll let you stand closer to the pot and I'll play my White Hole. You can play whatever you want."

The young kid made an exceptional shot, no one thought he could do it, and he won the White Hole. I wanted a White Hole. I never had one, Sadie never could find one, I could never win one, the kids with them were too big, too good.

The older kid tried to double or nothing, putting more marbles on the line, but the White Hole was the best marble going. The code of the playground is you can't turn down a game, everyone's locked in, but nothing the older kid had could match its value, and we were a lot of kids, he couldn't just take the little kid's marble. The small boy took his White Hole and the rest of the marbles and ran off the playground.

Sadie won and lost the family grief competition. Everyone mourned her the most, which meant she lost, her kids were counting their grief. Dad left the funeral service before it was over, rising dramatically from the pew, hysterically arching his back before fleeing the church. I don't even think the performance was a strategy to get more loot. He was overcome, his mother was dead. This is how Sadie finally won. Margaret whispered to me after the service, "I stayed through the whole thing. I loved my mother more than Will, you tell him that." Even I could tell Margaret really, truly thought she loved Sadie inside, and that quantifying the love was the only thing she knew how to do, the white hole of love sucking up all the evil expression within us until just the pure, true thing is left, and I saw the white. "I will," I promised, but I never did.

My cousin George biked to my house a day after Sadie finally got buried in the spring. Because of the infighting and larceny, the trustee put a hold on distribution of the estate until after Sadie went to the ground, thinking that this would be a cooling-off period. That period over, George told me that my father would never get the tractor. Lots of items can be stolen but stealing the tractor's stupid, it's too conspicuous.

"Your father's hasn't ridden the tractor as much as my father," he said. "And Will hasn't worked as hard at the Wasson place as my father. Working hard's what counts, you know."

Sadie lived in us. It took training to be this kind of soldier. Did George have to sit on the couch just as much I did, did he have to hear about entitlement? "My father's worth two Uncle Eugenes. If Eugene gets the tractor, it'll be a sin 'cause the tractor will just sit in the barn because your father is lazy." Sadie's policy was simple: if you don't defend yourself in this family, you're left with nothing. What would have happened if, on her deathbed, Sadie told each of her children how much she loved them?

I wonder if she did. I wonder. I only saw her the once, and I think she might have told me if she had the chance. "You're trespassing, you little fuck," I yelled. George was twenty pounds heavier than me, two full years older. "You know what trespassing is, asshole?" I said the word "asshole" with a voice rise that my father taught me. The day before, George and I biked around on the Wasson place's back trails. I made a fist and shook it in his face. "Go fuck yourself," I screamed, feeling my face tap into the old, hereditary power.

George picked up his bike, pleased. I had an idea about how to make him unhappy—I learned from Sadie. "Margaret's fucking the trustee to get the house. We all know it. You're mom's a whore."

George was suddenly less sure. "It's your mother that's the whore," he swore as he biked away.

I was eight years old. George was ten. Disagreements are temporary at that age. The next day George and I played marbles. I took his tenner after an easy approach to the pot, he should have defended it better. "George," I asked as I held his tenner in my hand, "do you think that Sadie had any marbles left over from her trips for us?" Sadie gave George marbles too. She gave all the male grandchildren marbles.

"I bet she's got a lot of them in there," George said.

Marbles are currency in a hierarchy of game: small pots to big pots, one-marble games to games involving glittering armadas of marbles. A player can lose every marble he has in less than five minutes or he can win every marble in the contest. Older kids make the younger kids marks but older kids have the best marbles. If I didn't play the older kids, I'd never win anything valuable. "George, when the trustee unlocks the house and lets our parents in, do you want to go looking for some marbles?" I asked.

My father proudly brought the dregs of the farmhouse in when the trustee made the final decisions. The objects Dad loved were never used. The footrest sat overturned next to the outdoor woodpile. Silver cutlery was hidden away in a hutch—not a single utensil ever touched a tongue. Vintage LPs from the swing era were shelved in the basement. A Catherine Karnes Munn original, covered in plastic, slouched against the attic wall.

For my father it was a moral victory that he won these things while also a conspicuous loss. All symbols need is to have outward, apparent value. They can be as empty as people are. Dad settled on a different symbol to get the same satisfaction he couldn't get from winning the farmhouse. Margaret got that and became the mythmaker.

It is hard to love without good examples. What was Sadie's example? Whenever we met, she gave me a stash of marbles. When I visited her in the hospital, she had nothing to give except her words and I chase them to this day. I confess that before I even set foot in the room, I hoped she would give me marbles for visiting her.

I give marbles to my son. I give dolls to my daughter. I have the music in me, too, but none of the hatred or the control. Thirty years later, my own father and mother died with a will. My brothers and sisters came to terms with the physical facts of our parents' lives. Dad granted each of us one thing that used to be Sadie's, doled out in a separate Sadie clause in the will.

We had their staggered sickbeds to gather around and dramatize ourselves, Dad dead in the spring, Mom dead in the winter. We ushered our children towards those sickbeds. My kids didn't cry. When I think back to when I was eight years old, turning away my cousin from my house, marbles bulging in my pockets, I realize the problem began with Sadie but it didn't end with her. The problem is that love will take the worst way if you let it, the white hole of an excuse, the belief that loving is worth it, no matter how the love happens. I told my son and daughter to say whatever they wanted, I wouldn't listen. I left the room, the ten-year-old girl and three-year-old ambling to their grandfather's bed and, seven months later, to their grandmother's.

Out of a bizarre respect, I replaced my cutlery with Sadie clause silver cutlery. Now my wife, daughter, and son use those utensils every day. When the things we eat and drink with become sacred, they become too good for us. Though the utensils are too good to put in the dishwasher, they tarnish in time. Baking soda and water puts the shine back on them, a satisfying clunk sounding every time I drop a newly clean one in the utensil drawer, a kind of interment.

THE FIELD OUR OWN

Straggler leaves fall on the October field. Rows of corn stand sentinel, stalks broken from the harvest. Father rented the field out to our cousins, the Bridges. At first they were good about the soil, harrowing and tilling it to the point of fine-grained sand, but since the corn was harvested they let the field sit. If the field didn't see the harrows turn stalks to ground soon, the field would petrify from frost and suffer next year. Worse, we would be called lazy in this country. Cars driving past on the highway would think, *That crew's too fucking lazy to care for the ground.* But the ground was lifeblood, was all we had.

Father cursed not doing the harrowing himself. For at the end of the day, when my father tracked the lines he made with ploughs, harrows, and planters, he couldn't boast about being a rich man, but he could boast about straight lines. Father picks a point in the distance and drives straight for it with determination. Straight means he can boast about work in terms of insult. "I'm not afraid of work," he'd say when the day was done. "Are you afraid of work, boy?"

"No," I say, making the responsorial psalm.

Complaining about work this way in this country signals that father is a hard worker. Hereabouts, this is the best thing said about a man. My father cursed the Bridges every day in October over the supper hour. Because it can mean weakness to discuss a debt, father has to be careful. If he mentions the neglected field to his cousins, he first has to travel to their farm, their land. He'll be seen as a nag.

"They'll call me woman," he shouts as he cut the corn from the cob. Dentured, he cuts everything he eats. "But if I do nothing about the field, I'll look weak to the Bridges and slothful to everyone who drives the Trans-Canada." All father could do was curse the Bridges as if they were still rivals from the one-room schoolhouse.

I like the rotting stalks that saw nips of frost already, their green-yellow bodies singed into grey at the tips. I stand as tall as their height. Father rented the field for five hundred dollars, cash up front, figuring the cousins who ridiculed him as often as they could in school would still be trouble. But the Bridges signed the one-page contract that named the price and they paid the lump sum in advance. As part of the contract, my father stipulated that the Bridges would harrow the field down at the end of the year.

We have four fields. The front field is largest, flattest, and richest—fertile sand, coagulable in the rain. Front field is pure flood plain, nestled against the deep and broad Saint John River that floods its banks every year, bathing the front field with overflow. The field is so fine my father can't pick up a rock there for blame, he can't throttle stone with his fists. This ground will grow anything but stone, but the ground won't grow anything cheaper than people will pay.

Last year ruined my father—it cost too much for tractor diesel, grease, seeds, fertilizer, spray, and hired men, too much to haul produce all the way to the market in Saint John. This year the Royal Bank of Canada supervised father's efforts to rent out the land he'd been forced to mortgage.

Having bled on the ground before, I never thought the land could be lost. While hired men hoed corn last spring, I gathered fiddleheads from the erratic cricks irrigating the back three fields. Fiddleheads grow in shadow as limp and coiled whips. I dropped them into a plastic bowl. Mother would steam them, and at supper Father would drench the fiddleheads with vinegar. After taking out his teeth, he'd rend them with his gums. I had no idea father couldn't pay the men who tended the farm. We lost them when fiddlehead season was done. Father had to do everything himself then, with me of course.

Over dinner tonight father roars about the front field again. "Fuckin' Bridges drive up and down the Trans Canada in their fucking piece of shit Ford and they honk their Christless horn and wave like they're sure I'm an asshole. An *asshole*. That field's been six weeks sitting and they know their obligations. Fuck them. If they don't harrow tomorrow, I'll borrow Johnny Gregson's Massey and take care of the goddamn field myself." In the field of the relationship with his cousins, the only manly option available is to shame them. If father still owned a tractor, he would have harrowed the field already and been happy he could tell people about the cheating Bridges. But if he still owned a tractor, he would never have rented out the land.

Like the fields, our old farmhouse has an antique trough system. When it rains, I hear each individual drop hit the roof, sluice the trough, and splash the downspout. Father taught me it's best to harrow the land wet, but not too wet. Too wet and the tractor's engulfed in mud. The evening sun slung low beneath spent rainclouds, silhouetting the field's dead corn against the sky. It's pointless to talk of anything other than the front field—a bad sign.

When he drinks, father turns cruel about the bank manager. After a few snorts, father raises his hands to choke his own neck and juts out his belly as if he were Mr. Kenny, CA. Father strains and mock-defecates and whomps his belly until I have to laugh. If I ever ask father to talk in voices, to pretend, he'll refuse. He only does such things on his own time—if I ask him to perform, to his mind I'm mocking him.

I eat quickly and leave mother with him. In my room, the rain flowing through the eavestrough drowns out his sound. Every now and then, I hear a single shouted word: *No*.

The next morning, father is gone. Mother stands in the kitchen with a bruise enveloping the right side of her face. Dishes from last night's meal sparkle in the drying rack. Her curled hair seems like a doily obscuring a half-disaster. Mother's split face of blood and beauty asks, "Sleep good last night?"

"The rain put me to sleep," I say. The dining room table is set— Red River oatmeal and brown sugar, the usual. I sit down and scoop oatmeal into my glass bowl. The brown sugar dusts the oatmeal in large, boulder-like crumbles, but the sugar soon coagulates into rich brown veins running through the meal.

Mother sits down across from me and bares her teeth. "Do you know why the Bridges boys are always on your father's mind?"

"He says they cheat him, he's always saying that."

"No, it's simple. With your father it's always simple! Niall and Irwin used to throw dirt in Will's hair, against his face, they shoved mud down his shirt. They were bigger. He couldn't fight back. That's how it works." Mother needs to colour in her half of me too, and with mother and father the kicking only gets worse. I get up to grab my bookbag.

"What, you don't want your food, the food I made you? Why ever not? Well, Will sat in his little seat at school and every day the teacher asked him why he was so dirty. Your father, he wouldn't say anything, HE WAS A COWARD THE DAY HE WAS BORN! One day Niall raised his hand to answer the teacher's question. Niall said your father was an animal. 'Will rolls around in the dirt to get the flies off,' he said." I ran out the door and through the field. "Niall and Irwin still call your father the Dirt King TO HIS FACE!" With each footfall, my thought: *bus, come, bus, come.*

When I come home from school that day, father is stuck in the middle of the front field. He's driving Johnny Gregson's little Massey. Behind him a too-small set of borrowed harrows brings him shame again—the bank forced father to sell all our equipment at the end of the previous year, not just the blood red Massey Ferguson. Father's Massey was a good tractor with power steering, front and back hydraulic, and power takeoff. The thing could pull a large harrow to properly tackle the front field. Today, father looks like a fierce, ridiculous hobbyist.

With the throttle full on, father pitches the tractor forward, then jerks it into reverse, switching back and forth from high to low gear, anything to get the tiny Massey out. Father seethes, wrenching the steering wheel round and round with the harrows hydraulic lifted all the way up so they won't drag to keep him stuck. There is no way he can get free. I stand near the highway, at the end of the dirt laneway, afraid to get close when he's this wild, watching every wheel-turn and gear-pull that mires him more. He knows he's beat, that's why he keeps going. The only people in this country with a machine big enough to pull him out are the Bridges.

At that moment, the Bridges turn off the highway in their shining Ford pickup. I move out of the way, but they don't want to drive down the coagulated laneway. A dirty truck means you are a picker, a hireling. A clean truck means high rank in the hierarchy of work, means that the truck driver is entitled to complain about other people's laziness. The Bridges sit in the truck and watch my father's frenzied motionlessness.

Bookbag bouncing on my back, I run into the field to the weak tractor and wave my arms until father notices me. He throttles down only low enough so his shout can be heard: "The *fuck* do you want?" I point at the gleaming Ford.

Surprised, father puts the tractor in neutral but shoves the throttle up all the way. He leans forward in the cracked rubber seat, glaring at the truck as if it, specifically, is responsible for him being stuck. Love and pride find cool expression on father's face, but hatred is white hot, demonically animate. There is nothing for a man like him to think other than that the Bridges, in their air-conditioned Ford, are laughing at him.

Things are even for now. My father tried to shame his cousins by harrowing the field before they did, but my father failed and now he needs their help. There is enough shame for everyone, all that has to be decided is the resolution. Who will make the first move?

The blue Ford backs up onto the highway and drives away. When it is out of sight, my father finally throttles down. I realize: with the tractor throttled up, the Bridges can't parley from a distance. My feet sink in muck sucking at my runners. Father never should have tried this piece of land, it is too wet. The rest of the field is fine but leaving a small oasis of dead corn gives the Bridges an excuse to not harrow the field. I imagine tall, sneaky Niall saying, "It's too wet Will, too wet! Even you couldn't get it done you see, boy! Now why did you get *impatient*? We were going to do it, you just got impatient now." Worse, Niall could say to everyone in the country: "Look, Dirt King can't take care of his own field! Dirt King needs us to take care of everything for him. Baby, just like he was in school."

Somehow father had chased them away. "What are you going to do about the tractor?" I ask.

He looks out at the river. "I don't know," he says. He shuts the tractor off and takes the key out, dropping the harrows down. Heat and ozone radiate from the Massey. Four or five more passes with the harrows would finish the field—less than two minutes' work. The brittle stalks jut from a small island of ground. Father enters the house, and thoroughly checks the kitchen cabinets—no alcohol. He switches out of his work clothes and dresses too fine for anything hereabouts. "You're coming, boy," he commands. We take off together in the old Cordoba, dark blue like the river. His level low, we head to Gagetown to find the bootlegger.

"Go ahead, boy, you can drink the pop," he says. The pop is his chaser for later.

I didn't answer. I had ideas of contamination, of *growing up just like him* as mother sometimes said. The Cordoba we got second hand, a luxury coupe with Corinthian leather interior. Whenever I touch the leather with my thighs and arms, I recall a Sunday service when the preacher read Corinthians 13:11: *When I was a child, I spoke as a child, I felt as a child.* The car's stacked headlights and boatish handling make it look like a floating rectangle, a bobbing block. To squire and cavort, father requires a lethargic car powered by a V8 engine, a big car of brimstone and fire.

Father tells me stories about his childhood. Truck driving, farming, competing with his cousins: he fucked the Bridges' sister in the Bridges' top mow until Uncle Buster chased him away with a brandished pitchfork. Father boasts about the sister but never mentions to me his title, Dirt King.

I know these stories already and Gagetown is still fifty kilometres away, but part of being a child is knowing stories by heart and wanting the tale told anyway. My dad is still good, his level is low. Father's face is like the sun on Sunday, bright and expectant, hopeful the bootlegger will be home. The bootlegger is always home.

For the past week the river had risen, approaching its banks but not cresting them. The Emergency Measures Organization advocates evacuation but EMO knows most of the farmers won't leave. Farmers here were born in their houses and figure they will die in them too. A codger interviewed on CKHJ FM radio says, "They can float me on out in a casket, I'm not leaving until then!"

I squint at the sun, wondering if it is as high as it will ever go. A road sign announces we are ten kilometres away from *GAGETOWN, THE OLDEST SETTLEMENT IN NEW BRUNSWICK!* Pleasure craft in the distance rig out their buffers, tying together near green buoys on this side of Middle Island.

The bootlegger's clapboard two-story has a long approach. Father disappears up a long lane for a few minutes. Father and the old suspendered bootlegger leave the back of the house and enter a cellar. Dad comes out with three Mason jars of yellow liquid.

I expect Al Capone from the Untouchables television show, a man with a forked-tongue and tail, someone stronger than my father. But the bootlegger is small, kyphotic, and careful with his step. Father says the bootlegger had been in the hospital with liver trouble, had learned how to quit drinking. Perhaps the bootlegger is stronger than my father, the bootlegger a backwoods magus whose power is distilled into Mason jars. "All right Will, all right boy! How's Ann?" the bootlegger says.

"She's great," father says, handing over two twenty dollar bills.

The Cordoba waves sinusoidally along the middle of the road. When sober, father takes corners properly. When drinking, his arcs are proportional to intake. Grandiloquent swaths, lazy swerves and sidebars—seatbelt buckled, I am companionship and audience. The Pepsi bottle rests between his legs. Father finds the Mason jar lip difficult to drink from, the shine slops out and soaks his shirt.

In a few days, the river might jump its banks to flood basements. The only means of transportation will be by boat, and some of those boats will hit backfield junk, hulls punctured by old car metal. Today the river is tame, a blue blanket for rest. Father's stories start to slur as the Cordoba's velocity jerks slower and faster. Father follows his swigs with the Pepsi chaser. His level gets higher, his face slackening. My father sings a line with the radio, "*Cause there's something in a Sunday that makes a body feel alone.*"

Father never tries to scare me with words, he doesn't need to. I can die every second I'm around him. He drives drunk, he rages, he needs to break whatever lies in his path. Or he lovingly lifts me up with his flat, sideboard-sized hands and puts me on his shoulders to better see the river.

We pass an overflowing Baptist church, its tower bell ringing—a funeral, everyone dressed in black. The men coming out are old and look like the bootlegger. The women appear happy. *Maybe the dead person was bad*, I think. *Maybe the dead person was a bootlegger.* The Cordoba grazes the roadside. Was father supposed to go to this funeral, is that why he's dressed fancy?

We keep going. Father sings Johnny Cash and Conway Twitty tunes. The signal he's at the most dangerous level comes when he cries at maudlin lyrics. I hold the two-litre Pepsi as I watch Father's face shift like a clump of dirt squeezed in the fist. It's time to stop the car. This is the end of father's middle period—an acknowledgement that the Highway Patrol can catch him.

I climb on his lap and we move again. Father works the pedals as I keep the car between the white and yellow lines. We drive through small villages where people, if they look out their windows or from their porches, can see a kid at the wheel, playing with a real toy.

I park the Cordoba in the centre of the driveway. I get off his lap, exiting through the driver's side door, but as I scoot off, a Mason jar falls out and smashes on the dirt laneway, the alcohol pooling and running in slow rivulets to the river. Father staggers out of the car. "Your fault," he slurs, "your fucking fault!"

Boats like dark shapes meander down the moonlit river. Cars race past on the highway. What did other people think when they saw us? Does anyone see us? No one ever intervenes in our lives. If I had parked closer to the door, or offered first to take the Mason jar in the house, I might not have lost the shine.

Muscle memory: I run behind the house and deeper into the fields, hopping over the rows. Father catches me just as I make it to the edge of the woods next to the crick, the best place in season to get fiddleheads.

Breathing blood, but with nothing broken, I wake to see a lone tent out on Middle Island. A bonfire blazes as a family of three sings "Will The Circle Be Unbroken." The Cordoba looks like a dead, mud-splattered fish, its wheel wells looming like gunwales. I creep inside the house, listening for father's apneic snore, hoping it won't stop.

On the way to my room, mother loudly calls out from the master bedroom. "I hope you sleep good. No rain tonight." As quick as I can, I take off my mud-covered clothes and fall asleep.

The Skidder is a monstrous device built for hauling trees in the woods. Woodsmen cut down trees with chainsaws, removing branches once the tree is felled. The Skidder pushes the logs together so woodsmen can wrap chains around the width of log bundles. The Skidder then pulls the log bundle out of the forest. The intended use of the Skidder means that the Skidder can go almost anywhere. The Bridges are the only ones along the river to own one—they bought it second hand in Saint John. Scratched, dented, and prone to wheezy roars, the big orange machine moves anything. When we farmed, father hired it on average twice a year to yank the Massey out of mud holes. The Bridges loved to send a hired man with the Skidder and he would link a chain around the tractor's front axle. The Skidder freed the Massey as easily as the water flowed down the river. Once the hired man was paid, the Skidder marauded off. The Bridges' hired man used to work for father.

Father wakes in the clothes he wore to the bootleggers, but the finery is stained now, his shirt torn at the sleeves. The blue Ford truck comes back at noon, but flanked by another truck, a dirty one. Unlike the previous visit, the Bridges waste no time. Two men exit each truck: Niall, the eldest, holds a forty of Captain Morgan in his hand. He walks in front of Irwin, his younger, smaller brother. Two men in their twenties follow their middle-aged masters to the mid-point of the front field. The four men wear gum rubbers—they are prepared. They stop ten feet from the tractor. Seeing the men from the kitchen window, I call out to father. "You'd better come with me boy," he says. Father put me out of the house first and slams the door behind him as loud as he can.

"Friday wasn't a good day to harrow this field," Niall shouts to my Dad from fifty feet away.

I walk beside father now. We continue to close the distance to the Massey, Niall and his men an oddly respectful distance from the tractor.

"We've been waiting months for it to dry out enough. *Months*, Will, *months*. That's the problem with this land. Too wet. You're lucky we rented it and didn't ask for money back. It's so wet, we might not even use this field next year. If we do use it I think the price should be lower, right Irwin?" Like pride and love in this country, shame comes in the form of threats. Without rent money we'd have nothing. For some reason I remember the taste of fiddleheads, more texture than taste. The tongue unravels them.

"Right," Irwin says, a little uncomfortably.

"You two broke the agreement. You were supposed to turn this soil over. All you did was use it and then you left it." Father stands with his fists at his sides. Negotiations depend upon the controlled, forceful appearance of how far one will go. "And I've been staring at it since, cursing you both for being lazier than *cut cats*." Father speaks the last two words with a rise in his voice and a quickened pace.

Niall smiles, having received the ultimate insult. The hired men behind him are loose. The forty-ouncer is near empty. "Smart talk from the Dirt King stuck in his shitty dirt. How many times have I pulled you out when no man would have been stupid enough to do what you do? I've pulled your tractor out of *ponds* before, Will. Here you are, a Dirt King in the field I pay you for, trying to make me the fool."

"You didn't *buy* this field from me. You *rented* it from me. And you didn't do what you said you'd do, and I always do what I say. So who's the fool, you lazy fucking fool."

"Have a drink, Will," says the hired man behind Niall.

"Yeah, Willy, have a drink," says the hired man behind Irwin.

Father's gaze remains locked on Niall's face. He can't afford to be distracted. The group of men could beat him, shove his face in the dirt. Is he afraid? He looks ridiculous, standing in the field that was once his father's in a ruined fancy suit. "Pull out that tractor you lazy fuckers," Father says.

"Will, a drink," says Irwin imploringly. Thin, intent on corrugations in the ground, Irwin doesn't seem to want these negotiations to go very far. I feel like Irwin.

"Yeah, Will! Great idear, Irwin! A great *idear*! Now why didn't I think of that! Come with us Will and we'll have a drink. We'll go to Casey's," Niall says. He turns to his brother. "Irwin, we'll drink at Casey's. You look like you need a drink too."

The offer of a drink implies that everyone can worry about the front field later. The Bridges might even buy enough alcohol to trick father. They could say that they had paid their debt and father would have to pay them for the Skidder. If father didn't pay them, the tractor would stay stuck, Johnny Gregson would want it back, cars going down the highway would laugh about the Dirt King and his mired tractor.

But the Bridges brought four men. If Niall had come alone and offered father a drink, father would have taken the bottle. But this was four against one man and a boy. The Bridges mean to intimidate father into drinking. Father said, sure, "This field has sat too long."

"Have a drink, Will."

"Have a drink, Willy."

"C'mon, Will. A little nip."

"Have a swalley."

Coated with grime, the hired men appear too stupid or lazy to earn a living year-round. They live only for alcohol, working just enough to get liquored. Men like these two are often paid in alcohol. If Niall isn't around to oversee them, they loaf. Cut cats.

On the gunmetal blue river, pleasure craft amble towards the shadow of the Burton Bridge. The other fields in Sheffield had long been harrowed. What did people driving along the highway think of the standoff out here, a newly-harrowed field with its small patch of untouched ground, dead corn sticking up around a little tractor, five men and a boy squaring off?

The audience for shame is as vast or small as a car travelling down the highway late in the evening. Boats peek over the heaped highway asphalt. Father looks at me, mud clinging to his leather shoes, fists steady and clenched at his sides. We are all stuck. Niall sways slightly, the bottle at an angle in his hand. Father looks Niall in the face and says through a smile, "I don't want a drink. Maybe you've had too much of that shit. I want you to turn this soil."

FUCKING SHIT ICE

For Corey Andrew Neilson

At ten years old, my brother hears in his head the phrase *It all comes down to this*. Reg Cook, the alcoholic coach of the Oromocto Atom AAA Eagles, still coming down from the last night's drinking session with my father, waves Corey to the bench with eight seconds left in regulation play.

"Eight seconds are left in the game. The fucking team is all about you. I play *you*, you little fuck," Coach Cook says, pumping his index finger into Corey's chest, "*you* and *you* and *you*. You're *my* ice hog. You get all the ice time because you are the best. You know you're the best. We need a goal, you dumbass. What?" Coach Cook puts his hands to his face, flutters his fingers, affects an effete voice. "You didn't know? This is the championship game! We depended on you all fucking year because you are the best player. You score the goals. I put you out there because you score them. That's the deal. If we lose then it's your fucking fault." Sweating and shaky, Coach Cook coughs, his voice brackish and hoarse. He screams the rest of his inspirational speech at the little boy, for all to hear. Kids on the bench and parents in the stands hear Coach Cook during the timeout totally lose his shit.

Coach Cook bellows, "You owe me a goal you chintzy fuck. They hand out bullshit silver medals at centre ice for second place wimps but winners get gold. Don't you want a trophy, Corey?"

With tears in his eyes, Corey says, "Yes. I want a trophy."

Coach Cook roars, "Go score, I put you out there to score, go and fucking score." Before the puck even drops, my father jumps over the protective glass, launching himself into the Eagles' bench, using his fists to end Coach Cook's decade-long tenure with the Oromocto Eagles. The ref blows his whistle to get this minor hockey mess over and done. Corey's eyes dry now, he carries the puck in the offensive zone, feeling like he can undress every player, pass them like pylons. In his head he hears Harry Neale from Hockey Night in Canada talk about "time and space." Corey is just nine years old but, as if he were a physicist-alchemist, he creates time and space. Nearing the far faceoff dot, he keeps the goalie close to the post. Five seconds elapse. With three seconds left in the game, Corey has a low-percentage shot available to him and he considers that shot. Will the result give good rebound? Already he's able to think one play ahead, an advantage over the respond-and-react anklers out there. Corey decides: *fake swing wide, fake pass to the wing, cut back, wraparound.* Corey's behind guy gamely circles. His winger's a chump. Corey hears Bob Cole say again in his head *It all comes down to this.* Corey can't look at the goalie—to look is to telegraph is to lose. *Trophy.*

Everyone in the rink knows that there is only one player on the Eagles who can tie the score. Coach Cook didn't lie, he spoke the truth. Corey needs everyone to disbelieve in him, that's the trick. He makes like he'll pass the puck, therefore giving away the game. But Corey keeps the faith by keeping possession of the puck, reversing and curling his stick. Corey shoots right handed, he was made for this play, it all comes down to this. He catches the goalie off balance. Like everyone else, the goalie expects the puck to go slot-side to the curling winger. The puck's in. A pockmarked goal judge turns on the green light. Teammates pile on my brother—Corey, the tie-game hero. Thinking back, I can't remember who won that game.

"Hey, Pelly. Look at this. I mean, *look* at these fucking cans. Holy. Fucking. Shit."

Cornie hands Pelly the porno mag. Now everyone's interested. Ballsy says, "Pass that sticky magazine over here when you're done with your fucking fingers,"

The Wolverhampton Wolves are seated on the bus according to a self-policed hierarchy: best players lounge in back, rookies and the unpopular take the cheap seats up front. I'm in England because I haven't seen my brother play hockey in ten years. The last time I watched him, he was a last-minute call-up with the Portland Pirates. Now he's the new player-coach of the Wolverhampton Wolves. "Just like Paul Newman in *Slapshot*," he explains. *If you're like Paul Newman*, I think, *then who are the Hanson Brothers?* Corey runs this team. He decides who can play and who can't. And, just like the old days, he's the best player the team has. He plays himself a lot. The Wolves are on a streak. Corey tells me on the transatlantic phone call, "Winning's not a coincidence. It never is. Winning is me."

Guys prepare for games differently. Some players make a covenant with their iPod. For Cornie and Pelly, it's porn. For others, it's cards. Ballsy asked me if I want to play euchre, but not out of friendliness. These guys would fleece me, say it's bonus pay from Coach. Ballsy hands me the porno mag making the rounds. "Fucking *look* at them!" I say, laughing. It's true. They are impressive. I hand the mag back to Pelly, whose real name is Pelletier, his hand out, impatient.

Is Pelletier, the star centreman my brother acquired just before the season started, working out? Pelletier was the leading scorer for the Quad City Mallards of the ECHL last year, but they cut him three games before the end of the regular season because of his attitude. I'd ask my brother but it's the agora here, everyone would hear me. There are a lot of things I can't talk about right now, things I want to know. Pelletier fiercely wins money from his jock colleagues at euchre.

Another forbidden question: How's Joanne? I don't know why I'm thinking about Corey's wife now, but I do want to know if he remains in love. Questions like mine are ridiculous, always have been.

I represent my brother and his players would lose respect for him. Who talks about love on the hockey bus? Love is an away game.

Before my brother lies down in the bus aisle to get some sleep, he asks if I need anything. "No," I say. Everyone is locked in their personal trance: the bus moves rhythmically, iPods are caressed, cards get shuffled, reshuffled, dealt. I haven't been on a team bus since high school hockey, when I was consigned to the front rows of the bus for being the kind of guy that asks too many questions. I observe instead and create a list of rules. Rule #1 of hockey road trips is: all team bus rides are the same, anywhere, for all time.

"Corey, if you fucking snore again like last bus ride, I'm going to pour this shit down your whistling mouth," Pelly says. "Lap lap lap," he says, his tongue hanging out, "down your mouth." Now Pelly's mouth is open, gagging, guzzling, gulping. "You hear?"

My brother slowly turns to Pelly. Pelletier is good, a really good player, but his problem, why he never made it to the show, is because he's a little guy. Way, way too little. Corey is 6'5". Lap lap lap will never happen. I understand what's going on between them—a challenge, assertion of authority, Pelly's testing Coach Corey's resolve. Pelly knows he's good, he's put on the ice to score goals. He thinks he can't get fired from this team, that Corey needs him too much. He might be right. Corey is probably doomed without Pelletier. This makes the standoff interesting.

Before the team left Wolverhampton, I checked out the Wolves' home dressing room. Pelletier's locker was plastered with pictures of three beautiful women, nude and in various positions on top of a Wolverhampton Wolves' jersey. The team photographer took the photos—his company logo was displayed in the left hand corner of all the posters. Pelletier had been with the team just *twenty fucking days*. Unbelievable.

My brother very slowly and exaggeratedly reclined on the floor, holding Pelly's eyes the whole time. He didn't say a word. Without verbally putting Pelly in a corner, the message was: *You try that, you fuck*. This helps me formulate rule #2 of hockey road trips: there is at least one shithead on every bus.

Before Coach Cook called the timeout and orated for the whole rink, the Eagles played against a team from the Miramichi. A father from the other team wearing a Fredericton Express jacket screams *Fill The Net* after his kid scores a goal. *Fill The Net Fill The Net Fill The Net* he barks at his son. The team's other asshole fathers take up the *Fill The Net* chant. It's only 1-0, but the other side wants to *Fill The Net*.

This angers everybody on our team, mothers and fathers included. Wanting to win is natural but chants to fill the net in Atom hockey are bullshit, the kids are just nine and ten years old. So my father gets the rest of our side's fathers to scream *Fill The Net* right back. It's gutsy since we don't have a goal yet. Our fathers stomp and clap, exhorting the Eagles to *Fill The Net, Fill The Net*. This command is meant as instruction to only one child—Corey. When people scream fill the net, they mean my brother. He's the only logical candidate.

Corey's team scores five unanswered goals. Corey pots four of them, all wraparounds, and assists on the other goal. Coach Cook restrains his players at goal five, telling them to take it easy. The glass fogs up in the old Renous barn. The home squad is hopeless but there is still ten minutes left to play. Our team's mothers and fathers don't want Corey to take it easy, though. They heard *Fill The Net* and now, bloodthirsty, they chant *Fill The Net* and won't stop. Mothers bash two-litre pop bottles filled with pennies against their knees. My father improvises to antagonize Mr. Fill The Net even more. He starts chanting Hat Trick Squared whenever Corey takes the ice and the other fathers get behind the chant. Dad makes a square with his arms above his head and starts dancing an Irish jig.

Like the best players at any level, Corey responds to crowd energy. Cheering works on him and that makes this game dangerous. Corey hears fathers incite him to score six goals. He has no choice. He decides to score two more goals in the hardest way possible. *Double Hat Trick Hat Trick* reaches him all the way down the ice, in the far corner of the opposing zone. Parents of the opposing team think this is fucking wrong, wait till we get in the parking lot, we'll break the arms of the square moron.

Corey could skate straight to the net and shoot top right corner over the goalie's blocker, he knows he'll score. Their goalie is shit. Instead, he skates behind the net and waits, faking left and right, making the goalie strain his neck to see which way the wraparound will come. Four goals by wraparound and Corey wants to punish this sieve with another one. In a second he goes in the opposite direction of the rubbernecking goalie and lifts the puck in on his backhand. Everyone watching the game, players and parents both, *knew* Corey would try the wraparound. He had done it four times before. Wraparound is his signature move. Coach Cook benches him after the fifth goal. "Nice work," Coach says, "but it's getting brutal out there. We need you for the next game."

Corey snores like Dad did. Pelly plays cards while Corey saws. Pelly bitches about the noise and making eyes at his drink, lap lap lap he mouths with the lolling tongue, but he never gets up with the coffee. He watches Corey a little too close, especially when the snoring stops, checking to see if Corey notices the mocking. Pelly takes Ballsy's money and says, "I bet they have free fucking skaters on the ice when we get there. Fucking ice's going to be shit."

Belfast's opposing rink is small, offering most fans a good view, except for the obstructed seats. Belfast's a small-market team with far fewer seats than Wolverhampton's National Ice Centre. The owner is unambitious—only two concession stands offer popcorn, hot dogs, and beer. Pelly's right—free skaters careen on the ice. Pelly's even more offended that the free skaters suck. "Fucking English can't skate," he says to Ballsy over the PA system blare. Ballsy's a Brit, Pelly's an import, born in Gatineau.

Corey uses the dry-erase whiteboard to itemize the strengths and weaknesses of Belfast's best players. "Watch out for Hunter, a tricky bastard. All skill if you try to kill him with hits." He diagrams a new breakout the Wolves worked on in practice all week: RD to LD, hard wrap, blow the zone. Last year's head coach, the guy who held the job before Corey, was a one-year wonder—lost the job despite a winning record. The team came second in the league. That'd never happen in Canada. Corey loses me as he talks trap—I never was good enough to play the game as one plays chess. I see human behaviour and it's like I'm in *The Matrix*, lines of green code telling me what people want and what they only think they want. Corey sees men on skates and his brain turns into a supercomputer.

Thibodeau the assistant player-coach calls to me, "Hey, Coach Brother, you got anything inspirational to say? Haw." Say nothing, my human-behaviour program says. Disregard: I say, "I memorized the speech in *Any Given Sunday* by heart. Wanna hear that?" Silence.

Corey widens his eyes, rescues me like he always did on the ice. "Fuck boys let's fill the net," he says, slamming the black marker down on the whiteboard ledge, "and play tenacious D." His pre-game speech is over. The men in the dressing room shout joyous, boyish *C'mon guys* and *Fuck let's do this blokes* and *Yeahs*.

The porn magazine comes back out and circulates again. Still impressive. I leave—isn't there some secret pro ritual they need to do? Say Fill The Net with their hands on their cocks or something? I walk into the dry, cold rink air. I notice a few free skaters wear their own skates, but most wear all the same kind—a strange deep blue. Rentals? One moron in black CCMs pushes hard around and around the perimeter. He stops to snow a babe in the blue buckles, but it makes her happy. He puts his arm around her. What is she doing with him?

The Wolves lose. I wished they would win so I could feel what an all-grown-up, professional win was like, hear Ballsy call out "Team

Party" on the bus. But the mood is funereal after this one-goal loss. I had been on teams that lost but my skin in the game was nil, I was never the best player, the coach never leaned over and told me that I, personally and completely, was responsible for losses, that losing is my fucking fault.

The Wolves are a pro team, paid to play. Corey cuts off Thibodeau mid-assessment and explains hockey math to me: "The reasons for a win matter less than the reasons for a loss. It's simple: something went wrong out there. After a loss, the assistant coaches and I sit at the front of the bus. The players go to the back. We evaluate play to find the reasons for the loss, but most of the time it's pretty fucking obvious what went wrong. Somebody fucked up, or somebody didn't produce. When we win, I let them enjoy it, I let them cheat and steal from each other and drink as much as they want all the way back to Wolverhampton."

Thibodeau resumes his run-down. "I give English a 3-. Not good enough tonight. Guys got by him and it hurt us. He wasn't brutal but he cost us."

"OK," Corey says, pencilling in a sheet. "Ballsy gets a 4-. Good offensive play, but still a problem in our end. But good chances though, so."

Players are scored on a five-point scale. What about Pelly? He scored the team's only goal tonight, a wraparound. Corey played him for most of the last ten minutes of the third period.

Rule #3 is spoken aloud by Corey. "I say this all the fucking time. Give good puck to the best offensive player. In that regard, all these assholes sucked, they get 1- for that. Give the fucking puck to Pelly, keep telling the guys that." Thibodeau and the other assistant nod. They know they are being told to distribute the command but also that they are being evaluated on the same terms. "Pelly gets a 4," Corey said, writing the number on the sheet.

Pelletier undressed guys, took high-percentage shots, set up shop behind their goalie's net. At the crowd's intake-of-breath moment, the puck bounced as Pelly skated behind Belfast's net, the goalie hopelessly out of position. For some reason I thought of the fool churning around the ice during the free skate to impress his impressive girlfriend, liable to smack into some poor ankler kid. *Wraparound,* too easy, Wolverhampton has tied the game.

Thibodeau pauses, then brings up Pelly's attitude. "Listen guys. There are leaders on this team. Guys that say things and make the mood. Pelly's body language was fucking shit. When a pass missed him he'd do the *Aww* move and guys on the bench would bash themselves and say, "Better passes, fuck guys we need to make better passes." It was that way the whole fucking game. Corey, did you put him on the ice at the end of the game for so long because you got sick of the asshole whining on the bench? Christ fuck."

"I'd give his play a full 5. He was our best offensive player tonight. But Pelletier acts like it too. So that's why the 4, not a 4+ or a 5. I'll take care of it."

As Corey talks, Pelletier is deep in a euchre game. Catching me looking, he yells to the front of the bus, "Hey, Corey, how about a movie? Put a movie on."

The other guys join in. "Yeah, Corey, a movie."

"We haven't seen a move in a long time."

"Let's watch Coach Carter."

"Fuck Ballsy, you got any porny DVDs? Can we put one in Corey?"

The assistant coaches shake their heads. Thibodeau mutters *No fucking movies.*

Corey smiles like he has the puck on his stick. "Hey, Pelletier. I'm glad you asked if you could watch a movie. You've got great timing. We just lost a game we should have won. Belfast is a fucking balls hockey club and we lost. This team only scored one goal and you bitched the whole game. Our payroll is three times theirs. I know I don't pay you to care, Pelly, but I do pay you to win fucking games and we lost. We lost because you didn't score enough. No movie."

The bus stays quiet until Pelletier smiles at Ballsy and says, "Coach'd put on Cinderella anyway. Hey Ballsy. No need for you this hand. I'm going alone."

Back home in New Brunswick last summer, I needed a collapsible crib for my infant son. They had red ones on sale at the Canadian Tire. Mom said to set it up in Corey's old room. I opened the door to the room and the shrine shine hit me: ribbons, trophies, pictures of Corey at centre ice shaking hands with tournament officials, mayors, MPs, premiers. One of the trophies was all the way back from Mites. Fucking five-year-olds play Mites! If I ever got a trophy, it was because I was incidental, someone else won the game for me. A coach would lean over and tell Corey, "This is your goal, we need a goal and it's going to be your goal, right now." Victory. I got a trophy that way.

I counted the gold trophies. Each trophy represented an accepted assignment. There wasn't enough room for all that shit on the shelf. Mom packed extra hardware in boxes sitting in the middle of the room. I pushed the heavy boxes to the side of the room to set up the crib.

My brother's goal with the new Wolverhampton job is to win the division title. He tells me it isn't like North American hockey here in England, playoffs are less important than having the most points at the end of the season. "I have to find a way to get guys to focus on every game," he says, worried. The usual mentality is to win when it counts, but this brand of hockey averages out the pressure over an entire season.

"Hey little awesome dude, drooly man, time to go to sleep in the real church of hockey. Close your eyes or you'll go blind," I whisper to my son as I set him down on the soft crib mat. What did I sarcastically say to Corey when he came home from obscure hockey greatness? "Did you like the parade at the airport?" Looking at the bright metal shining down on the sleeping boy, I couldn't help it, I felt my son was receiving a blessing.

When the Wolves are done hanging up their gear in the National Ice Centre home dressing room, my brother and I are alone. I feel like I'm his teammate again on the Oromocto Eagles. "What are you going to do about Pelletier's attitude?" I ask. "Pelly will just push and push until there's an explosion."

Corey looks like Coach Cook at that moment, Coach Cook tapping a player's shoulder and saying, *Your turn, now.* "Pelly's our leading scorer."

"But he's a shithead. What would you have done if he poured the coffee in your mouth?"

"You ask stupid questions. I win games. He didn't do it. He didn't do it because he was afraid of me. And I'm not afraid of him. That's how it works. I win games and he knows if he doesn't help us do that then he's a fucking shit player and he's gone. Simple."

Love is an away game. Love is never simple. "How's Joanne?" I ask, wishing he were winning that game.

"She's fine," he says. We're fine," he adds, his facial expression changing from cool anger into a little boy's bewilderment, desperate to score.

BURNING ROCK
NABOKOV

THE GREAT NEWFOUNDLAND NOVEL

The Sub-Committee of Cabinet which was created some weeks ago to study the subject of centralization and relocation of population in Newfoundland held a special meeting in the Cabinet chamber yesterday afternoon. I had the pleasure of being present and a thorough discussion took place. It was decided that the time had come for the Government to set up a special short-term organization to conduct an intensive research campaign to gather and compile all the facts that must be known before the Government can lay down the foundations of a strong centralization program. In recent weeks the special Sub-Committee of Cabinet was in touch with certain Welfare Officers throughout Newfoundland and obtained from them certain information as to the settlements which, in the opinion of these Welfare Officers, might be regarded as settlements that had no great future.

– Joey Smallwood, October 1957

And as life snapped we saw/ A pinhead light dwindle and die...
— V. Nabokov, *Pale Fire*

The thing about Vladimir is—he loves his wife, Vera. She's his protector and minder, his muse and, above all, his love. Every book Vladimir writes, he writes for Vera. Even *Lolita*, that scandalous nymphet of a book.

After *Lolita* is stupidly rejected by Alfred A. Knopf, Vladimir's fundamentally unserious publisher, Alfred A.'s wife Blanche tries to paper over the rejection. Vera sees through this tactic, knowing that if the great publisher himself were to reject her husband, the rejection would be more brutal—and more difficult. *The wimp,* Vera thinks. *Alfred probably tasked his ditz with writing me, hoping gentle ladyfolk will diffuse the stupidity of this rejection.* Blanche invites the Nabokovs for dinner as her courtly, crafty first sortie. In her note, Blanche expresses great regret and embarrassment at being *forced* to reject the book because of the philistine tastes of America's book-burning public. The philistines duly dispensed with, Blanche writes at length about the wayward antics of Coco, her addled son. Blanche attempts to displace the nature of her note from hard rejection into a shared future with the Knopf publishing house. "Come, Vladimir and Vera," the note seems to say, "*Lolita* is unpublishable, be so kind as to give us a mulligan on your genius. Nevertheless, we must break bread together and discuss our disappointing children!" The end of the note says, *Dinner, 8 PM, Ritz Carlton, Cheever will be joining us. We very much hope you will come.*

Vladimir and Vera have only one child, Dmitri. Dmitri has never disappointed either of his parents in life. While Coco snorts cocaine in flop houses, Dmitri touches ivory in concert halls. Coco has a limp from third-degree burns on his left leg sustained during a very bad experience in a disreputable house in the Lower East Side. Dmitri is lithe, muscular, a dancer. Vera's no fool. She's the one who picks up the daily mail from the post box. She reads the importunate pleas for her husband's time, presence, willingness to comment, his availability for blurbs. Reject an obvious masterpiece like *Lolita* and insult Dmitri by implication? *Blanche Knopf, you jealous failure*! Vera thinks, her mind snapping like a whip.

Vera too thinks *Lolita* to be unspeakable. But *Lolita* is unspeakable *poetry.* When she samples the text, which isn't often, she understands that her husband wants all of her, at every age. In response to Blanche's philistine note, Vera strikes the Knopf name from her address book permanently, covering it with black marker. Vera never says another word to that publishing house in her life—therefore, Vladimir doesn't, either. Vera, the gatekeeper, closes the Nabokovian gate forever.

Seven years later (what Vladimir calls "the itch"), *Pale Fire* is released by Knopf's rival, Putnam. This, Vladimir's greatest novel, uses the thematic conceit of a 999-line poem written by the major—and fictional—poet John Shade. Vladimir spent years on the construction of the poem itself, making sure he packed in as much allusive sneakery as he could. A lot of the tricks are aphrodisiacal in the Nabokov household—Vladimir dresses in a centurion costume some evenings, standing on a stool, declaiming a few lines of Shade's opus. Vladimir's passionate recitals incite Vera to rush to the bedroom closet for her lion tamer outfit. Vladimir recites a line, Vera wields her whip in unison—*snap*. Vladimir beats his chest, shoves his fist in the air, relishes the risqué bits. Vladimir designed the stanzaic medleys of wenches, thirst, shame, and pain—*snap*—to get Vera in the mood. Loving Vladimir, Vera also loves to tame him on these nights. Utterly her creature despite his wild breast-beating, Vladimir eventually whispers into her post-coital ear: "Your ruby ring made life and laid down the law." In response, Vera wiggles the red birthstone on her engagement ring. "Vladimir, you are incorrigible," she says, pinching his cheek. Vera and Vladimir are both White Russians.

A few weeks after the magnificent reaction to *Pale Fire*, Vera receives—amongst a heap of importunate, inconsiderate correspondence—a curious invitation from a far-flung Canadian university. An English professor by the name of John Shade—sharing the name of the pretentious protagonist of *Pale Fire*—makes the following request:

Dear Mr. Nabokov,

A writer of your stature is far beyond what I can reasonably expect to attract to our Writer-in-Residence program at Memorial University, yet I feel that the hospitality and conviviality of Newfoundland would benefit you in the way I have seen it benefit those less talented than yourself. If this place can refine the talents of the mediocre, I wonder what would happen if a genius came here to write. This is, I suppose, an entirely selfish invitation—you could go anywhere you pleased, and here I am, wishing to poach you from the confines of Cornell!

The nitty-gritty: a second floor apartment would be made available to you on Duckworth Street. You would have office space at Memorial, though I'd not expect you to keep hours nor to maintain any sort of professional relationship with the University. You'd not have to create or recycle a talk.

At this point, Vera yawns. Shade is right about one thing. Universities from Europe, North America, and South America regularly make such invitations to her husband. Even Russia and China make occasional offers. Some schools promise trinkets like stag heads and gold chalices and intricate carpets, but all offers are generous and the schools make few demands in exchange for the simple presence of her husband. *Why bother with the obscure coast of Canada?* she asks herself. Vera smooths her cotton dress and wishes with a lioness's child-protecting ferocity that everyone, everywhere, leave her husband alone. But out of politeness, she reads the final paragraphs:

Yes, my selfishness is ludicrous, absurd. What I want, or hope for, is that by coming here you'll see in Quidi Vidi or Cape Spear what will become that mythical beast called The Great Newfoundland Novel. Perhaps my desire is not selfish at all, but one that would benefit all your readers.

A confession: I am from away. I come from Upper Zembla, a small town in New Brunswick, just up the road from Middle Zembla. Educated on the mainland, I got a job in St. John's through hard luck and small prospects. But the things I've seen here have changed how I *see*: this place transcends the mediocre by transforming the mediocre into the flesh and blood and pulse of life, the kind you experienced on your father's knee before fleeing St. Petersburg. That feeling you got then, of power and security and limitless love, of recognizing butterflies and questing for a novel species, the feeling that died when your father was assassinated, the feeling you believe you've lost.

How do I know that you still think of home? We all do, I admit it. But home is the secret of here! Newfoundland is no exile, it becomes home because it is abandoned, neglected, despoiled, fled—and beloved. The people who leave can never be free, the people who come can never leave. It is the great taproot. Come.

The much lesser,

Dr. John Shade

Dr. Shade stuffed squalid pamphlets about the Avalon Peninsula, Gros Morne, and ancient Viking settlements in the package. Vera brushes her manicured hands against the glossy brochures. Christ— Vladimir would like the Viking thing, big burning pyres and horn helmets, screaming out loud *L'Anse aux Meadows* and beating his chest. *Snap.* But why the enclosed postcard of Muddy Hole? The place looks derelict, like a decrepit ghost town.

Vera tosses the papers in the garbage. Vladimir descends from the second floor where he's writing the prologue to *Speak, Memory*—a memoir of his love for Vera which, true to form, never mentions Vera at all, save in the most intimate of codes. Vladimir is sweating it out lately, less interested even in the taming evenings.

"I can't get the words down, Vera. I keep thinking about common butterflies, common as shit." Vladimir's morning porridge clung to the corners of his mouth, looking a little like Coco the last time Vera gave him change at Times Square. "I need my metaphors to light into the rare—the kinds I've always been seeking, like when in childhood I caught an insect Master Prokofiev hadn't seen before. But the damn thing flew out of our net when I got careless. God, I was excited then. A thousand novels in me at that moment. I can't even remember the look of that butterfly now—or of anything new and novel. I'm washed up, Vera, an effete prose hack! I just remember goddamn sulphurs and I write dully, sulphurically, pretending I'm moved by novel species."

It might be good to get Vladimir beating his chest again, even if it takes a silly Viking helmet to do it, Vera thinks. Vera mentions Shade's letter, Newfoundland. "Vera, my darling," Vladimir says, "you are the light of my life! I'm saved!" Vladimir takes his wife into his arms. Shade's letter and pamphlets wing to the ground, making *flit, flit* sounds as they hit the parquet. "We're going!" Vladimir declares. He climbs the stairs ecstatically, taking the first step while clicking his heels, and immediately writes this rash response to John Shade:

Dear. Mr. Shade,

I am glad to accept the generosity of Newfoundland. I will come and see how I can profit from your country. America bores me. I detest its cigarettes and suffragettes and holy writs in the form of politics. The television screen here is impossibly small, it shrinks with each day. I want simple streets and bright colours (how you spell it, yes?) and an escape from revolutionary mystiques that encourage rebellions without a clue.

I gag to read of beat poets and California and the best minds of generations pretending to be naked when they are indeed naked, pretending to be mad when they are indeed mad, mad as an ad, pretending to be starving when they prefer to be starving for what they call art. Which they promptly rhyme with fart. All hail glossies and the advent of calendars, beautiful men and women fetchingly arrayed by Madison Avenue! America has been the same, the same since Whitman. Myself, myself, my stateside song the cloying song of innumerable individuals in lonely unison.

I sing: begone, Cornell. I'm coming to St. John's. I would like to see your Joey Smallwood, my one request. I do appreciate strong arms, if not policy.

Sincerely,

Vladimir Nabokov

Shade writes back, *thrilled, shocked*, to inform the Nabokovs that the meeting with Smallwood will occur a short time after landing on the island. Shade adds, "He's in the fish mafia now, though. The little guy makes laws and grants permits for factories and in terms of money they're the same thing. Do be careful. I had to kiss his ring a month after I arrived on the island, and the kiss cemented certain... responsibilities."

Vera reads this in the kitchen after picking up the mail, just back from hearing about the carnal exploits of the university president at Sirinox, a favourite haunt of gossipy Cornell faculty wives. Deciding this fact is useful to apprise Vladimir of, she calls up to her newly-invigorated husband banging madly on the typewriter. Vera reads aloud Dr. Shade's response to Vladimir, stroking his hand.

But how to tell him she can't go? Dmitri is busy playing piano in various repertory theatres in nearby New York City and Vera has never missed a performance in her life. Not to mention that her friends—Russian émigré or Virginians, they all seemed to be one, or the other, or the same at once, both—can't come with her. Vera refers to this issue in private as her "glamour deficit."

At smoky Sirinox, the wives puff out big smoke signals of bitchiness while Vera smiles, explaining her predicament. Margaret Wells, the daughter of a slim Virginian tobacco tycoon, builds up the courage to speak. Margaret's but a girl, barely twenty-three, married to a randy colleague of Vladimir's, a middle-aged lecturer in Medieval English and a serial despoiler of Ivy League youth.

Margaret gasps out rapid-fire pieces of horrifying information. "They eat salt cod there, and hard tack, and when flush with cash they ingest cod tongues. My dear, you won't *survive* on that diet! Fish! Fish! Fish, fish, fish, and tack! Vera, really! Imagine! Trading New York for Newfoundland?"

Everyone, everywhere, even the green wife of a fantastic prick, wants to outdo my husband's alliterative, punning genius, Vera thinks. But Vera knows that her husband, a hypnotic hero of hortatory, high-performance English, can't be bested by *the chiennes jaloux* of Cornell. *Salt cod sounds good*, Vera thinks, looking the pretty, immature nincompoop up and down. *Like caviar, only grown up.* "Margaret, how do you know all this?" Vera asks. The gossipy wives, presented with the new tasty tidbit of the possible evacuation of a Great Writer, a Great Writer who is also a writer of porn, sit quietly as Margaret, in her way, tries to dissuade Vera from abandoning the group.

"Father, Mother, and I navigated Newfoundland for a whole detestable week last summer. Father was invited by the king of that place, the priest of that place, or some such title. President? Premier? Prime Minister? Potentate? Plenipotentiary?"

Margaret desperately withstood the gale-force of Vera's unspoken condescension. "Joey Smothersomethingorother asked Father to erect tobacco farms on the island, offering tax breaks and a subsidized work force. That might have worked. But it rained the whole beastly time. The wind blew, it blew, it didn't stop blowing, because it *couldn't,* I think, the wind just *is* there, it blows! The sea-smell cracked open my nostrils. The temperature never went above fifty degrees. Father said, 'Margaret, the only tobacco that will grow here is the wacky-tabacky, darling, in the closets of people desperate to get out of the weather.'

Margaret makes scare quotes for the marijuana slang. *So, so hip,* Vera thinks. *So cool.* "Father told the little prince no on the tarmac as we were about to board our jet. With a big stogie stuck between his lips, the petite patrician said, 'You are hereby excommunicated from this great land of this great dominion of this great people. Get lost, cancer-causer.' They're crazy out there, Vera! From the top on down."

Another Russian-Virginian, Rebecca, takes a puff on a cigarette, expels smoke like a stack, and says, "Darling Vera, now how will you ever have a cultured evening all the way out there in Nowherenewland?"

This argument gains traction. As lively as it is in Newfoundland kitchens, a rock in the Atlantic can't compete with Broadway plays or the gold-encrusted apparel of Fifth Avenue. Nor with Vera's White Russians who drink hefty amounts of white Russians in manicured hands, or the nouveau riche wives of Virginian industrialists making their killings by killing. *I must tell my genius husband that he will go to Duckworth Street alone,* Vera thinks with regret. *Yet still in unison, as Vladimir says to me as he leaves for his solo butterfly hunts.*

Vladimir misses Vera on the flight. John Shade promised everything— that the air would call words forth from Vladimir's typewriter, words flying onto the page. Vladimir wants to set foot in the windy, rocky country and realize that Newfoundlanders are his people, his true aristocrats in vernacular and puns. Vladimir arrives in St. John's on a connecting flight from Hoboken. But John Shade couldn't promise Vladimir that his wife would come too, there are limits to all boundless offers.

In the airport foyer, a matinee man holds a sign with **Humbert Humbert B'ye** marked in red letters. *Humbert Humbert?* Vladimir thinks. *I killed that character with a cause of death fitting for a pretentious soliloquizer and despoiler of premature beauty.* Humbert Humbert died of coronary thrombosis, not just any old heart attack.

If you're Dr. Shade, then you're an asshole, Vladimir thinks. Vladimir did not want to be greeted with the name of his most pathetic creation, a narcissistic prole prone to reframe sexual perversity as the tragedy of a romantic with a demographic problem.

The matinee man with the placard stands still. BETSY, a MR. CHIPS, and the PARTY OF MORTIMER LILL meet their chaperones and chauffeurs, get greeted and whisked away. Vladimir stops in front of the matinee man and looks down at his muddy gum rubbers. *God— the people of Newfoundland practise a strange form of diplomacy!* Vladimir thinks. Vladimir waits for Shade to acknowledge his presence, the presence which Memorial University paid generously simply to have in proximity.

The man with the placard coughs with every revolution of an adjacent baggage carousel. An unclaimed red bag sits on the carousel, moving steadily around, then hiding behind the wall where personnel invisibly unload luggage. The red bag doggedly comes back into view after disappearing. Who would claim the red bag? Who? "Are you John Shade?" Vladimir asks, unwilling to waste any more time.

The man with the placard leans forward a little, intently tracking the red bag as it rides the carousel.

"Sir," Vladimir asked the man, "Is that your bag?"

The man replies, "Comfortably robed, I would settle down in the rich post-meridian shade after my own demure dip, and there I would sit, with a dummy book or a bag of bonbons, or both, or nothing but my tingling glands, and watch her gambol, rubber-capped, bepearled, smoothly tanned, as glad as an ad."

Christ. I wrote that. Vladimir looks more closely at the man. Quite tall, with broad shoulders and an athletic mien, soft dark hair and a filmic lantern jaw, Vladimir realizes he's looking through a red-eye haze at *his* Humbert Humbert. If only Vera were here! She'd know what to do. She'd ignore this goof and take Vladimir to their quarters downtown using the address Dr. Shade sent them after they accepted the university's offer, the address Vladimir promptly lost upon boarding the plane. *I lose everything! I need Vera,* he thinks. *Vera, my minder, my temptress, the reason I write, my favourite word, I am her creature.* She wouldn't have lost the address, scribbled as it was onto blank space in the upper margin of the *St. John Telegram*'s obituary page. *Now who could be dying memorably in that poor provincialist principality?* Vladimir thought then, believing Vera would accompany him, that Vera would know, that Vera knows everything.

Humbert Humbert takes the red bag off the carousel and hands it to Vladimir, saying, "I give you glad tidings of great Madison ads.

You need a strong arm to carry this bag. Joey Smallwood says, *Hello!*"
Hubert Humbert drops his advertisement for *Lolita* and runs away.

Vladimir opens the red bag. Inside is a bottle of Screech wrapped
in a glossy photo of an enervated-looking Hon. Joey Smallwood about
to bite the head off a codfish. Written on the inside of the rolled-up
photo are a time, one month from the present, ten p.m., and a location,
THE SHIP INN, 265 Duckworth Street. Vladimir takes a long pull
from the Screech and calls a cab. *The great dictator is making me wait*,
Vladimir thinks. *I shall do as I always do. I will write every word for
my love, my life, my Vera. Where the fuck is Shade?*

Despite being without Vera, the first week was close to perfect for
Vladimir. He sat at his desk, looked out at the well-protected harbour,
and started to write a story about a ghost town. In the evenings he
took in George Street and took field notes about tolerance. But soon
being without Vera blights his pen and his thought until Vladimir
succumbs to Screech every day, all day, passing out at his desk where
a few dozen incoherent notecards are strewn. *Dr. John Shade is a
fool, a liar. The past month hasn't given me a useful word.* Giving
up on the prologue to *Speak, Memory*, Vladimir decides to write his
wife directly. Vladimir loves Vera. Needing her, he writes Vera every
day of his exile.

Dearest Vera,

I am a barbarian. I drink local rum and seethe. I daydream of
a dead child and a fire and I want to write a novel. I can't. I
miss you.

What's the point of writing a book when you're not around?
I've never had to ask myself that question before. But I do ask
now, every day. We've been together a long time. I try to get the
words down by pretending that they are being written to you.
But in a minute or two my gaze drifts to the ocean through the
window. The Atlantic is endless here, stabbed by rock, bleeding

profusely. Men stagger down the street nightly. I hear the most beautiful songs in the rooming house—women being fucked, odd sea shanties striking up like roosters in the morning. I just don't understand this place. I suffer culture shock, I have wifelessness, I may soon join the staggering midnight men on Duckworth Street.

Please, come and make sense of this hardscrabble for me. Let us sing in unison.

Bunny

After writing this letter to Vera, the last in a series, Vladimir joins the staggering men. Drunk, he opens his door and sees them swarm, black scamps walking arm in arm. He looks back at his desk and sees the useless notecards filled with drafted pleas to Vera for rescue. She isn't coming—why doesn't she answer his letters?

He looks at the lost men. *They are my kind*, he decides. He shoves a bottle of Screech into his coat pocket, something he can share with a friend. *What's the word for my current state?* he thinks. *Cancelled? Abandoned? No—outported.*

Drinking on Duckworth Street yet again one evening, Vladimir meets Greg Wells. Greg lost a daughter in a fire. "Terrible 'ting," he said. "Terrible when I lost Maggie. Burned to a crisp." Greg immigrated to St. John's from Muddy Hole as part of the resettlement program but he couldn't find work, so he drank. Vladimir tried to find out more about Maggie but Greg wouldn't talk more about her, except that she died in a fire, and that the blame was with Smallwood.

Outraged, Vladimir offered to write to Smallwood, to threaten to bleat the story to the *Telegram*. "I'll tell the people, Greg. I'll tell them about Maggie."

"No b'ye," Greg said. "The Smallwood, he never forgets. I'll never work again. Or worse. No b'ye, don't say a word. Our secret, b'ye." Greg clinks his pint against Vladimir's, and the two of them drink to silence. But Greg disappears, the rumour being that he has a job off the Grand Banks, or he's after being crazy and drowning in the harbour, or he's left town for Muddy Hole. Without Greg around to remind him to stay quiet, Vladimir went wild too, fixated on an image of a burning baby. Vladimir finally breaks his promise, sending letters to Joey Smallwood, the Primary Person of these Parts.

Dear Iosef,

I know about the burned baby of Muddy Hole. I know wells of what you dos.

Sincerely,

Vladimir

Smallwood surveys the Ship Inn crowd from his throne at the bar. *This is my Newfoundland*, he thinks, *but it's a Newfoundland still preferring the past.* The balding, slightly paunched Smallwood takes a deep breath and then a big jag from his glass of Screech on the bartop. He says, "Right. People fall all over themselves to drink their beer and rum and demand endless dole for what? To suck the life out of free enterprise, to drag down the rest of us working stiffs. These fucks in Muddy Hole give me grief. Stupid Muddy Hole fucks who don't know their own asses from where they live—brown and fucking desolate, no one should or will go there. Except them. Asses! Who the fuck in Muddy Hole is ever going to make something of themselves? Who the fuck decided Muddy Hole should be a place to fuck and have kids and fuck and have more kids? And fuck, who the fuck looked on that godforsaken part of earth two hundred years ago and felt Muddy Hole is a place to get busy building shacks to accommodate more stupid bums? Idiots—only idiots think this way. They sit their asses down on a rock and only later—once their asses are good and fat and stuck in the mud—do they realize they're *fucked*. But with their asses down, they scheme to keep their asses planted.

Solidarity for the asses! Workers of the world, put down your asses! Unite! One ass down means that another ass can go down, one ass an excuse for more all sticking and plunking of asses because the real assholes, working assholes like me," Smallwood raps out in delirious vernacular, pointing slowly at every single man in the bar, "pay these asses to stay sitting! Fucking ass plantations! By, for, and of the asses! I FUCKING HATE Muddy Hole."

Smallwood stops for another pull of Screech, taking a moment to recover and catch his breath. His paunch is bigger, his shirt unfurled from his beltline like a sail is unfurled to take advantage of prevailing winds, the sweat from his brow more drenching, his voice loud enough to rattle the bones of dead sailors dashed on the coast's rocky promontories. He's not done. Thundering to the entire room as if they were the citizens of every outport drain on the treasury, "I fucking hate Grole. I fucking hate Exploits and I hate Sops Island. All of them ten fucking families strong, all of them fucking and all of them on the fucking dole."

Nabokov staggers into the bar to find a strange peaked man on a gold stool wearing a priest's collar. Vladimir feels sick, but this place is open, warm, and promises company. "I will free the stuck asses of my people," Smallwood roars. "I will bring them to the promised land of civilization. They will come to St. John's or else." *That's a good Newfoundland place name,* Vladimir thinks. *Fucking Else. Population: asses.*

Smallwood drinks the rest of his glass, then demands the forty-ouncer from the barkeep. Vladimir isn't as tolerant of rum. When he partakes, his fiction veers into places where it, too, prefers to sit its ass down and baroquely demand that the reader feed it grapes.

Vladimir realizes this is the fish-biting man in the photo from the red bag on the airport carousel. This is Joey Smallwood! Vladimir instantly feels sympathy for the indolents in the outports of Newfoundland. Swaying from side to side, he decides he has always been writing for the outports of Newfoundland. He is their champion!

Vladimir thinks of Vera. If Vera were here, she would forbid him liquor just as John Shade, Vladimir's fictional creation, was forbidden liquor. Vera is his minder, his protector, his muse—but his muse is very far away.

Vladimir tries to focus. As Russian Literary Ambassador, he must acquit himself well. He focuses on Smallwood's nose like a fisherman heeds the signal of the lighthouse. *Smallwood's nose is too small,* Vladimir thinks. *Large enough to let air in, but the air can't escape the nose, the nose keeps air in. Air can only foghorn through the mouth.*

Focusing fails. Vladimir imagines Smallwood snorting huge bumps of cocaine, the drug shimmering through arteries, going straight to Smallwood's brain. As Smallwood rants, his audience standing room only now at the Ship, spilling out onto the street, Vladimir takes the lounge menu from a rack and writes out Smallwood's name in Cyrillic: смаллвуд. Methodically, Vladimir rips the letters from the page, arranging the letters on the bar into white lines.

Smallwood addresses every man and woman in the Ship by name. He orders everyone a drink. Apologizing for the current postal strike, he calls it a "Canadian problem." As he preaches his gospel of the Liberal government's five year plan for relocation of the kulaks, Vladimir imagines Smallwood taking every one of the Cyrillic letters up his small, small nose. Vladimir, experiencing a severe case of delirium tremens, is terrified he will get snorted too. He yells out, "Joe S., leave the poor people alone!"

Smallwood's nose magnifies in Vladimir's eyes, growing until it looks like it can suck up all the oxygen in the Ship. Smallwood's face turns a shade of hell. Vladimir wishes he wore a Viking helmet. Smallwood beats his breast, declaiming, "The plopped asses will martyr themselves on barren rock because their asses are their *brains.* They won't fucking move an inch. Someone, it just takes one, will die there and I'll look heartless."

Outside the Ship, a white limousine pulls up. Humbert Humbert leaves the car and smokes, hazes of grey sucked into his mouth, blown out his nose. The crowd at the Ship could lynch Vladimir or declare him a hero.

"You know this guy?"

"Isn't he a Wells?"

"A stranger!"

Vladimir is convinced the small man on the stool is a child-killing Cossack from Ossetia. "Cossack," Vladimir drawls with an insulting tone.

"What? Yes, the cod must be sick to death of being used by Muddy Holians for the dole. Fish one fish, get a stack of cash to last. Even the fucking fish are embarrassed." Smallwood slides off the stool and takes a menacing step towards Vladimir. "All I'm trying to do is get the fuckers to forget the fish a little more, to forget to beg a little more, to expect to expect less. So I'll make them do what's good for them, the lazy fucks."

"Still a Cossack, *Cossack*!" Vladimir slurs, bashing his hands on the table with each word. Smallwood takes a cod from a red bag under the gold stool. "Kiss the cod now, and forever hold your peace," he says. Then he clubs Vladimir in the head with the fish. From the ground, Vladimir sees Smallwood rise above the barstool, over the bar, and into the rafters. A halo glints over Smallwood's head. Smallwood's nostrils emit scraps of paper, paper that looks like little flies. Smallwood becomes a giant nose. Vladimir is sucked up in the angry snort of white limousine leaving the Ship.

The postal strike ends when the union rank and file lose enough money to want to work again and the federal government saves enough in unpaid wages to painlessly increase the carrier's salaries. Though he relentlessly brands the issue as a "Canadian problem" before it's solved, Smallwood claims credit for resolving the dispute on the radio call-in shows. The men and women living in the outports grit their teeth as he asks, "So, did you all get your cheques?"

Vera receives twenty letters from her husband in a single day. In the kitchen, missing the sound of typing upstairs, she reads the first letter:

> Dear Vera,
>
> Where are you to, b'ye? Why won't you answer? I can't see sometimes, not sure if it's the wrong stuff I'm drinking. Smallwood makes us angry! He is a puppetmaster, dangling money at the end of a fishing line, then yanking the bait back. We chase the bait and never close our mouths around the money. God I cannot sleep. I have nightmares about a child trapped in an inferno. O Vera I love you please save me, I will never find the butterfly.
>
> Bunny

The letters are out of order, but that doesn't matter—they are all consistent, the same note on different scraps of paper. Before he left, devastated that she would abandon him, Vladimir called Vera a Cossack and refused to let her drive him to the airport. He refused her pleas to call as soon as he set foot on the island, to write her every day, even just short notes with one word: love. "I am going into exile from you," he said. "I hope you are happy with the idle vamps and divorcées of the faculty club."

Vladimir is losing his mind! she thinks now. *Why did we have to leave on such bad terms? He can't do without me. He couldn't help himself when he left, his outburst was a plea.* Vera left for Newfoundland in the evening. For the next week, the postman stuffs the Nabokov mailbox with more letters until no more fit, letters falling out of the box and littering the stoop.

Scraps of wallpaper fall like little flies across Vladimir's vision. A mix of sleet and ash drips from holes in the ceiling of a doorless, burnt-out shack. His face numb, his mouth and nose encrusted by ice, Vladimir thinks the holes in the ceiling are apertures for butterflies. *Flit, flit—* sounds like Vera's whip, yet not quite.

Butterflies fancy themselves the resplendent regal messengers of quivering kings and queens, airborne and deep-thirsted enjoyments, insects one watches in pleasantness. *Small things are fastest,* Vladimir thinks, liking to imbue small, dead things with an overabundance of life.

A ghost village looms out the open window. He scrapes ice from his nose and stands to see fishing boats bobbing at a decrepit dock. A small church opposite makes a little noise with its cracked bell, the bell sounding with the movement of the perpetual wind, or, Vladimir suspects, the wind whipping through the crack against the clapper. Covered in snow, the corner of the shack is bathed in light from the open roof above, the floor white, the holes in the ceiling rimmed in black.

Other dilapidated buildings appear to be in a lesser state of ruin. Vladimir leaves the shack, finding a sign on the squat church. CHRIST'S CHURCH, MUDDY HOLE.

Scraps of snow blow over the tougher crust, *flit, flit.* If there's any mud here, it's deeper than the strata where Vladimir stands. Some of the snow is black—ash from the adjacent shack. Perhaps *I* have no great future, Vladimir thinks, whitened, blackened, frozen, and alone. He walks downhill towards the rotted dock. When did fishermen last tend this dock? Was it five years ago, or ten? The Atlantic wears away at the pilings, scraps of wood flecking off with each forceful wave. The splinters and chunks are greenish-black, dead bits eroding from the white crust of pulsing surf.

In contrast to the dock, the dories seem newly-built, so bright they might even *be* new. The brown ropes mooring them fray from a hundred thousand days of hard salt weather. But the boats sleep on the ocean's breast beautifully, each boasting a bold name written in Cyrillic. The farthest boat, a subtle green elegance, is вэра: *The Vera.*

Vladimir steps into вэра to see what she's about. He sits aft, takes out a notecard, and tests if the hospitality of Newfoundland as promised by Dr. John Shade will finally come true, if the Celtic power of the place can successfully be tapped. On the card, he writes out the word маггиэ.

Yes. Vladimir does feel different somehow.

Humbert Humbert holds another sign—чарлоттэ хазэ б'е in Cyrillic. But when Smallwood sees the elegant white-haired woman step down onto the tarmac, he tells his chauffeur to lose the sign. Men and women stream off the international flight but there is only one Vera—distinguished and elegant in a green shawl covering a white dress. Smallwood knows he has a tough customer on his hands. Time for charm. "Good morning, Mrs. Nabokov. Let's get straight to business, come to my car." Once inside, Smallwood says, "Hum, take us to VOCM." As the limousine races downtown, Smallwood explains, "Mrs. Nabokov—Vera, if I may—my plan is public address, to get the word out through the radio stations. I've already taken to the airwaves to inform all of Newfoundland that Vladimir is missing. I am personally, on behalf of all Newfoundlanders, very sorry about your husband's disappearance. Perhaps it would help if you spoke to the people of Newfoundland—they're good people, they'd look for Vladimir. Tell them what they should look for."

"I will tell your people about my husband," Vera says.

"But of course," Smallwood replies, sounding like a character of Vladimir's, intent on getting the last word.

In front of the microphone, thousands of lines of Russian poetry flit through her mind. Able to speak several languages, how she feels requires no translator. *It's my fault he's gone*, she thinks. He reached out for her over and over again—his letters begged her to come. *Should I tell the people of Newfoundland about how smart a man he is, and how true? About how we first met, how I wore a mask, how I wouldn't let him slip it off? How he had to see my face on the second date? No—the pedestrian details. Appearance, build, sound of voice.*

Smallwood, hating to wait, takes in a deep whistle of air through his nose, readying his voice. Vera blurts out, "Vladimir—I hope you can hear me. I will never leave this place until I find you. Where are you, my darling? The leader of this Newfoundland thinks you are a great man. Please, everyone who hears me: Vladimir is *sick*, he might speak *Russian* to you, he needs your *help*. He loves butterflies." Perfect and white-headed above the radio desk, Vera resembles a downy pile of snow.

Smallwood seamlessly takes over the public address, concluding with his personal phone number in case Vladimir's spotted. "A very great man," Smallwood confirms, "we are honoured to have him here and he must be found." Leaving VOCM, Smallwood says to Vera, "Mrs. Nabokov, please stay with me for this night at least? My wife Clara will show you great hospitality."

"Hum, is it?" Vera asks, ignoring Smallwood. "Hum, drop me on Duckworth Street," she commands. Vera turns to Smallwood and barks, "I am not going to sleep until I find my husband. He is my life, my light."

Before Vladimir can further his thoughts about Maggie or butterflies, both a species of pale fire or of ash, he notices a ridiculously small dory at the end of the dock. A man stands inside the dory wearing a yellow wharf jacket. From a distance, he looks a little like Robert Frost. Old, bent, thin, querulous, superior Frost.

The man in the dory holds a notecard, the same lined kind Vladimir uses to draft his novels. On the notecard is scrawl too small to discern at this distance. Vladimir calls to the man: "You will catch your death out there—Frost? Is it you?" The man in the dory doesn't speak. Vladimir stamps his feet to improve circulation. "Hey, Frost. Ha hah hah. I got here by the boat not taken!" Vladimir leaves вэра and carefully negotiates the groaning, unstable dock, small gulls pecking at the sides. After a few minutes of creeping, Vladimir makes it close enough to see two words written in Cyrillic on the notecard: иван шадэ б'е.

Is this Nabokov's creation, John Shade the poet, or Dr. John Shade, the academic who invited him to come to Newfoundland? He speaks: "In the words of the men of this place, a *shade* is a case or covering of a sword, dagger, or knife. A leather case that sealers would wear around their waists."

Vladimir sees no shade or scabbard at the man's waist. Is that a seal at the man's feet? The black object looks to be the size of a baby seal. The boat is otherwise empty, no oars, lifejackets, or buckets. Shade stands in the boat with ease. Vladimir is nauseated by the huge ocean around him rolling like black fire: sibilants of crisp claps, water brushing the dory, then scouring and slapping it against the doomed dock. Vladimir climbs in the dory, wanting to choke Shade, but the force of the water keeps Vladimir off balance. Vladimir sits down, not wanting to fall overboard.

Shade turns to face the prow. Vladimir imagines Charon in a yellow slicker, his scythe cunningly shrunk and concealed in the so-called shade of this place. The man unties a mooring. Vladimir looks back at Muddy Hole and realizes that, though abandoned, it's far more permanent than he; up on the slope it would take a hundred thousand years to slide into the ocean. Shade and Vladimir drift out to sea.

The music starts softly, drifting down the hill, echoing off the algaed rocks and bouncing out over the ocean, the rhythmic sibilance eventually reaching Vladimir and his guide, still within hailing distance from the shore. *Is it the sound of the sea itself?* Vladimir thinks, having entered into the body of the sea, but as the sound increases in volume he's certain it comes from Muddy Hole.

Captain John Shade the poet, or the professor, the one, or the other, or the same at once, both, is undeterred. His back is turned to Vladimir, he keeps his right hand on the tiller. The music swells with the sea.

Vladimir turns back to the shore. The ragged ghost citizens of Muddy Hole, children with tin flutes, men with accordions, and women with drums, flare in a pale fire Vladimir knows from burning his first drafts. The orange ghosts play a lurching waltz, a tunelessly beautiful melody with an other-life in timing. The ghost citizens of Muddy Hole gently burn, their instruments afire too, as is the rock beneath their burning feet.

Vladimir hears a tapping sound: turning back to the limitless sea ahead, Vladimir sees John Shade has changed his position. Shade looks at the pale fire too, tapping his foot against the black object in the bottom of the boat. Parts of the black object crumble, falling away in dust.

The ghosts on shore spin, their instruments incorporated into the dance. No man or woman may sit and play, they must rather move as part of a gay marching band, a Celtic military unit. "Are the people on the shore bards?" Vladimir asks John Shade. Though the song lurches, the ghosts play in perfect unison.

Shade shakes his head. "No. They are just poor, ordinary, good people. Even good people flicker, sometimes do the wrong thing. The good people on the rocky shore make music for this black corpse at my feet. Her name is Maggie, just two years old." Vladimir looks down at the burnt corpse that fragments with each buffeting wave from the ocean. "A Wells kid," Shade continues. "One family of ten chose to remain here, despite the premier's wishes. Smallwood's policy was that a whole community had to leave before any resettlement money would be paid. All or nothing with Smallwood, that's his way. One night Simms, a father of five with thin, sick children, got drunk and threw a Molotov right through the kitchen window, starting a blaze. Everyone in the house got out but Maggie, the wee one in the crib. You can see Maggie's mother there, in the front. She has the shawl on, the dress underneath." Vladimir peers at a pregnant woman throwing her arms and drum into the air. The ghostly pale fire leaps from her to the others, making a snapping sound as it arcs out.

The people of Muddy Hole dance in and through the fire. Vladimir looks further back to the shack where he slept the night. The building is now as black as the ocean, a huge cloud of its ash streaking into the sky. As the song ends, a man with an immense blue accordion dances with the pregnant woman playing a green whistle. It's Greg Wells, dancing with his wife. *So he did die then*, Vladimir thought. *Smallwood killed him. Just like he killed me.*

The melody decelerates, but in legato. The new speed and style makes the ghosts lurch backward while still keeping close together, fire blazing into further fire. Players come to the dock and with a single, unified shout, they throw their instruments into the ocean, the pale fire flaring underneath the enveloping marble top. Children climb onto the backs of their fathers, the women helping the aged climb back up the hill, filing past the church and then out of Vladimir's view.

"When the Wells home burned and Maggie died, Muddy Hole got its money. The Wells family left," Shade says. Vladimir raises his hand in a salute to silence, to not saying and singing another word. With his arm raised in the air, he looks back down at the burnt baby. *Flit, flit,* the corpse is nearly disintegrated.

Another sound strikes up over the ocean noise: the beating of wings. An orange cloud flies from the ash plume of the shack, over the church, and moves quickly towards the sea, past the dock and towards the dory. The sound increases, flit, flit, snap, snap, *SNAP*.

A mass of butterflies—the rare variety from Vladimir's childhood, the kind he lost and Master Prokofiev beat him for losing—shrouds the dory. Using his talent for imbuing dead things with superabundant life, Vladimir likens the work of the master's hands on his body long ago to the frantic clap of butterfly wings against his present face, his chest, his hands. At seventy years of age, Vladimir more than anything wants to name a novel species of butterfly after his wife, Vera.

As orange butterflies strafe the dory, Shade intones: "I do not consider myself a true artist, save in one matter: I can only do what a true artist can do—pounce upon a forgotten butterfly of revelation, wean myself abruptly from the habit of things, see the web of the world, and the warp and the weft of that web."

He *is* John Shade—*his* John Shade, the very great poet! Vladimir watches Shade take the notecard and fold it, capturing a butterfly that Vladimir uses as the rarest substance of fiction: the mystery of death, the hauntings of ghosts, the longing of love. This substance would constitute every lovely word he would write, every superabundant word of it novel, every word Newfoundland.

ACKNOWLEDGEMENTS

I express my gratitude to the editors of the following periodicals listed in alphabetical order:

"Sitting" won second place in *Matrix*'s 2009 Litpop contest and was published in *The Antigonish Review*

"The Alcoholic Physician" is in palimpsest at the *Canadian Medical Association Journal*

"Freight" was published in the *Fiddlehead*

"Prawn" was published in *Geist*

"Gorblimey!" appeared as a chapbook with Jackpine Press

"The Entirely Beautiful" was published in the *Malahat Review*

"Will" and "The Field Our Own" were published in *Queen's Quarterly*

"Fucking Shit Ice" was published in *Riddle Fence*

In the story "The Entirely Beautiful," the lines from W. H. Auden's poem "Lullaby" are from the Edward Mendelson-edited *Collected Poems of W.H. Auden*. My copy is the Knopf Doubleday trade paperback from 1991.

In the story "The Great Newfoundland Novel," there is a quote from Nabokov's *Lolita* on p. 251 that appears in the form of a line of dialogue by Smallwood's chauffeur Humbert Humbert. My copy of Lolita is the Knopf Doubleday trade paperback of 1989.

The line of dialogue attributed to John Shade on p. 265 is also a quote from – the actual? – John Shade of Nabokov's *Pale Fire*. My copy is the Vintage International edition of 1989.

The stories in *Will* have benefited from the attention of the following friends, colleagues, institutions, and enemies (not listed in that order, but in alphabetical order):

Douglas Glover, Adam Honsinger, Nicholas McArthur, Cordelia Strube, Russell Smith, and Michael Winter. I also thank the instructors and fellow students at the University of Guelph Creative Writing MFA.

DISCLAIMER

All references to media in this work are deliberately distorted invocations meant to adhere to my own imposed narrative line. Nicole Kidman didn't get her hair pulled in *Malice*, for example (I do wonder if Alec Baldwin ever wanted to, though.) Michael Jackson, a million dollars, can you feel me, holla.

The use of historical figures is similarly loose. McCrae's field hospital was never "overrun," for example, and the Nabokov story is brazenly duplicitous (and often wrong) about details in a style faithful to Kinbote, but too much of this explaining, including purposefully mixed-up Newfoundland pseudo-history and Fredericton geography, and I'll appear to presume you're less intelligent than you are.